Benjamin Franklin

Works of the Late Doctor Benjamin Franklin

Consisting of his Life, Written by himself; Together with Essays, Humorous, Moral

and Literary, Chiefly in the Manner of the Spectator

Benjamin Franklin

Works of the Late Doctor Benjamin Franklin
Consisting of his Life, Written by himself; Together with Essays, Humorous, Moral and Literary, Chiefly in the Manner of the Spectator

ISBN/EAN: 9783337093709

Printed in Europe, USA, Canada, Australia, Japan

Cover: Foto ©Raphael Reischuk / pixelio.de

More available books at **www.hansebooks.com**

W O R K S

OF THE LATE

DOCTOR BENJAMIN FRANKLIN:

CONSISTING OF

HIS LIFE, WRITTEN BY HIMSELF,

TOGETHER WITH

ESSAYS, HUMOROUS, MORAL & LITERARY,

CHIEFLY IN THE MANNER OF

THE SPECTATOR.

————

—DUBLIN:—

PRINTED FOR P. WOGAN, P. BYRNE, J. MOORE,
AND W. JONES.

————

1793.

PREFACE.

THE volume that is here prefented to the Public, confifts of two parts: the Life of Dr. Franklin; and a Collection of Mifcellaneous Effays, the work of that author.

It is already known to many, that Dr. Franklin amufed himfelf, towards the clofe of his life, with writing memoirs of his own hiftory. Thefe memoirs were brought down to the year 1757. Together with fome other manufcripts they were left behind him at his death, and were confidered as conftituting a part of his pofthumous property. It is a little extraordinary that, under thefe circumftances, interefting as they are, from the celebrity of the character of which they treat, and from the critical fituation of the prefent times, they fhould fo long have been with-held from the Public. A tranflation of them appeared in France near two years ago, coming down to the year 1731. There can be no fufficient reafon, that what has thus been fubmitted to the perufal of Europe, fhould not be made acceffible to thofe to whom Dr. Franklin's language is native. The hiftory of his life, as far as page 149 of the prefent volume, is tranflated from that publication.

The

The ſtyle of theſe memoirs is uncommonly pleaſing.
The ſtory is told with the moſt unreſerved ſincerity, and
without any falſe colouring or ornament. We ſee, in
every page, that the author examined his ſubject with
the eye of a maſter, and related no incidents, the ſprings
and origin of which he did not perfectly underſtand.
It is this that gives ſuch exquiſite and uncommon perſpicuity to the detail and delight in the review. The
tranſlator has endeavoured, as he went along, to conceive the probable manner in which Dr. Franklin expreſſed his ideas in his Engliſh manuſcript, and he hopes
to be forgiven if this enquiry ſhall occaſionally have ſubjected him to the charge of a ſtyle in any reſpect bald or
low: to imitate the admirable ſimplicity of the author,
is no eaſy taſk.

The Eſſays, which are now, for the firſt time, brought
together from various reſources, will be found to be
more miſcellaneous than any of Dr. Franklin's that have
formerly been collected, and will therefore be more generally amuſing. Dr. Franklin tells us, in his Life,
that he was an aſſiduous imitator of Addiſon, and from
ſome of theſe papers it will be admitted that he was not
an unhappy one. The public will be amuſed with following a great philoſopher in his relaxations, and ob-
ſerving in what reſpects philoſophy tends to elucidate
and improve the moſt common ſubjects. The editor
has purpoſely avoided ſuch papers as, by their ſcienti-
fical nature, were leſs adapted for general peruſal.
Theſe he may probably hereafter publiſh in a volume
by themſelves.

He

He subjoins a letter from the late celebrated and amiable Dr. Price, to a gentleman in Philadelphia, upon the subject of Dr. Franklin's memoirs of his own life.

" Hackney, June 19, 1790.

" DEAR SIR,

" I am hardly able to tell you how kindly I take the letters with which you favour me. Your last, containing an account of the death of our excellent friend Dr. Franklin, and the circumstances attending it, deserves my particular gratitude. The account which he has left of his life will show, in a striking example, how a man, by talents, industry, and integrity, may rise from obscurity to the first eminence and consequence in the world; but it brings his history no lower than the year 1757, and I understand that since he sent over the copy, which I have read, he has been able to make no additions to it. It is with a melancholy regret I think of his death; but to death we are all bound by the irreversible order of nature, and in looking forward to it, there is comfort in being able to reflect—that we have not lived in vain, and that all the useful and virtuous shall meet in a better country beyond the grave.

" Dr. Franklin, in the last letter I received from him, after mentioning his age and infirmities, observes, that it has been kindly ordered by the Author of nature, that, as we draw nearer the conclusion of life, we are furnished with more helps to wean us from it, among which one of the strongest is the loss of dear friends. I was delighted with the account you gave in your letter of the honour shewn to his memory at Philadelphia, and

by

by Congrefs; and yefterday I received a high additional
pleafure, by being informed that the National Affembly
of France had determined to go into mourning for him.
—What a glorious fcene is opened there! The annals
of the world furnifh no parallel to it. One of the ho-
nours of our departed friend is, that he has contributed
much to it.

> " I am, with great refpect,
>
> Your obliged and very
>
> humble fervant,
>
> RICHARD PRICE."

                       New

CONTENTS.

LIFE

OF

DOCTOR BENJAMIN FRANKLIN, &c.

MY DEAR SON,

I HAVE amufed myfelf with collecting fome little anecdotes of my family. You may remember the enquiries I made, when you were with me in England, among fuch of my relations as were then living; and the journey I undertook for that purpofe. To be acquainted with the particulars of my parentage and life, many of which are unknown to you, I flatter myfelf, will afford the fame pleafure to you as to me. I fhall relate them upon paper: it will be an agreeable employment of a week's uninterrupted leifure, which I promife myfelf during my prefent retirement in the country. There are alfo other motives which induce me to the undertaking. From the bofom of poverty and obfcurity, in which I drew my firft breath and fpent my earlieft years, I have raifed myfelf to a ftate of opulence and to fome degree of celebrity in

B

the

the world. A conftant good fortune has attended me through every period of life to my
prefent advanced age; and my defcendants may
be defirous of learning what were the means of
which I made ufe, and which, thanks to the
affifting hand of Providence, have proved fo
eminently fuccefsful. They may alfo, fhould
they ever be placed in a fimilar fituation, derive
fome advantage from my narrative.

When I refleĉt, as I frequently do, upon the
felicity I have enjoyed, I fometimes fay to myfelf, that, were the offer made me, I would engage to run again, from beginning to end, the
fame career of life. All I would afk fhould be
the privilege of an author, to correĉt, in a fecond
edition, certain errors of the firft. I could wifh,
likewife, if it were in my power, to change fome
trivial incidents and events for others more favourable. Were this however denied me, ftill
would I not decline the offer. But fince a repetition of life cannot take place, there is nothing
which, in my opinion, fo nearly refembles it, as
to call to mind all its circumftances, and, to render their remembrance more durable, commit
them to writing. By thus employing myfelf,
I fhall yield to the inclination, fo natural in old
men, to talk of themfelves and their exploits,
and may freely follow my bent, without being
tirefome to thofe who, from refpeĉt to my age,
might think themfelves obliged to liften to me ;
as they will be at liberty to read me or not as they
pleafe. In fine—and I may as well avow it, fince
nobody would believe me were I to deny it—I
fhall perhaps, by this employment, gratify my
vanity. Scarcely indeed have I ever heard or
read the introduĉtory phrafe, " *I may fay without
vanity,*" but fome ftriking and charaĉteriftic inftance of vanity has immediately followed. The
                                        generality

generality of men hate vanity in others, however
ftrongly they may be tinctured with it themfelves: for myfelf, I pay obeifance to it where-
ever I meet with it, perfuaded that it is advantageous, as well to the individual whom it governs,
as to thofe who are within the fphere of its influence. Of confequence, it would in many cafes,
not be wholly abfurd, that a man fhould count
his vanity among the other fweets of life, and
give thanks to Providence for the bleffing.

And here let me with all humility acknowledge, that to Divine Providence I am indebted
for the felicity I have hitherto enjoyed. It is
that Power alone which has furnifhed me with
the means I have employed, and that has crowned them with fuceefs. My faith in this refpect
leads me to hope, though I cannot count upon it,
that the divine goodnefs will ftill be exercifed
towards me, either by prolonging the duration
of my happinefs to the clofe of life, or by giving me fortitude to fupport any melancholy reverfe, which may happen to me, as to fo many
others. My future fortune is unknown but to
him in whofe hand is our deftiny, and who can
make our very afflictions fubfervient to our benefit.

One of my uncles, defirous, like myfelf, of
collecting anecdotes of our family, gave me fome
notes, from which I have derived many particulars
refpecting our anceftors. From thefe I learn,
that they had lived in the fame village (Eaton in
Northamptonfhire), upon a freehold of about
thirty acres, for the fpace at leaft of three hundred years. How long they had refided there
prior to that period, my uncle had been unable
to difcover; probably ever fince the inftitution
of furnames, when they took the appellation of

Franklin,

Franklin, which had formerly been the name of a particular order of individuals*

This petty estate would not have sufficed for their subsistence, had they not added the trade of blacksmith, which was perpetuated in the family down to my uncle's time, the eldest son having been uniformly brought up to this employment: a custom which both he and my father observed with respect to their eldest sons.

In the researches I made at Eaton, I found no account of their births, marriages, and deaths, earlier than the year 1555; the parish register not extending farther back than that period.

* As a proof that Franklin was anciently the common name of an order or rank in England, see Judge Fortescue, *De laudibus legum Angliæ*, written about the year 1412, in which is the following passage, to shew that good juries might easily be formed in any part of England:

" Regio etiam illa, ita resperfa refertaque est *possessoribus*
" *terrarum* et agrorum, quod in ea, villula tam parva reperiri
" non poterit, in qua non est *miles*, *armiger*, vel pater-familias,
" qualis ibidem *franklin* vulgariter nuncupatur, magnis di-
" tatus possessionibus, nec non libere tenentes et alii *valecti*
" plurimi, suis patrimoniis sufficientes, ad faciendum jura-
" tum, in forma prænotata."

" Moreover the fame country is fo filled and replenished
" with landed menne, that therein fo fmall a thorpe cannot
" be found wherein dwelleth not a knight, an efquire, or fuch
" a houfeholder as is there commonly called a *franklin*, en-
" riched with great poffeffions; and alfo other freeholders
" and many yeomen, able for their livelihoodes to make a jury
" in form aforementioned."

Old Translation.

Chaucer too calls his country gentleman a *franklin*, and after describing his good housekeeping, thus characterises him:

This worthy franklin bore a purfe of filk,
Fix'd to his girdle, white as morning milk.
Knight of the fhire, firft juftice at th' affize,
To help the poor, the doubtful to advife.
In all employments, generous, juft he prov'd,
Renown'd for courtefy, by all belov'd.

This

This regifter informed me, that I was the youngeft fon of the youngeft branch of the family,
counting five generations. My grandfather,
Thomas, who was born in 1598, lived at Eaton
till he was too old to continue his trade, when
he retired to Banbury in Oxfordfhire, where his
fon John who was a dyer, refided, and with
whom my father was apprenticed. He died, and
was buried there : we faw his monument in 1758.
His eldeft fon lived in the family houfe at Eaton,
which he bequeathed, with the land belonging to
it, to his only daughter; who, in concert with
her hufband, Mr. Fifher of Wellinborough, afterwards fold it to Mr. Efted, the prefent proprietor.

My grandfather had four furviving fons, Thomas, John, Benjamin, and Jofias. I fhall give
you fuch particulars of them as my memory will
furnifh, not having my papers here, in which
you will find a more minute account, if they are
not loft during my abfence.

Thomas had learned the trade of blackfmith
under his father; but poffeffing a good natural
underftanding, he improved it by ftudy, at the
folicitation of a gentleman of the name of Palmer,
who was at that time the principal inhabitant of
the village, and who encouraged in like manner
all my uncles to cultivate their minds. Thomas
thus rendered himfelf competent to the functions
of a country attorney; foon became an effential
perfonage in the affairs of the village; and was
one of the chief movers of every public enterprize, as well relative to the county as the town
of Northampton. A variety of remarkable incidents were told us of him at Eaton. After enjoying the efteem and patronage of lord Halifax,
he died, January 6, 1702, precifely four years
before I was born. The recital that was made us
of his life and character, by fome aged perfons

of

of the village, ftruck you, I remember. as extraordinary, from its analogy to what you knew
of myfelf. "Had he died," faid you, "juft
"four years later, one might have fuppofed a
"tranfmigration of fouls."

John, to the beft of my belief, was brought
up to the trade of a wool-dyer.

Benjamin ferved his apprenticefhip in London
to a filk-dyer. He was an induftrious man: I
remember him well; for, while I was a child, he
joined my father at Bofton, and lived for fome
years in the houfe with us. A particular affection had always fubfifted between my father and
him; and I was his godfon. He arrived to a
great age. He left behind him two quarto volumes of poems in manufcript, confifting of little fugitive pieces addreffed to his friends. He
had invented a fhort-hand, which he taught me,
but having never made ufe of it, I have now
forgotten it. He was a man of piety, and a conftant attendant on the beft preachers, whofe fermons he took a pleafure in writing down according to the expeditory method he had devifed.
Many volumes were thus collected by him. He
was alfo extremely fond of politics, too much fo
perhaps for his fituation. I lately found in London a collection which he had made of all the
principal pamphlets relative to public affairs, from
the year 1641 to 1717. Many volumes are
wanting, as appears by the feries of numbers;
but there ftill remain eight in folio, and twenty-
four in quarto and octavo. The collection had
fallen into the hands of a fecond-hand bookfeller,
who, knowing me by having fold me fome books,
brought it to me. My uncle, it feems, had left
it behind him on his departure for America, a-
bout fifty years ago. I found various notes of
his writing in the margins. His grandfon, Samuel, is now living at Bofton.

Our

Our humble family had early embraced the Reformation. Theyremained faithfully attached during the reign of Queen Mary, when they were in danger of being molefted on account of their zeal againft popery. They had an Englifh Bible, and, to conceal it the more fecurely, they conceived the project of faftening it, open, with packthreads acrofs the leaves, on the infide of the lid of a clofe-ftool. When my great-grandfather wifhed to read to his family, he reverfed the lid of the clofe-ftool upon his knees, and paffed the leaves from one fide to the other, which were held down on each by the packthread. One of the children was ftationed at the door, to give notice if he faw the proctor (an officer of the fpiritual court) make his appearance: in that cafe, the lid was reftored to its place, with the Bible concealed under it as before. I had this anecdote from my uncle Benjamin.

The whole family preferved its attachment to the Church of England till towards the clofe of the reign of Charles II. when certain minifters, who had been ejected as nonconformifts, having held conventicles in Northamptonfhire, they were joined by Benjamin and Jofias, who adhered to them ever after. The reft of the family continued in the epifcopal church.

My father, Jofias, married early in life. He went, with his wife and three children, to New England, about the year 1682. Conventicles being at that time prohibited by law, and frequently difturbed, fome confiderable perfons of his acquaintance determined to go to America, where they hoped to enjoy the free exercife of their religion, and my father was prevailed on to accompany them.

My father had alfo by the fame wife four children born in America, and ten others by a fecond

cond wife, making in all feventeen. I remember to have feen thirteen feated together at his
table, who all arrived to years of maturity, and
were married. I was the laft of the fons, and
the youngeft child, excepting two daughters.
I was born at Bofton in new England. My mother, the fecond wife, was Abiah Folger, daughter of Peter Folger, one of the firft colonifts of
New England, of whom Cotton Mather makes
honourable mention, in his Ecclefiaftical Hiftory
of that province, as " *a pious and learned Englifh-
man,*" if I rightly recollect his expreffions. I
have been told of his having written a variety of
little pieces; but there appears to be only one in
print, which I met with many years ago. It
was publifhed in the year 1675, and is in familiar
verfe, agreeably to the tafte of the times and
the country. The author addreffes himfelf to the
governors for the time being, fpeaks for liberty
of confcience, and in favour of the anabaptifts,
quakers, and other fectaries, who had fuffered
perfecution. To this perfecution he attributes
the wars with the natives, and other calamities
which afflicted the country, regarding them as
the judgments of God in punifhment of fo odious an offence, and he exhorts the government
to the repeal of laws fo contrary to charity. The
poem appeared to be written with a manly freedom and a pleafing fimplicity. I recollect the fix
concluding lines, though I have forgotten the
order of words of the two firft; the fenfe of
which was, that his cenfures were dictated by
benevolence, and that, of confequence, he wifhed to be known as the author; becaufe, faid he,
I hate from my very foul diffimulation:

From Sherburne *, where I dwell,
   I therefore put my name,
Your friend, who means you well,
              PETER FOLGER.

* Town in the Ifland of Nantucket.

My

My brothers were all put apprentice to different trades. With refpect to myfelf, I was fent, at the age of eight years, to a grammar fchool. My father deftined me for the church, and already regarded me as the chaplain of the family. The promptitude with which from my infancy I had learned to read, for I do not remember to have been ever without this acquirement, and the encouragement of his friends, who affured him that I fhould one day certainly become a man of letters, confirmed him in this defign. My uncle Benjamin approved alfo of the fcheme, and promifed to give me all his volumes of fermons, written, as I have faid, in the fhort-hand of his invention, if I would take the pains to learn it.

I remained however fcarcely a year at the grammar fchool, although, in this fhort interval, I had rifen from the middle to the head of my clafs, from thence to the clafs immediately above, and was to pafs, at the end of the year, to the one next in order. But my father, burthened with a numerous family, found that he was incapable, without fubjecting himfelf to difficulties, of providing for the expence of a collegiate education; and confidering befides, as I heard him fay to his friends, that perfons fo educated were often poorly provided for, he renounced his firft intentions, took me from the grammar fchool, and fent me to a fchool for writing and arithmetic, kept by a Mr. George Brownwel, who was a fkilful mafter, and fucceeded very well in his profeffion by employing gentle means only, and fuch as were calculated to encourage his fcholars. Under him I foon acquired an excellent hand; but I failed in arithmetic, and made therein no fort of progrefs.

At

At ten years of age, I was called home to affift my father in his occupation, which was that of foap-boiler and tallow-chandler; a bufinefs to which he had ferved no apprenticefhip, but which he embraced on his arrival in New England, becaufe he found his own, that of a dyer, in too little requeft to enable him to maintain his family. I was accordingly employed in cutting the wicks, filling the moulds, taking care of the fhop, carrying meffages, &c.

This bufinefs difpleafed me, and I felt a ftrong inclination for a fea life; but my father fet his face againft it. The vicinity of the water, however, gave me frequent opportunities of venturing myfelf both upon and within it, and I foon acquired the art of fwimming, and of managing a boat. When embarked with other children, the helm was commonly deputed to me, particularly on difficult occafions; and, in every other project, I was almoft always the leader of the troop, whom I fometimes involved in embarraffments. I fhall give an inftance of this, which demonftrates an early difpofition of mind for public enterprifes, though the one in queftion was not conducted by juftice.

The mill-pond was terminated on one fide by a marfh, upon the borders of which we were accuftomed to take our ftand, at high water, to angle for fmall fifh. By dint of walking, we had converted the place into a perfect quagmire. My propofal was to erect a wharf that fhould afford us firm footing; and I pointed out to my companions a large heap of ftones, intended for the building a new houfe near the marfh, and which were well adapted for our purpofe. Accordingly, when the workmen retired in the evening, I affembled a number of my playfellows, and by labouring diligently, like ants, fometimes

four

four of us uniting our ftrength to carry a fingle
ftone, we removed them all, and conftructed our
little quay. The workmen were furprifed the
next morning at not finding their ftones, which
had been conveyed to our wharf. Enquiries were
made refpecting the authors of this conveyance;
we were difcovered; complaints were exhibited
againft us; many of us underwent correction on
the part of our parents; and though I ftrenuoufly defended the utility of the work, my father
at length convinced me, that nothing which was
not ftrictly honeft could be ufeful.

It will not, perhaps, be uninterefting to you
to know what fort of a man my father was. He
had an excellent conftitution, was of a middle
fize, but well made and ftrong, and extremely
active in whatever he undertook. He defigned
with a degree of neatnefs, and knew a little of
mufic. His voice was fonorous and agreeable;
fo that when he fung a pfalm or hymn, with the
accompaniment of his violin, as was his frequent
practice in an evening, when the labours of the
day were finifhed, it was truly delightful to hear
him. He was verfed alfo in mechanics, and could,
upon occafion, ufe the tools of a variety of trades.
But his greateft excellence was a found underftanding and folid judgment, in matters of prudence, both in public and private life. In the
former indeed he never engaged, becaufe his
numerous family, and the mediocrity of his
fortune, kept him unremittingly employed in
the duties of his profeffion. But I very well
remember, that the leading men of the place
ufed frequently to come and afk his advice refpecting affairs of the town, or of the church to
which he belonged, and that they paid much de-
ference to his opinion. Individuals were alfo in
the

the habit of confulting him in their private affairs, and he was often chofen arbiter between contending parties.

He was fond of having at his table, as often as poffible, fome friends or well-informed neighbours capable of rational converfation, and he was always careful to introduce ufeful or ingenious topics of difcourfe, which might tend to form the minds of his children. By this means he early attracted our attention to what was juft, prudent, and beneficial in the conduct of life. He never talked of the meats which appeared upon the table, never difcuffed whether they were well or ill dreffed, of a good or bad flavour, high-feafoned or otherwife, preferable or inferior to this or that difh of a fimilar kind. Thus accuftomed, from my infancy, to the utmoft inattention as to thefe objects, I have always been perfectly regardlefs of what kind of food was before me; and I pay fo little attention to it even now, that it would be a hard matter for me to recollect, a few hours after I had dined, of what my dinner had confifted. When travelling, I have particularly experienced the advantage of this habit; for it has often happened to me to be in company with perfons, who, having a more delicate, becaufe a more exercifed tafte, have fuffered in many cafes confiderable inconvenience; while, as to myfelf, I have had nothing to defire.

My mother was likewife poffeffed of an excellent conftitution. She fuckled all her ten children, and I never heard either her or my father complain of any other diforder than that of which they died: my father at the age of eighty-feven, and my mother at eighty-five. They are buried together at Bofton, where, a few years ago, I placed a marble over their grave, with this infcription:

" Here

" Here lie
" JOSIAS FRANKLIN and ABIAH his wife : They
" lived together with reciprocal affection for fifty-
" nine years ; and without private fortune, with-
" out lucrative employment, by affiduous labour
" and honeft induftry, decently fupported a nu-
" merous family, and educated, with fuccefs,
" thirteen children, and feven grand-children.
" Let this example, reader, encourage thee dili-
" gently to difcharge the duties of thy calling,
" and to rely on the fupport of Divine Provi-
" dence.
" He was pious and prudent,
" She difcreet and virtuous.
" Their youngeft fon, from a fentiment of filial
" duty, confecrates this ftone
" To their memory."

I perceive, by my rambling digreffions, that I
am growing old. But we do not drefs for a
private company as for a formal ball. This de-
ferves perhaps the name of negligence.

To return. I thus continued employed in my
father's trade for the fpace of two years ; that is
to fay, till I arrived at twelve years of age.
About this time my brother John, who had ferved his apprenticefhip in London, having quitted
my father, and being married and fettled in bufinefs on his own account at Rhode Ifland, I was
deftined, to all appearance, to fupply his place,
and be a candle-maker all my life : but my diflike
of this occupation continuing, my father was
apprehenfive, that, if a more agreeable one were
not offered me, I might play the truant and efcape to fea ; as, to his extreme mortification, my
brother Jofias had done. He therefore took me
fometimes to fee mafons, coopers, braziers, join-
ers, and other mechanics, employed at their
work ;

work; in order to difcover the bent of my inclination, and fix it if he could upon fome occupation that might retain me on fhore. I have
fince, in confequence of thefe vifits, derived no
fmall pleafure from feeing fkilful workmen handle
their tools; and it has proved of confiderable
benefit, to have acquired thereby fufficient knowledge to be able to make little things for myfelf,
when I have had no mechanic at hand, and to
conftruct fmall machines for my experiments,
while the idea I have conceived has been frefh
and ftrongly impreffed on my imagination.

My father at length decided that I fhould be a
cutler, and I was placed for fome days upon trial
with my coufin Samuel, fon of my uncle Benjamin, who had learned this trade in London, and
had eftablifhed himfelf at Bofton. But the pre-
mium he required for my apprenticefhip difplea-
fing my father, I was recalled home.

From my earlieft years I had been paffionately
fond of reading, and I laid out in books all the
little money I could procure. I was particularly
pleafed with accounts of voyages. My firft acquifition was Bunyan's collection in fmall feparate volumes. Thefe I afterwards fold in order to
buy an hiftorical collection by R. Burton, which
confifted of fmall cheap volumes, amounting in
all to about forty or fifty. My father's little library was principally made up of books of practical and polemical theology. I read the greateft
part of them. I have fince often regretted, that
at a time when I had fo great a thirft for knowledge, more eligible books had not fallen into my
hands, as it was then a point decided that I fhould
not be educated for the church. There was alfo
among my father's books Plutarch's Lives, in
which I read continually, and I ftill regard as
advantageoufly employed the time I devoted to
them.

them. I found befides a work of De Foe's, entitled, an Effay on Projects, from which, perhaps, I derived impreffions that have fince influenced fome of the principal events of my life.

My inclination for books at laft determined my father to make me a printer, though he had already a fon in that profeffion. My brother had returned from England in 1717, with a prefs and types, in order to eftablifh a printing-houfe at Bofton. This bufinefs pleafed me much better than that of my father, though I had ftill a predilection for the fea. To prevent the effects which might refult from this inclination, my father was impatient to fee me engaged with my brother. I held back for fome time; at length however I fuffered myfelf to be perfuaded, and figned my indentures, being then only twelve years of age. It was agreed that I fhould ferve as apprentice to the age of twenty-one, and fhould receive journeyman's wages only during the laft year.

In a very fhort time I made great proficiency in this bufinefs, and became very ferviceable to my brother. I had now an opportunity of procuring better books. The acquaintance I neceffarily formed with bookfellers' apprentices, enabled me to borrow a volume now and then, which I never failed to return punctually and without injury. How often has it happened to me to pafs the greater part of the night in reading by my bed-fide, when the book had been lent me in the evening, and was to be returned the next morning, left it might be miffed or wanted!

At length, Mr. Matthew Adams, an ingenious tradefman, who had a handfome collection of books, and who frequented our printing-houfe, took notice of me. He invited me to fee his library,

brary, and had the goodnefs to lend me any books I was defirous of reading. I then took a ftrange fancy for poetry, and compofed feveral little pieces. My brother, thinking he might find his account in it, encouraged me, and engaged me to write two ballads. One, called the Lighthoufe Tragedy, contained an account of the fhipwreck of captain Worthilake and his two daughters; the other was a failor's fong on the capture of the noted pirate called *Teach*, or *Black-beard*. They were wretched verfes in point of ftyle, mere blind-men's ditties. When printed, he difpatched me about the town to fell them. The firft had a prodigious run, becaufe the event was recent, and had made a great noife.

My vanity was flattered by this fuccefs; but my father checked my exultation, by ridiculing my productions, and telling me that verfifiers were always poor. I thus efcaped the misfortune of being, probably, a very wretched poet. But as the faculty of writing profe has been of great fervice to me in the courfe of my life, and principally contributed to my advancement, I fhall relate by what means, fituated as I was, I acquired the fmall fkill I may poffefs in that way.

There was in the town another young man, a great lover of books, of the name of John Collins, with whom I was intimately connected. We frequently engaged in difpute, and were indeed fond of argumentation, that nothing was fo agreeable to us as a war of words. This contentious temper, I would obferve by the by, is in danger of becoming a very bad habit, and frequently renders a man's company infupportable, as being no otherwife capable of indulgence than by indifcriminate contradiction. Independently of the acrimony and difcord it introduces into converfation, it is often productive of diflike, and

and even hatred, between perſons to whom friendſhip is indiſpenſably neceſſary.   I acquired it by
reading, while I lived with my father, books of
religious controverſy. I have ſince remarked,
that men of ſenſe ſeldom fall into this error;
lawyers, fellows of univerſities, and perſons of
every profeſſion educated at Edinburgh, excepted.

Collins and I fell one day into an argument
relative to the education of women; namely,
whether it were proper to inſtruct them in the
ſciences, and whether they were competent to
the ſtudy.   Collins ſupported the negative, and
affirmed that the taſk was beyond their capacity.
I maintained the oppoſite opinion, a little perhaps for the pleaſure of diſputing. He was naturally more eloquent than I; words flowed co-
piouſly from his lips; and frequently I thought
myſelf vanquiſhed, more by his volubility than
by the force of his arguments. We ſeparated
without coming to an agreement upon this point;
and as we were not to ſee each other again for
ſome time, I committed my thoughts to paper,
made a fair copy, and ſent it him.   He anſwer-
ed, and I replied.   Three or four letters had been
written by each, when my father chanced to
light upon my papers and read them.   Without
entering into the merits of the cauſe, he embraced the opportunity of ſpeaking to me upon my
manner of writing.   He obſerved, that though I
had the advantage of my adverſary in correct
ſpelling and pointing, which I owed to my occupation, I was greatly his inferior in elegance
of expreſſion, in arrangement, and perſpicuity.
Of this he convinced me by ſeveral examples.
I felt the juſtice of his remarks, became more
attentive to language, and reſolved to make every effort to improve my ſtyle.   Amidſt theſe

C   refolves

refolves an odd volume of the Spectator fell into my hands. This was a publication I had never feen. I bought the volume, and read it again and again. I was enchanted with it, thought the ftyle excellent, and wifhed it were in my power to imitate it. With this view I felected fome of the papers, made fhort fummaries of the fenfe of each period, and put them for a few days afide. I then, without looking at the book, endeavoured to reftore the effays to their true form, and to exprefs each thought at length, as it was in the original, employing the moft appropriate words that occurred to my mind. I afterwards compared my Spectator with the original; I perceived fome faults, which I corrected: but I found that I wanted a fund of words, if I may fo exprefs myfelf, and a facility of recollecting and employing them, which I thought I fhould by that time have acquired, had I continued to make verfes. The continual need of words of the fame meaning, but of different lengths for the meafure, or of different founds for the rhyme, would have obliged me to feek for a variety of fynonymes, and have rendered me mafter of them. From this belief, I took fome of the tales of the Spectator and turned them into verfe; and after a time, when I had fufficiently forgotten them, I again converted them into profe.

Sometimes alfo I mingled all my fummaries together; and a few weeks after, endeavoured to arrange them in the beft order, before I attempted to form the periods and complete the effays. This I did with a view of acquiring method in the arrangement of my thoughts. On comparing afterwards my performance with the original, many faults were apparent, which I corrected; but I had fometimes the fatisfaction to

think,

think, that, in certain particulars of little importance, I had been fortunate enough to improve the order of thought or the ſtyle: and this encouraged me to hope that I ſhould ſucceed, in time, in writing decently in the Engliſh language, which was one of the great objects of my ambition.

The time which I devoted to theſe exerciſes, and to reading, was the evening after my day's labour was finiſhed, the morning before it began, and Sundays when I could eſcape attending divine ſervice. While I lived with my father, he had inſiſted on my punctual attendance on public worſhip, and I ſtill indeed conſidered it as a duty; but a duty which I thought I had no time to practiſe.

When about ſixteen years of age, a work of Tryon fell into my hands, in which he recommends vegetable diet. I determined to obſerve it. My brother, being a batchelor, did not keep houſe, but boarded with his apprentices in a neighbouring family. My refuſing to eat animal food was found inconvenient, and I was often ſcolded for my ſingularity. I attended to the mode in which Tryon prepared ſome of his diſhes, particularly how to boil potatoes and rice, and make haſty puddings. I then ſaid to my brother, that if he would allow me per week half what he paid for my board, I would undertake to maintain myſelf. The offer was inſtantly embraced, and I ſoon found that of what he gave me I was able to ſave half. This was a new fund for the purchaſe of books; and other advantages reſulted to me from the plan. When my brother and his workmen left the printing-houſe to go to dinner, I remained behind; and diſpatching my frugal meal, which frequently conſiſted of a biſcuit only, or a ſlice of bread and

C 2

a bunch

a bunch of raisins, or a bun from the pastrycook's, with a glass of water, I had the rest of the time, till their return, for study; and my progress therein was proportioned to that clearness of ideas, and quickness of conception, which are the fruit of temperance in eating and drinking.

It was about this period that, having one day been put to the blush for my ignorance in the art of calculation, which I had twice failed to learn while at school, I took Cocker's Treatise of Arithmetic, and went through it by myself with the utmost ease. I also read a book of Navigation by Seller and Sturmy, and made myself master of the little geometry it contains, but I never proceeded far in this science. Nearly at the same time I read Locke on the Human Understanding, and the Art of Thinking by Messrs. du Port Royal.

While labouring to form and improve my style, I met with an English Grammar, which I believe was Greenwood's, having at the end of it two little essays on rhetoric and logic. In the latter I found a model of disputation after the manner of Socrates. Shortly after I procured Xenophon's work, entitled, Memorable Things of Socrates, in which are various examples of the same method. Charmed to a degree of enthusiasm with this mode of disputing, I adopted it, and renouncing blunt contradiction, and direct and positive argument, I assumed the character of a humble questioner. The perusal of Shaftsbury and Collins had made me a sceptic; and being previously so as to many doctrines of Christianity, I found Socrates's method to be both the safest for myself, as well as the most embarrassing to those against whom I employed it. It soon afforded me singular pleasure; I incessantly practised it; and became very adroit in obtaining, even from persons of superior understanding, concessions of

which

which they did not forefee the confequences.
Thus I involved them in difficulties from which
they were unable to extricate themfelves, and
fometimes obtained victories, which neither my
caufe nor my arguments merited.

This method I continued to employ for fome
years; but I afterwards abandoned it by degrees,
retaining only the habit of exprefling myfelf
with modeft diffidence, and never making ufe,
when I advanced any propofition which might
be controverted, of the words *certainly*, *undoubtedly*, or any others that might give the appearance of being obftinately attached to my opinion.
I rather faid, I imagine, I fuppofe, or it appears to
me, that fuch a thing is fo or fo, for fuch and fuch
reafons; or it is fo, if I am not miftaken. This
habit has, I think, been of confiderable advantage to me, when I have had occafion to imprefs
my opinion on the minds of others, and perfuade
them to the adoption of the meafures I have fuggefted. And fince the chief ends of converfation
are, to inform or to be informed, to pleafe or to
perfuade, I could wifh that intelligent and well-
meaning men would not themfelves diminifh the
power they poffefs of being ufeful, by a pofitive
and prefumptuous manner of exprefling themfelves, which fcarcely ever fails to difguft the
hearer, and is only calculated to excite oppofition, and defeat every purpofe for which the faculty of fpeech has been beftowed upon man.
In fhort, if you wifh to inform, a pofitive and
dogmatical manner of advancing your opinion
may provoke contradiction, and prevent your
being heard with attention. On the other hand, if
with a defire of being informed, and of benefiting
by the knowledge of others, you exprefs yourfelf
as being ftrongly attached to your own opinions,
modeft

modeſt and ſenſible men, who do not love diſ-
putation, will leave you in tranquil poſſeſſion of
your errors.   By following ſuch a method, you
can rarely hope to pleaſe your auditors, concili-
ate their good-will, or work conviction on thoſe
whom you may be deſirous of gaining over to
your views.   Pope judiciouſly obſerves,

> Men muſt be taught as if you taught them not,
> And things unknown propos'd as things forgot.

And in the ſame poem he afterwards advices us,

> To ſpeak, though ſure, with ſeeming diffidence.

He might have added to theſe lines, one that he
has coupled elſewhere, in my opinion, with leſs
propriety.   It is this:

> For want of decency is want of ſenſe.

If you aſk why I ſay with *leſs propriety*, I muſt
give you the two lines together:

> Immodeſt words admit of *no defence*,
> For want of decency is want of ſenſe.

Now want of ſenſe, when a man has the misfortune to be ſo circumſtanced, is it not a kind of
excuſe for want of modeſty? And would not the
verſes have been more accurate, if they had been
conſtructed thus:

> Immodeſt words admit *but this defence*,
> That want of decency is want of ſenſe.

But I leave the deciſion of this to better judges
than myſelf.

    In 1720, or 1721, my brother began to print
a new public paper. It was the ſecond that made
its appearance in America, and was entitled the
New-England Courant. The only one that exiſted before was the *Boſton News Letter.* Some of
his friends, I remember, would have diſſuaded
                                            him

him from this undertaking, as a thing that was
not likely to fucceed ; a fingle newfpaper being,
in their opinion, fufficient for all America.   At
prefent, however, in 1771, there are no lefs than
twenty-five.   But he carried his project into execution, and I was employed in diftributing the
copies to his cuftomers, after having affifted in
compofing and working them off.

Among his friends he had a number of literary characters, who, as an amufement, wrote
fhort effays for the paper, which gave it reputation and increafed its fale.   Thefe gentlemen
frequently came to our houfe.   I heard the converfation that paffed, and the accounts they gave
of the favourable reception of their writings with
the public.   I was tempted to try my hand a-
mong them ; but, being ftill a child as it were,
I was fearful that my brother might be unwilling
to print in his paper any performance of which
he fhould know me to be the author.   I therefore contrived to difguife my hand, and having
written an anonymous piece, I placed it at night
under the door of the printing-houfe, where it
was found the next morning.   My brother communicated it to his friends, when they came as
ufual to fee him, who read it, commented upon it within my hearing, and I had the exquifite
pleafure to find that it met with their approbation, and that, in the various conjectures they
made refpecting the author, no one was mentioned who did not enjoy a high reputation in the
country for talents and genius.   I now fuppofed
myfelf fortunate in my judges, and began to fufpect that they were not fuch excellent writers as
I had hitherto fuppofed them.   Be that as it may,
encouraged by this little adventure, I wrote and
fent to the prefs, in the fame way, many other
pieces, which were equally approved ; keeping
the

the fecret till my flender ftock of information and knowledge for fuch performances was pretty completely exhaufted, when I made myfelf known.

My brother, upon this difcovery, began to entertain a little more refpeẗ for me; but he ftill regarded himfelf as my mafter, and treated me like an apprentice. He thought himfelf entitled to the fame fervices from me as from any other perfon. On the contrary, I conceived that, in many inftances, he was too rigorous, and that, on the part of a brother, I had a right to expeẗ indulgence. Our difputes were frequently brought before my father; and either my brother was generally in the wrong, or I was the better pleader of the two, for judgment was commonly given in my favour. But my brother was paffionate, and often had recourfe to blows; a circumftance which I took in very ill part. This fevere and tyrannical treatment contributed, I believe, to imprint on my mind that averfion to arbitrary power, which during my whole life I have ever preferved. My apprenticefhip became infupportable to me, and I continually fighed for an opportunity of fhortening it, which at length unexpeẗedly offered.

An article inferted in our paper, upon fome political fubjeẗ which I have now forgotten, gave offence to the Affembly. My brother was taken into cuftody, cenfured, and ordered into confinement for a month, becaufe, as I prefume, he would not difcover the author. I was alfo taken up, and examined before the council; but, though I gave them no fatisfaẗion, they contented themfelves with reprimanding, and then difmiffed me; confidering me probably as bound, in quality of apprentice, to keep my mafter's fecrets.

The

The imprifonment of my brother kindled my refentment, notwithftanding our private quarrels. During its continuance the management of the paper was entrufted to me, and I was bold enough to infert fome pafquinades againft the governors; which highly pleafed my brother, while others began to look upon me in an unfavourable point of view, confidering me as a young wit inclined to fatire and lampoon.

My brother's enlargement was accompanied with an arbitrary order from the houfe of affembly, " That James Franklin fhould no longer " print the newfpaper entitled the *New-England* " *Courant*." In this conjuncture, we held a confultation of our friends at the printing-houfe, in order to determine what was proper to be done. Some propofed to evade the order, by changing the title of the paper : but my brother forefeeing inconveniences that would refult from this ftep, thought it better that it fhould in future be printed in the name of Benjamin Franklin ; and to avoid the cenfure of the affembly, who might charge him with ftill printing the paper himfelf, under the name of his apprentice, it was refolved that my old indentures fhould be given up to me, with a full and entire difcharge written on the back, in order to be produced upon an emergency; but that, to fecure to my brother the benefit of my fervice, I fhould fign a new contract, which fhould be kept fecret during the remainder of the term. This was a very fhallow arrangement. It was, however, carried into immediate execution, and the paper continued, in confequence, to make its appearance for fome months in my name. At length a new difference arifing between my brother and me, I ventured to take advantage of my liberty, prefuming that he would not dare to produce the new

contract.

contract. It was undoubtedly dishonourable to avail myself of this circumstance, and I reckon this action as one of the first errors of my life; but I was little capable of estimating it at its true value, embittered as my mind had been by the recollection of the blows I had received. Exclusively of his passionate treatment of me, my brother was by no means a man of an ill temper, and perhaps my manners had too much of impertinence not to afford it a very natural pretext.

When he knew that it was my determination to quit him, he wished to prevent my finding employment elsewhere. He went to all the printing-houses in the town, and prejudiced the masters against me; who accordingly refused to employ me. The idea then suggested itself to me of going to New-York, the nearest town in which there was a printing-office. Farther reflection confirmed me in the design of leaving Boston, where I had already rendered myself an object of suspicion to the governing party. It was probable, from the arbitrary proceedings of the Assembly in the affair of my brother, that, by remaining, I should soon have been exposed to difficulties, which I had the greater reason to apprehend, as, from my indiscreet disputes upon the subject of religion, I began to be regarded, by pious souls, with horror, either as an apostate or an atheist. I came therefore to a resolution; but my father, in this instance, siding with my brother, I presumed that if I attempted to depart openly, measures would be taken to prevent me. My friend Collins undertook to favour my flight. He agreed for my passage with the captain of a New-York sloop, to whom he represented me as a young man of his acquaintance, who had had an affair with a girl of bad character, whose parents wished to compel me to marry her, and

that

that of confequence I could neither make my appearance nor go off publicly. I fold part of my books to procure a fmall fum of money, and went privately on board the floop. By favour of a good wind, I found myfelf in three days at New-York, nearly three hundred miles from my home, at the age only of feventeen years, without knowing an individual in the place, and with very little money in my pocket.

The inclination I had felt for a fea-faring life was entirely fubfided, or I fhould now have been able to gratify it; but having another trade, and believing myfelf to be a tolerable workman, I hefitated not to offer my fervices to the old Mr. William Bradford, who had been the firft printer in Pennfylvania, but had quitted that province on account of a quarrel with George Keith, the governor. He could not give me employment himfelf, having little to do, and already as many perfons as he wanted; but he told me that his fon, printer at Philadelphia, had lately loft his principal workman, Aquila Rofe, who was dead, and that if I would go thither, he believed that he would engage me. Philadelphia was a hundred miles farther. I hefitated not to embark in a boat in order to repair, by the fhorteft cut of the fea, to Amboy, leaving my trunk and effects to come after me by the ufual and more tedious conveyance. In croffing the bay we met with a fquall, which fhattered to pieces our rotten fails, prevented us from entering the Kill, and threw us upon Long Ifland.

During the fquall a drunken Dutchman, who like myfelf was a paffenger in the boat, fell into the fea. At the moment that he was finking, I feized him by the fore-top, faved him, and drew him on board. This immerfion fobered him a little, fo that he fell afleep, after having taken
from

from his pocket a volume, which he requeſted me to dry. This volume I found to be my old favourite work, Bunyan's Voyages, in Dutch, a beautiful impreſſion on fine paper, with copper-plate engravings; a dreſs in which I had never ſeen it in its original language. I have ſince learned that it has been tranſlated into almoſt all the languages of Europe, and next to the Bible, I am perſuaded, it is one of the books which has had the greateſt ſpread. Honeſt John is the firſt, that I know of, who has mixed narrative and dialogue together; a mode of writing very engaging to the reader, who, in the moſt intereſting paſſages, finds himſelf admitted as it were into the company, and preſent at the converſation. De Foe has imitated it with ſucceſs in his Robinſon Cruſoe, his Moll Flanders, and other works; as alſo has Richardſon in his Pamela, &c.

In approaching the iſland, we found that we had made a part of the coaſt where it was not poſſible to land, on account of the ſtrong breakers produced by the rocky ſhore. We caſt anchor and veered the cable towards the ſhore. Some men, who ſtood upon the brink, hallooed to us, while we did the ſame on our part; but the wind was ſo high, and the waves ſo noiſy, that we could neither of us hear each other. There were ſome canoes upon the bank, and we called out to them, and made ſigns to prevail on them to come and take us up; but either they did not underſtand us, or they deemed our requeſt impracticable, and withdrew. Night came on, and nothing remained for us but to wait quietly the ſubſiding of the wind; till when we determined, that is, the pilot and I, to ſleep if poſſible. For that purpoſe we went below the hatches along with the Dutchman, who was drenched with water. The ſea broke over the boat, and reached

us

us in our retreat, so that we were presently as completely drenched as he.

We had very little repose during the whole night: but the wind abating the next day, we succeeded in reaching Amboy before it was dark, after having passed thirty hours without provisions, and with no other drink than a bottle of bad rum, the water upon which we rowed being salt. In the evening I went to bed with a very violent fever. I had somewhere read that cold water, drank plentifully, was a remedy in such cases. I followed the prescription, was in a profuse sweat for the greater part of the night, and the fever left me. The next day I crossed the river in a ferry-boat, and continued my journey on foot. I had fifty miles to walk, in order to reach Burlington, where I was told I should find passage-boats that would convey me to Philadelphia. It rained hard the whole day, so that I was wet to the skin. Finding myself fatigued about noon, I stopped at a paltry inn, where I passed the rest of the day and the whole night, beginning to regret that I had quitted my home. I made besides so wretched a figure, that I was suspected to be some runaway servant. This I discovered by the questions that were asked me; and I felt that I was every moment in danger of being taken up as such. The next day, however, I continued my journey, and arrived in the evening at an inn, eight or ten miles from Burlington, that was kept by one Dr. Brown.

This man entered into conversation with me while I took some refreshment, and perceiving that I had read a little, he expressed towards me considerable interest and friendship. Our acquaintance continued during the remainder of his life. I believe him to have been what is called an itinerant doctor; for there was no

town

town in England, or indeed in Europe, of which he could not give a particular account. He was neither deficient in underftanding or literature, but he was a fad infidel; and, fome years after, wickedly undertook to travefty the Bible in bur-lefque verfe; as Cotton has traveftied Virgil. He exhibited, by this means, many facts in a very ludicrous point of view, which would have gi-ven umbrage to weak minds, had his work been publifhed, which it never was.

I fpent the night at his houfe, and reached Burlington the next morning On my arrival, I had the mortification to learn that the ordinary paffage-boats had failed a little before. This was on a Saturday, and there would be no other boat till the Tuefday following. I returned to the houfe of an old woman in the town who had fold me fome ginger-bread to eat on my paffage, and I afked her advice. She invited me to take up my abode with her till an opportunity offered for me to embark. Fatigued with having travelled fo far on foot, I accepted her invitation. When fhe underftood that I was a printer, fhe would have perfuaded me to ftay at Burlington, and fet up my trade: but fhe was little aware of the capital that would be neceffary for fuch a pur-pofe! I was treated while at her houfe with true hofpitality. She gave me, with the utmoft good-will, a dinner of beef-fteaks, and would accept of nothing in return but a pint of ale.

Here I imagined myfelf to be fixed till the Tuefday in the enfuing week; but walking out in the evening by the river fide, I faw a boat with a number of perfons in it approach. It was going to Philadelphia, and the company took me in. As there was no wind, we could only make way with our oars. About midnight, not per-ceiving the town, fome of the company were of
opinion

opinion that we muſt have paſſed it, and were unwilling to row any farther; the reſt not knowing where we were, it was reſolved that we ſhould ſtop. We drew towards the ſhore, entered a creek, and landed near ſome old paliſades, which ſerved us for fire-wood, it being a cold night in October. Here we ſtayed till day, when one of the company found the place in which we were to be Cooper's Creek, a little above Philadelphia; which in reality we perceived the moment we were out of the creek. We arrived on Sunday about eight or nine o'clock in the morning, and landed on Market-ſtreet wharf.

I have entered into the particulars of my voyage, and ſhall in like manner deſcribe my firſt entrance into this city, that you may be able to compare beginnings ſo little auſpicious, with the figure I have ſince made.

On my arrival at Philadelphia I was in my working dreſs, my beſt clothes being to come by ſea. I was covered with dirt; my pockets were filled with ſhirts and ſtockings; I was unacquainted with a ſingle ſoul in the place, and knew not where to ſeek for a lodging. Fatigued with walking, rowing, and having paſſed the night without ſleep, I was extremely hungry, and all my money conſiſted of a Dutch dollar, and about a ſhilling's worth of coppers, which I gave to the boatmen for my paſſage. As I had aſſiſted them in rowing, they refuſed it at firſt; but I inſiſted on their taking it. A man is ſometimes more generous when he has little, than when he has much money; probably becauſe, in the firſt caſe, he is deſirous of concealing his poverty.

I walked towards the top of the ſtreet, looking eagerly on both ſides, till I came to Market-ſtreet, where I met a child with a loaf of bread. Often had I made my dinner on dry bread. I

enquired

enquired where he had bought it, and went ftraight to the baker's fhop which he pointed out to me. I afked for fome bifcuits, expecting to find fuch as we had at Bofton; but they made, it feems, none of that fort at Philadelphia. I then afked for a three penny loaf. They made no loaves of that price. Finding myfelf ignorant of the prices, as well as of the different kinds of bread, I defired him to let me have three penny-worth of bread of fome kind or other. He gave me three large rolls. I was furprized at receiving fo much: I took them, however, and having no room in my pockets, I walked on with a roll under each arm, eating the third. In this manner I went through Market-ftreet to Fourth-ftreet, and paffed the houfe of Mr. Read, the father of my future wife. She was ftanding at the door, obferved me, and thought, with reafon, that I made a very fingular and grotefque appearance.

I then turned the corner, and went through Chefnut-ftreet, eating my roll all the way; and having made this round, I found myfelf again on Market-ftreet wharf, near the boat in which I had arrived. I ftepped into it to take a draught of the river water; and finding myfelf fatisfied with my firft roll, I gave the other two to a woman and her child, who had come down the river with us in the boat, and was waiting to continue her journey. Thus refrefhed, I regained the ftreet, which was now full of well dreffed people, all going the fame way. I joined them, and was thus led to a large Quaker's meeting-houfe near the Market-place. I fat down with the reft, and after looking round me for fome time, hearing nothing faid, and being drowfy from my laft night's labour and want of reft, I fell into a found fleep. In this ftate I continued

till

till the affembly difperfed, when one of the congregation had the goodnefs to wake me. This
was confequently the firft houfe I entered or in
which I flept at Philadelphia.

I began again to walk along the ftreet by the
river fide; and looking attentively in the face of
every one I met, I at length perceived a young
quaker whofe countenance pleafed me. I accofted him, and begged him to inform me where a
ftranger might find a lodging. We were then
near the fign of the Three Mariners. They receive travellers here, faid he, but it is not a houfe
that bears a good character; if you will go with
me, I will fhew you a better one. He conducted me to the Crooked Billet, in Water-ftreet.
There I ordered fomething for dinner, and during my meal a number of curious queftions were
put to me; my youth and appearance exciting
the fufpicion of my being a runaway. After
dinner my drowfinefs returned, and I threw myfelf upon a bed without taking off my clothes,
and flept till fix o'clock in the evening, when I
was called to fupper. I afterwards went to bed
at a very early hour, and did not awake till the
next morning.

As foon as I got up I put myfelf in as decent
a trim as I could, and went to the houfe of Andrew Bradford the printer. I found his father
in the fhop, whom I had feen at New-York.
Having travelled on horfeback, he had arrived
at Philadelphia before me. He introduced me to
his fon, who received me with civility, and gave me
fome breakfaft; but told me he had no occafion
at prefent for a journeyman, having lately procured one. He added, that there was another
printer newly fettled in the town, of the name
of Keimer, who might perhaps employ me; and
that in cafe of refufal, I fhould be welcome to

D   lodge

lodge at his houfe, and he would give me a little work now and then, till fomething better fhould offer.

The old man offered to introduce me to the new printer. When we were at his houfe: "Neighbour," faid he, " I bring you a young man in the printing bufinefs; perhaps you may have need of his fervices."

Keimer afked me fome queftions, put a compofing ftick in my hand to fee how 1 could work, and then faid, that at prefent he had nothing for me to do, but that he fhould foon be able to employ me. At the fame time taking old Bradford for an inhabitant of the town well-difpofed towards him, he communicated his project to him, and the profpect he had of fuccefs. Bradford was careful not to difcover that he was the father of the other printer; and from what Keimer had faid, that he hoped fhortly to be in poffeffion of the greater part of the bufinefs of the town, led him by artful queftions, and by ftarting fome difficulties, to difclofe all his views, what his hopes were founded upon, and how he intended to proceed. 1 was prefent, and heard it all. I inftantly faw that one of the two was a cunning old fox, and the other a perfect novice. Bradford left me with Keimer, who was ftrangely furprized when I informed him who the old man was.

I found Keimer's printing materials to confift of an old damaged prefs, and a fmall caft of wornout Englifh letters, with which he was himfelf at work upon an elegy on Aquila Rofe, whom I have mentioned above, an ingenious young man, and of an excellent character, highly efteemed in the town, fecretary to the affembly, and a very tolerable poet. Keimer alfo made verfes, but they were indifferent ones. He could not be faid to write in verfe, for his method was to fet the

lines

lines as they flowed from his mufe; and as he worked without copy, had but one fet of letter-cafes, and the elegy would probably occupy all his type, it was impoffible for any one to affift him. I endeavoured to put his prefs in order, which he had not yet ufed, and of which indeed he underftood nothing: and having promifed to come and work off his elegy as foon as it fhould be ready, I returned to the houfe of Bradford, who gave me fome trifle to do for the prefent, for which I had my board and lodging.

In a few days Keimer fent for me to print off his elegy. He had now procured another fet of letter-cafes, and had a pamphlet to reprint, upon which he fet me to work.

The two Philadelphia printers appeared deftitute of every qualification neceffary in their profeffion. Bradford had not been brought up to it, and was very iliterate. Keimer, though he underftood a little of the bufinefs, was merely a compofitor, and wholly incapable of working at the prefs. He had been one of the French prophets, and knew how to imitate their fupernatural agitations. At the time of our firft acquaintance he profeffed no particular religion, but a little of all upon occafion. He was totally ignorant of the world, and a great knave at heart, as I had afterwards an opportunity of experiencing.

Keimer could not endure that, working with him, I fhould lodge at Bradford's. He had indeed a houfe, but it was unfurnifhed; fo that he could not take me in. He procured me a lodging at Mr. Read's, his landlord, whom I have already mentioned. My trunk and effects being now arrived, I thought of making, in the eyes of Mifs Read, a more refpectable appearance

than

than when chance exhibited me to her view, eating my roll, and wandering in the ftreets.

From this period I began to contract acquaintance, with fuch young people of the town as
were fond of reading, and fpent my evenings
with them agreeably, while at the fame time I
gained money by my induftry, and, thanks to
my frugality, lived contented. I thus forgot
Bofton as much as poffible, and wifhed every
one to be ignorant of the place of my refidence,
except my friend Collins, to whom I wrote, and
who kept my fecret.

An incident however arrived, which fent me
home much fooner than I had propofed. I had
a brother-in-law, of the name of Robert Holmes,
mafter of a trading floop from Bofton to Delaware. Being at Newcaftle, forty miles below
Philadelphia, he heard of me, and wrote to inform me of the chagrin which my fudden departure from Bofton had occafioned my parents,
and of the affection which they ftill entertained
for me, affuring me that, if I would return every thing fhould be adjufted to my fatisfaction;
and he was very preffing in his entreaties. I anfwered his letter, thanked him for his advice,
and explained the reafons which had induced
me to quit Bofton, with fuch force and clearnefs,
that he was convinced I had been lefs to blame
than he had imagined.

Sir William Keith, governor of the province,
was at Newcaftle at the time. Captain Holmes,
being by chance in his company when he received my letter, took occafion to fpeak of me, and
fhewed it him. The governor read it, and appeared furprized when he learned my age. He
thought me, he faid, a young man of very promifing talents, and that, of confequence, I ought
to be encouraged; that there were at Philadelphia

phia none but very ignorant printers, and that if I were to fet up for myfelf, he had no doubt of my fuccefs; that, for his own part, he would procure me all the public bufinefs, and would render me every other fervice in his power. My brother-in-law related all this to me afterwards at Bofton; but I knew nothing of it at the time; when one day Keimer and I being at work together near the window, we faw the governor and another gentleman, colonel French of Newcaftle, handfomely dreffed, crofs the ftreet, and make directly for our houfe. We heard them at the door, and Keimer, believing it to be a vifit to himfelf, went immediately down: but the governor enquired for me, came up ftairs, and, with a condefcenfion and politenefs to which I had not at all been accuftomed, paid me many compliments, defired to be acquainted with me, obligingly reproached me for not having made myfelf known to him on my arrival in the town, and wifhed me to accompany him to a tavern, where he and colonel French were going to tafte fome excellent Madeira wine.

I was, I confefs, fomewhat furprifed, and Keimer appeared thunderftruck. I went however with the governor and the colonel to a tavern at the corner of Third ftreet, where, while we were drinking the Madeira, he propofed to me to eftablifh a printing-houfe. He fet forth the probabilities of fuccefs, and himfelf and colonel French affured me that I fhould have their protection and influence in obtaining the printing of the public papers of both governments: and as I appeared to doubt whether my father would affift me in this enterprize, Sir William faid that he would give me a letter to him, in which he would reprefent the advantages of the fcheme, in a light which he had no doubt would determine
him.

him. It was thus concluded that I should return to Boston by the first vessel, with the letter
of recommendation from the governor to my
father. Meanwhile the project was to be kept
secret, and I continued to work for Keimer as
before.

The governor sent every now and then to in-
vite me to dine with him. I considered this as
a very great honour; and I was the more sensible of it, as he conversed with me in the most
affable, familiar, and friendly manner imaginable.

Towards the end of April 1724, a small vessel
was ready to sail for Boston. I took leave of
Keimer, upon the pretext of going to see my parents. The governor gave me a long letter, in
which he said many flattering things of me to my
father; and strongly recommended the project
of my settling at Philadelphia, as a thing which
could not fail to make my fortune.

Going down the bay we struck on a flat, and
sprung a leak. The weather was very tempes-
tuous, and we were obliged to pump without
intermission; I took my turn. We arrived
however safe and found at Boston, after about a
fortnight's passage.

I had been absent seven complete months, and
my relations, during that interval, had received
no intelligence of me; for my brother-in-law,
Holmes, was not yet returned, and had not written about me. My unexpected appearance sur-
prized the family; but they were all delighted
at seeing me again, and, except my brother,
welcomed me home. I went to him at the printing-house. I was bettter dressed than I had ever
been while in his service: I had a complete suit
of clothes, new and neat, a watch in my pocket,
and my purse was furnished with nearly five
pounds

pounds fterling in money. He gave me no very civil reception; and having eyed me from
head to foot, refumed his work.

The workmen afked me with eagernefs where
I had been, what fort of a country it was, and
how I liked it. I fpoke in the higheft terms of
Philadelphia, the happy life we led there, and
expreffed my intention of going back again. One
of them afking what fort of money we had, I
difplayed before them a handful of filver, which
I drew from my pocket. This was a curiofity
to which they were not accuftomed, paper being
the current money at Bofton. I failed not after
this to let them fee my watch; and at laft, my
brother continuing fullen and out of humour, I
gave them a fhilling to drink, and took my leave.
This vifit ftung my brother to the foul; for when,
fhortly after, my mother fpoke to him of a reconciliation, and a defire to fee us upon good
terms, he told her that I had fo infulted him before his men, that he would never forget or for-
give it; in this, however, he was miftaken.

The governor's letter appeared to excite in my
father fome furprife; but he faid little. After
fome days, captain Holmes being returned, he
fhowed it him, afking him if he knew Keith,
and what fort of a man he was: adding, that,
in his opinion, it proved very little difcernment
to think of fetting up a boy in bufinefs, who for
three years to come would not be of an age to be
ranked in the clafs of men. Holmes faid every
thing he could in favour of the fcheme; but my
father firmly maintained its abfurdity, and at laft
gave a pofitive refufal. He wrote, however, a civil letter to Sir William, thanking him for the protection he had fo obligingly offered me, but refufing to affift me for the prefent, becaufe he
thought me too young to be entrufted with the
conduct

conduct of so important an enterprise, and which would require so considerable a sum of money.

My old comrade Collins, who was a clerk in the post-office, charmed with the account I gave of my new residence, expressed a desire of going thither; and while I waited my father's determination, he set off before me, by land, for Rhode Island, leaving his books, which formed a handsome collection in mathematics and natural philosophy, to be conveyed with mine to New-York, where he purposed to wait for me.

My father, though he could not approve Sir William's proposal, was yet pleased that I had obtained so advantageous a recommendation as that of a person of his rank, and that my industry and œconomy had enabled me to equip myself so handsomely in so short a period. Seeing no appearance of accommodating matters between my brother and me, he consented to my return to Philadelphia, advised me to be civil to every body, to endeavour to obtain general esteem, and avoid satire and sarcasm, to which he thought I was too much inclined; adding, that, with perseverance and prudent œconomy, I might, by the time I became of age, save enough to establish myself in business; and that if a small sum should then be wanting, he would undertake to supply it.

This was all I could obtain from him, except some trifling presents, in token of friendship from him and my mother. I embarked once more for New-York, furnished at this time with their approbation and blessing. The sloop having touched at Newport in Rhode Island, I paid a visit to my brother John, who had for some years been settled there, and was married. He had always been attached to me, and he received me with great affection. One of his friends, whose

name

name was Vernon, having a debt of about thirty-six pounds due to him in Penfylvania, begged me to receive it for him, and to keep the money till I fhould hear from: accordingly he gave me an order for that purpofe. This affair occafioned me, in the fequel, much uneafinefs.

At Newport we took on board a number of paffengers; among whom were two young women, and a grave and fenfible quaker lady with her fervants. I had fhown an obliging forwardnefs in rendering the quaker fome trifling fervices, which led her, probably, to feel an intereft in my welfare; for when fhe faw a familiarity take place, and every day increafe, between the two young women and me, fhe took me afide and faid: " Young man, I am in pain for thee. Thou haft no parent to watch over thy conduct, and thou feemeft to be ignorant of the world, and the fnares to which youth is expofed. Rely upon what I tell thee: thofe are women of bad characters; I perceive it in all their actions. If thou doft not take care, they will lead thee into danger. They are ftrangers to thee, and I advife thee, by the friendly intereft I take in thy prefervation, to form no connection with them." As I appeared at firft not to think quite fo ill of them as fhe did, fhe related many things fhe had feen and heard, which had efcaped my attention, but which convinced me that fhe was in the right. I thanked her for her obliging advice, and promifed to follow it.

When we arrived at New-York, they informed me where they lodged, and invited me to come and fee them. I did not however go, and it was well I did not; for the next day, the captain, miffing a filver fpoon and fome other things which had been taken from the cabin, and knowing thefe women to be proftitutes, procured a

fearch

fearch warrant, found the ftolen goods upon them, and had them punifhed. And thus, after having been faved from one rock concealed under water, upon which the veffel ftruck during our paffage, I efcaped another of a ftill more dangerous nature.

At New-York I found my friend Collins, who had arrived fome time before. We had been intimate from our infancy, and had read the fame books together; but he had the advantage of being able to devote more time to reading and ftudy, and an aftonifhing difpofition for mathematics, in which he left me far behind him. When at Bofton, I had been accuftomed to pafs with him almoft all my leifure hours. He was then a fober and induftrious lad; his knowledge had gained him a very general efteem, and he feemed to promife to make an advantageous figure in fociety. But, during my abfence, he had unfortunately addicted himfelf to brandy, and I learned, as well from himfelf as from the report of others, that every day fince his arrival at New-York he had been intoxicated, and had acted in a very extravagant manner. He had alfo played and loft all his money; fo that I was obliged to pay his expences at the inn, and to maintain him during the reft of his journey; a burthen that was very inconvenient to me.

The governor of New-York, whofe name was Burnet, hearing the captain fay that a young man who was a paffenger in his fhip had a great number of books, begged him to bring me to his houfe. I accordingly went, and fhould have taken Collins with me, had he been fober. The governor treated me with great civility, fhewed me his library, which was a very confiderable one, and we talked fome time upon books and authors. This was the fecond governor who had honoured

ed

ed me with his attention; and to a poor boy, as I was then, thefe little adventures did not fail to be pleafing.

We arrived at Philadelphia. On the way I received Vernon's money, without which we fhould have been unable to finifh our journey.

Collins wifhed to get employment as a merchant's clerk; but either his breath or his countenance betrayed his bad habit; for, though he had recommendations, he met with no fuccefs, and continued to lodge and eat with me, and at my expence. Knowing that I had Vernon's money, he was continually afking me to lend him fome of it; promifing to repay me as foon as he fhould get employment. At laft he had drawn fo much of this money, that I was extremely alarmed at what might become of me, fhould he fail to make good the deficiency. His habit of drinking did not at all diminifh, and was a frequent fource of difcord between us; for when he had drank a little too much, he was very headftrong.

Being one day in a boat together, on the Delaware, with fome other young perfons, he refufed to take his turn in rowing. You fhall row for me, faid he, till we get home.—No, I replied, we will not row for you.—You fhall, faid he, or remain upon the water all night.—As you pleafe.—Let us row, faid the reft of the company; what fignifies whether he affifts or not? But, already angry with him for his conduct in other refpects, I perfifted in my refufal. He then fwore that he would make me row, or would throw me out of the boat; and he made up to me. As foon as he was within my reach I took him by the collar, gave him a violent thruft, and threw him head foremoft into the river. I knew that he was a good fwimmer, and was therefore under

under no apprehensions for his life. Before he could turn himself, we were able, by a few strokes of our oars, to place ourselves out of his reach; and whenever he touched the boat, we asked him if he would row, striking his hands at the same time with the oars to make him let go his hold. He was nearly suffocated with rage, but obstinately refused making any promise to row. Perceiving at length that his strength began to be exhausted, we took him into the boat, and conveyed him home in the evening completely drenched. The utmost coldness subsisted between us after this adventure. At last the captain of a West-India ship, who was commissioned to procure a tutor for the children of a gentleman at Barbadoes, meeting with Collins offered him the place. He accepted it, and took his leave of me, promising to discharge the debt he owed me with the first money he should receive; but I have heard nothing of him since.

The violation of the trust reposed in me by Vernon, was one of the first great errors of my life; and it proves that my father was not mistaken when he supposed me too young to be intrusted with the management of important affairs. But Sir William, upon reading his letter, thought him too prudent. There was a difference, he said, between individuals: years of maturity were not always accompanied with discretion, neither was youth in every instance devoid of it. Since your father, added he, will not set you up in business, I will do it myself. Make out a list of what will be wanted from England, and I will send for the articles. You shall repay me when you can. I am determined to have a good printer here, and I am sure you will succeed. This was said with so much seeming cordiality, that I suspected not for an instant the sincerity of the
offer.

offer. I had hitherto kept the project, with which Sir William had inspired me, of settling in business, a secret at Philadelphia, and I still continued to do so. Had my reliance on the governor been known, some friend, better acquainted with his character than myself, would doubtless have advised me not to trust him; for I afterwards learned that he was universally known to be liberal of promises, which he had no intention to perform. But having never solicited him, how could I suppose his offers to be deceitful? On the contrary, I believed him to be the best man in the world.

I gave him an inventory of a small printing-office; the expence of which I had calculated at about a hundred pounds sterling. He expressed his approbation; but asked, if my presence in England, that I might choose the characters myself, and see that every article was good in its kind, would not be an advantage? You will also be able, said he, to form some acquaintance there, and establish a correspondence with stationers and booksellers. This I acknowledged was desirable. That being the case, added he, hold yourself in readiness to go with the Annis. This was the annual vessel, and the only one, at that time, which made regular voyages between the ports of London and Philadelphia. But the Annis was not to sail for some months. I therefore continued to work with Keimer, unhappy respecting the sum which Collins had drawn from me, and almost in continual agony at the thoughts of Vernon, who fortunately made no demand of his money till several years after.

In the account of my first voyage from Boston to Philadelphia, I omitted I believe a trifling circumstance, which will not perhaps be out of place here. During a calm which stopped us above

Block

Block-Ifland, the crew employed themfelves in fifhing for cod, of which they caught a great number. I had hitherto adhered to my refolution of not eating any thing that had poffeffed life ; and I confidered on this occafion, agreeably to the maxims of my mafter Tryon, the capture of every fifh as a fort of murder, committed without provocation, fince thefe animals had neither done, nor were capable of doing, the fmalleft injury to any one that fhould juftify the meafure. This mode of reafoning I conceived to be unanfwerable. Meanwhile I had formerly been extremely fond of fifh ; and when one of thefe cod was taken out of the frying-pan, I thought its flavour delicious. I hefitated fome time between principle and inclination, till at laft recollecting, that when the cod had been opened fome fmall fifh were found in its belly, I faid to myfelf, If you eat one another, I fee no reafon why we may not eat you. I accordingly dined on the cod with no fmall degree of pleafure, and have fince continued to eat like the reft of mankind, returning only occafionally to my vegetable plan. How convenient does it prove to be a *rational animal*, that knows how to find or invent a plaufible pretext for whatever it has an inclination to do!

I continued to live upon good terms with Keimer, who had not the fmalleft fufpicion of my projected eftablifhment. He ftill retained a portion of his former enthufiafm ; and being fond of argument, we frequently difputed together. I was fo much in the habit of ufing my Socratic method, and had fo frequently puzzled him by my queftions, which appeared at firft very diftant from the point in debate, yet neverthelefs led to it by degrees, involving him in difficulties and contradictions from which he was unable to extricate

tricate himfelf, that he became at laft ridiculoufly
cautious, and would fcarcely anfwer the moft
plain and familiar queftion without previoufly
afking me—What would you infer from that?
Hence he formed fo high an opinion of my talents for refutation, that he ferioufly propofed
to me to become his colleague in the eftablifhment of a new religious feƐt. He was to propa-
gate the doƐtrine by preaching, and I to refute
every opponent.

When he explained to me his tenets, I found
many abfurdities which I refufed to admit, unlefs he would agree in turn to adopt fome of my
opinions. Keimer wore his beard long, becaufe
Mofes had fomewhere faid, *Thou fhalt not mar the
corners of thy beard*. He likewife obferved the Sabbath ; and thefe were with him two very effential
points. I difliked them both ; but I confented to
adopt them, provided he would agree to abftain
from animal food. I doubt, faid he, whether my
conftitution will be able to fupport it. I affured
him, on the contrary, that he would find himfelf
the better for it. He was naturally a glutton, and
I wifhed to amufe myfelf by ftarving him. He
confented to make trial of this regimen, if I
would bear him company ; and in reality we continued it for three months. A woman in the
neighbourhood prepared and brought us our
viƐtuals, to whom I gave a lift of forty difhes ;
in the compofition of which there entered neither
flefh nor fifh. This fancy was the more agreeable to me, as it turned to good account ; for the
whole expence of our living did not exceed for
each eighteen-pence a week.

I have fince that period obferved feveral Lents
with the greateft ftriƐtnefs, and have fuddenly
returned again to my ordinary diet, without experiencing the fmalleft inconvenience ; which has
led

led me to regard as of no importance the advice commonly given, of introducing gradually such alterations of regimen.

I continued it cheerfully; but poor Keimer suffered terribly. Tired of the project, he sighed for the flesh-pots of Egypt. At length he ordered a roast pig, and invited me and two of our female acquaintance to dine with him; but the pig being ready a little too soon, he could not resist the temptation, and eat it all up before we arrived.

During the circumstances I have related, I had paid some attentions to Miss Read. I entertained for her the utmost esteem and affection; and I had reason to believe that these sentiments were mutual. But we were both young, scarcely more than eighteen years of age; and as I was on the point of undertaking a long voyage, her mother thought it prudent to prevent matters being carried too far for the present, judging that, if marriage was our object, there would be more propriety in it after my return, when, as at least I expected, I should be established in my business. Perhaps also she thought that my expectations were not so well founded as I imagined.

My most intimate acquaintance at this time were Charles Osborne, Joseph Watson, and James Ralph; young men who were all fond of reading. The two first were clerks to Mr. Charles Brockdon, one of the principal attornies in the town, and the other clerk to a merchant. Watson was an upright, pious and sensible young man: the others were somewhat more loose in their principles of religion, particularly Ralph, whose faith, as well as that of Collins, I had contributed to shake; each of whom made me suffer a very adequate punishment. Osborne was

fensible,

senfible, and fincere and affectionate in his friend-
fhips, but too much inclined to the critic in matters of literature. Ralph was ingenious and
fhrewd, genteel in his addrefs, and extremely
eloquent. I do not remember to have met with
a more agreeable fpeaker. They were both en-
amoured of the mufes, and had already evinced
their paffion by fome fmall poetical productions.

It was a cuftom with us to take a charming
walk on Sundays, in the woods that border the
Skuylkil. Here we read together, and afterwards
converfed on what we read. Ralph was difpofed
to give himfelf up entirely to poetry. He flattered himfelf that he fhould arrive at great eminence
in the art, and even acquire a fortune. The fub-
limeft poets, he pretended, when they firft began
to write, committed as many faults as himfelf.
Ofborne endeavoured to diffuade him, by affuring him that he had no genius for poetry, and
advifed him to ftick to the trade in which he had
been brought up. In the road of commerce, faid
he, you will be fure, by diligence and affiduity,
though you have no capital, of fo far fucceeding
as to be employed as a factor, and may thus, in
time, acquire the means of fetting up for yourfelf. I concurred in thefe fentiments, but at the
fame time expreffed my approbation of amufing
ourfelves fometimes with poetry, with a view to
improve our ftyle. In confequence of this it was
propofed, that, at our next meeting, each of us
fhould bring a copy of verfes of his own compofition. Our object in this competition was to benefit each other by our mutual remarks, criti-
cifms, and corrections; and as ftyle and expreffion were all we had in view, we excluded every
idea of invention, by agreeing that our tafk
fhould be a verfion of the eighteenth pfalm, in
which is defcribed the defcent of the deity.

E,   The

The time of our meeting drew near, when
Ralph called upon me, and told me that his performance was ready. I informed him that I had
been idle, and, not much liking the taſk, had
done nothing. He ſhowed me his piece, and
aſked what I thought of it. I expreſſed myſelf
in terms of warm approbation; becauſe it really
appeared to have conſiderable merit. He then
ſaid: Oſborne will never acknowledge the ſmall-
eſt degree of excellence in any production of mine.
Envy alone dictates to him a thouſand animad-
verſions. Of you he is not ſo jealous: I wiſh
therefore you would take the verſes, and produce
them as your own. I will pretend not to have
had leiſure to write any thing. We ſhall then
ſee in what manner he will ſpeak of them. I a-
greed to this little artifice, and immediately tran-
ſcribed the verſes to prevent all ſuſpicion.

We met. Watſon's performance was the firſt
that was read. It had ſome beauties, but many
faults. We next read Oſborne's, which was
much better. Ralph did it juſtice, remarking a
few imperfections, and applauding ſuch parts as
were excellent. He had himſelf nothing to ſhow.
It was now my turn. I made ſome difficulty;
ſeemed as if I wiſhed to be excuſed; pretended
that I had had no time to make corrections, &c.
No excuſe, however, was admiſſible, and the piece
muſt be produced. It was read and re-read.
Watſon and Oſborne immediately reſigned the
palm, and united in applauding it. Ralph alone
made a few remarks, and propoſed ſome alterations; but I defended my text. Oſborne agreed
with me, and told Ralph that he was no more
able to criticiſe than he was able to write.

When Oſborne was alone with me, he expreſſed himſelf ſtill more ſtrongly in favour of what
he conſidered as my performance. He pretended
　　　　　　　　　　　　　　　　　that

that he had put some restraint on himself before, apprehensive of my construing his commendation into flattery. But who would have supposed, said he, Franklin to be capable of such a composition? What painting, what energy, what fire! He has surpassed the original. In his common conversation he appears not to have a choice of words; he hesitates, and is at a loss: and yet, good God, how he writes!

At our next meeting Ralph discovered the trick we had played Osborne, who was rallied without mercy.

By this adventure Ralph was fixed in his resolution of becoming a poet. I left nothing unattempted to divert him from his purpose; but he persevered, till at last the reading of Pope * effected his cure: he became, however, a very tolerable prose writer. I shall speak more of him hereafter; but as I shall probably have no farther occasion to mention the other two, I ought to observe here, that Watson died a few years after in my arms. He was greatly regretted; for he was the best of our society. Osborne went to the islands, where he gained considerable reputation as a barrister, and was getting money; but he died young. We had seriously engaged, that whoever died first should return, if possible, and pay a friendly visit to the survivor, to give him an account of the other world; but he has never fulfilled his engagement.

The governor appeared to be fond of my company, and frequently invited me to his house. He always spoke of his intention of settling me in business, as a point that was decided. I was

---

* Probably the Dunciad, where we find him thus immortalized by the author:

Silence, ye wolves, while RALPH to Cynthia howls,
And makes night hideous; answer him, ye owls!

to

to take with me letters of recommendation to a number of his friends; and particularly a letter of credit, in order to obtain the neceffary fum for the purchafe of my prefs, types, and paper. He appointed various times for me to come for thefe letters, which would certainly be ready; and when I came, always put me off to another day.

Thefe fucceffive delays continued till the veffel, whofe departure had been feveral times deferred, was on the point of fetting fail; when I again went to Sir William's houfe, to receive my letters and take leave of him. I faw his fecretary, Dr. Bard; who told me that the governor was extremely bufy writing, but that he would be down at Newcaflle before the veffel, and that the letters would be delivered to me there.

Ralph, though he was married and had a child, determined to accompany me in this voyage. His object was fuppofed to be the eftablifhing a correfpondence with fome mercantile houfes, in order to fell goods by commiffion; but I afterwards learned, that, having reafon to be diffatisfied with the parents of his wife, he propofed to himfelf to leave her on their hands, and never return to America again.

Having taken leave of my friends, and interchanged promifes of fidelity with Mifs Read, I quitted Philadelphia. At Newcaflle the veffel came to anchor. The governor was arrived, and I went to his lodgings. His fecretary received me with great civility, told me on the part of the governor that he could not fee me then, as he was engaged in affairs of the utmoft importance, but that he would fend the letters on board, and that he wifhed me, with all his heart, a good voyage and fpeedy return. I returned, fomewhat aftonifhed, to the fhip, but ftill without entertaining the flighteft fufpicion.

Mr.

Mr. Hamilton, a celebrated barrifter of Philadelphia, had taken a paffage to England for himfelf and his fon, and, in conjunction with Mr. Denham a quaker, and Meffrs. Oniam and Ruffel, proprietors of a forge in Maryland, had agreed for the whole cabin, fo that Ralph and I were obliged to take up our lodging with the crew. Being unknown to every body in the fhip, we were looked upon as of the common order of people: but Mr. Hamilton and his fon (it was James, who was afterwards governor) left us at Newcaftle, and returned to Philadelphia, where he was recalled, at a very great expence, to plead the caufe of a veffel that had been feized; and juft as we were about to fail, colonel Finch came on board, and fhewed me many civilities. The paffengers upon this paid me more attention, and I was invited, together with my friend Ralph, to occupy the place in the cabin which the return of the Mr. Hamiltons had made vacant; an offer which we very readily accepted.

Having learned that the difpatches of the governor had been brought on board by colonel Finch, I afked the captain for the letters that were to be intrufted to my care. He told me that they were all put together in the bag, which he could not open at prefent; but before we reached England, he would give me an opportunity of taking them out. I was fatisfied with this anfwer, and we purfued our voyage.

The company in the cabin were all very fociable, and we were perfectly well off as to provifions, as we had the advantage of the whole of Mr. Hamilton's, who had laid in a very plentiful ftock. During the paffage Mr. Denham contracted a friendfhip for me, which ended only with his life: in other refpects the voyage was

by

by no means an agreeable one, as we had much
bad weather.

When we arrived in the river, the captain was
as good as his word, and allowed me to fearch in
the bag for the governor's letters.   I could not
find a fingle one with my name written on it, as
committed to my care; but I felected fix or feven,
which I judged from the direction to be thofe
that were intended for me; particularly one to
Mr. Bafket the king's printer, and another to a
ftationer, who was the firft perfon I called upon.
I delivered him the letter as coming from governor Keith.   " I have no acquaintance (faid he)
" with any fuch perfon;" and opening the letter,
" Oh, it is from Riddlefden!" he exclaimed.
" I have lately difcovered him to be a very ar-
" rant knave, and I wifh to have nothing to do
" either with him or his letters."   He inftantly
put the letter in my hand, turned upon his heel,
and left me to ferve fome cuftomers.

I was aftonifhed at finding thefe letters were
not from the governor.   Reflecting, and putting
circumftances together, I then began to doubt
his fincerity.   I rejoined my friend Denham, and
related the whole affair to him.   He let me at
once into Keith's character, told me there was
not the leaft probability of his having written a
fingle letter; that no one who knew him ever
placed any reliance on him, and laughed at my
credulity in fuppofing that the governor would
give me a letter of credit, when he had no credit
for himfelf.   As I fhowed fome uneafinefs refpecting what ftep I fhould take, he advifed me
to try to get employment in the houfe of fome
printer.   You may there, faid he, improve yourfelf in bufinefs, and you will be able to fettle
yourfelf the more advantageoufly when you return to America.

We

We knew already, as well as the stationer, attorney Riddlesden to be a knave. He had nearly ruined the father of Miss Read, by drawing him in to be his security. We learned from his letter, that he was secretly carrying on an intrigue, in concert with the governor, to the prejudice of Mr. Hamilton, who it was supposed would by this time be in Europe. Denham, who was Hamilton's friend, was of opinion that he ought to be made acquainted with it; and in reality, the instant he arrived in England, which was very soon after, I waited on him, and, as much from good-will to him as from resentment against the governor, put the letter into his hands. He thanked me very sincerely, the information it contained being of consequence to him; and from that moment bestowed on me his friendship, which afterwards proved on many occasions serviceable to me.

But what are we to think of a governor who could play so scurvy a trick, and thus grossly deceive a poor young lad, wholly destitute of experience? It was a practice with him. Wishing to please every body, and having little to bestow, he was lavish of promises. He was in other respects sensible and judicious, a very tolerable writer, and a good governor for the people; though not so for the proprietaries, whose instructions he frequently disregarded. Many of our best laws were his work, and established during his administration.

Ralph and I were inseparable companions. We took a lodging together at three and-sixpence a week, which was as much as we could afford. He met with some relations in London, but they were poor, and not able to assist him. He now, for the first time, informed me of his intention to remain in England, and that he had no
thoughts

thoughts of ever returning to Philadelphia. He
was totally without money; the little he had
been able to raife having barely fufficed for his
paffage. I had fifteen piftoles remaining; and to
me he had from time to time recourfe, while he
tried to get employment.

At firft, believing himfelf poffeffed of talents
for the ftage, he thought of turning actor; but
Wilkes, to whom he applied, frankly advifed
him to renounce the idea, as it was impoffible he
fhould fucceed. He next propofed to Roberts,
a bookfeller in Paternofter-row, to write a weekly paper in the manner of the Spectator, upon
terms to which Roberts would not liften. Laftly,
he endeavoured to procure employment as a co-
pyift, and applied to the lawyers and ftationers
about the temple; but he could find no vacancy.

As to myfelf, I immediately got engaged at
Palmer's, at that time a noted printer in Bartho-
lomew Clofe, with whom I continued nearly a
year. I applied very affiduoufly to my work;
but I expended with Ralph almoft all that I earned. Plays, and other places of amufement which
we frequented together, having exhaufted my
piftoles, we lived after this from hand to mouth.
He appeared to have entirely forgotten his wife
and child, as I alfo, by degrees, forgot my engagements with Mifs Read, to whom I never
wrote more than one letter, and that merely to
inform her that I was not likely to return foon.
This was another grand error of my life, which
I fhould be defirous of correcting were I to begin
my career again.

I was employed at Palmer's on the fecond edition of Woolafton's Religion of Nature. Some
of his arguments appearing to me not to be well
founded, I wrote a fmall metaphyfical treatife,
in which I animadverted on thofe paffages. It
was

was entitled, a Diſſertation on Liberty and Neceſſity, Pleaſure and Pain. I dedicated it to my friend
Ralph, and printed a ſmall number of copies.
Palmer upon this treated me with more conſide-
ration, and regarded me as a young man of talents; though he ſeriouſly took me to taſk for
the principles of my pamphlet, which he looked
upon as abominable. The printing of this work
was another error of my life.

While I lodged in Little Britain I formed acquaintance with a bookſeller of the name of Wil-
cox, whoſe ſhop was next door to me. Circulating libraries were not then in uſe. He had an
immenſe collection of books of all ſorts. We a-
greed that, for a reaſonable retribution, of which
I have now forgotten the price, I ſhould have
free acceſs to his library, and take what books I
pleaſed, which I was to return when I had read
them. I conſidered this agreement as a very great
advantage; and I derived from it as much benefit as was in my power.

My pamphlet falling into the hands of a ſur-
geon, of the name of Lyons, author of a book
entitled, Infallibility of Human Judgment, was
the occaſion of a conſiderable intimacy between
us. He expreſſed great eſteem for me, came
frequently to ſee me, in order to converſe upon
metaphyſical ſubjects, and introduced me to Dr.
Mandeville, author of the Fable of Bees, who
had inſtituted a club at a tavern in Cheapſide, of
which he was the ſoul: he was a facetious and
very amuſing character. He alſo introduced me,
at Batſon's coffee-houſe, to Dr. Pemberton, who
promiſed to give me an opportunity of ſeeing Sir
Iſaac Newton, which I very ardently deſired;
but he never kept his word.

I had brought ſome curioſities with me from
America; the principal of which was a purſe
made of the aſbeſtos, which fire only purifies.

Sir

Sir Hans Sloane hearing of it, called upon me, and invited me to his houfe in Bloomfbury-fquare, where, after fhowing me every thing that was curious, he prevailed on me to add this piece to his collection; for which he paid me very handfomely.

There lodged in the fame houfe with us a young woman, a milliner, who had a fhop by the fide of the Exchange. Lively and fenfible, and having received an education fomewhat above her rank, her converfation was very agreeable. Ralph read plays to her every evening. They became intimate. She took another lodging, and he followed her. They lived for fome time together; but Ralph being without employment, fhe having a child, and the profits of her bufinefs not fufficing for the maintenance of three, he refolved to quit London, and try a country fchool. This was a plan in which he thought himfelf likely to fucceed, as he wrote a fine hand, and was verfed in arithmetic and accounts But confidering the office as beneath him, and expecting fome day to make a better figure in the world, when he fhould be afhamed of its being known that he had exercifed a profeffion fo little honourable, he changed his name, and did me the honour of affuming mine. He wrote to me foon after his departure, informing me that he was fettled at a fmall village in Berkfhire. In his letter he recommended Mrs. T***, the milliner, to my care, and requefted an anfwer, directed to Mr. Franklin, fchool-mafter at N***.

He continued to write to me frequently, fending me large fragments of an epic poem he was compofing, and which he requefted me to criticife and correct. I did fo, but not without endeavouring to prevail on him to renounce this purfuit. Young had juft publifhed one of his

Satires.

Satires. I copied and sent him a great part of it; in which the author demonstrates the folly of cultivating the Muses, from the hope, by their instrumentality, of rising in the world. It was all to no purpose; paper after paper of his poem continued to arrive every post.

Meanwhile Mrs. T*** having lost, on his account, both her friends and her business, was frequently in distress. In this dilemma she had recourse to me; and to extricate her from her difficulties, I lent her all the money I could spare. I felt a little too much fondness for her. Having at that time no ties of religion, and taking advantage of her necessitous situation, I attempted liberties (another error of my life,) which she repelled with becoming indignation. She informed Ralph of my conduct; and the affair occasioned a breach between us. When he returned to London, he gave me to understand that he considered all the obligations he owed me as annihilated by this proceeding; whence I concluded that I was never to expect the payment of what money I had lent him, or advanced on his account. I was the less afflicted at this, as he was wholly unable to pay me; and as, by losing his friendship, I was relieved at the same time from a very heavy burden.

I now began to think of laying by some money. The printing-house of Watts, near Lincoln's-Inn Fields, being a still more considerable one than that in which I worked, it was probable I might find it more advantageous to be employed there. I offered myself, and was accepted; and in this house I continued during the remainder of my stay in London.

On my entrance I worked at first as a pressman, conceiving that I had need of bodily exercise, to which I had been accustomed in America,
where

where the printers work alternately as compofitors and at the prefs. I drank nothing but water. The other workmen, to the number of a-
bout fifty, were great drinkers of beer. I carried occafionally a large form of letters in each
hand, up and down ftairs, while the reft employed both hands to carry one. They were furprized to fee, by this and many other examples,
that the *American Aquatic,* as they ufed to call
me, was ftronger than thofe who drank porter.
The beer-boy had fufficient employment during
the whole day in ferving that houfe alone. My
fellow-preffman drank every day a pint of beer
before breakfaft, a pint with bread and cheefe for
breakfaft, one between breakfaft and dinner, one
at dinner, one again about fix o'clock in the afternoon, and another after he had finifhed his
day's work. This cuftom appeared to me abominable; but he had need, he faid, of all this
beer, in order to acquire ftrength to work.

I endeavoured to convince him that the bodily
ftrength furnifhed by the beer, could only be in
proportion to the folid part of the barley diffol-
ved in the water of which the beer was compofed ; that there was a larger portion of flour in
a penny loaf, and that confequently if he eat this
loaf, and drank a pint of water with it, he
would derive more ftrength from it than from a
pint of beer. This reafoning, however, did not
prevent him from drinking his accuftomed quantity of beer, and paying every Saturday night a
fcore of four or five fhillings a week for this cur-
fed beverage ; an expence from which I was wholly exempt. Thus do thefe poor devils continue
all their lives in a ftate of voluntary wretchednefs
and poverty.

At the end of a few weeks, Watts having occafion for me above ftairs as a compofitor, I quitted

ted the prefs. The compofitors demanded of me garnifh-money afrefh. This I confidered as an impofition, having already paid below. The mafter was of the fame opinion, and defired me not to comply. I thus remained two or three weeks out of the fraternity. I was confequently looked upon as excommunicated; and whenever I was abfent, no little trick that malice could fuggeft was left unpractifed upon me I found my letters mixed, my pages tranfpofed, my matter broken, &c. &c. all which was attributed to the fpirit that haunted the chapel *, and torment-ed thofe who were not regularly admitted. I was at laft obliged to fubmit to pay, notwith-ftanding the protection of the mafter; convinced of the folly of not keeping up a good underftand-ing with thofe among whom we are deftined to live.

After this I lived in the utmoft harmony with my fellow-labourers, and foon acquired confide-rable influence among them. I propofed fome alterations in the laws of the chapel, which I car-ried without oppofition. My example prevailed with feveral of them to renounce their abomina-ble practice of bread and cheefe with beer; and they procured, like me, from a neighbouring houfe, a good bafon of warm gruel, in which was a fmall flice of butter, with toafted bread and nutmeg. This was a much better breakfaft, which did not coft more than a pint of beer, namely, three-halfpence, and at the fame time preferved the head clearer. Thofe who continued to gorge themfelves with beer, often loft their credit with the publican, from neglecting to pay their fcore. They had then recourfe to me, to become fecurity for them; *their light*, as they

---

* Printing-houfes in general are thus denominated by the workmen: the *fpirit* they call by the name of *Ralph*.

ufed to call it, *being out*. I attended at the pay-
table every Saturday evening, to take up the little fum which I had made myfelf anfwerable for;
and which amounted to nearly thirty fhillings a
week.

This circumftance, added to my reputation of
being a tolerable good *gabber*, or, in other words,
fkilful in the art of burlefque, kept up my importance in the chapel. I had befides recommended myfelf to the efteem of my mafter by
my affiduous application to bufinefs, never obferving Saint Monday. My extraordinary quick-
nefs in compofing always procured me fuch work
as was moft urgent, and which is commonly beft
paid; and thus my time paffed away in a very
pleafant manner.

My lodging in Little Britain being too far from
the printing-houfe, I took another in Duke-ftreet
oppofite the Roman Catholic chapel. It was at
the back of an Italian warehoufe. The houfe
was kept by a widow, who had a daughter, a
fervant, and a fhop-boy; but the latter flept out
of the houfe. After fending to the people with
whom I lodged in Little Britain, to enquire into
my character, fhe agreed to take me in at the
fame price, three-and-fixpence a week; content-
ing herfelf, fhe faid, with fo little, becaufe of
the fecurity fhe fhould derive, as they were all
women, from having a man lodge in the houfe.

She was a woman rather advanced in life, the
daughter of a clergyman. She had been educated a Proteftant; but her hufband, whofe memory fhe highly revered, had converted her to
the Catholic religion. She had lived in habits
of intimacy with perfons of diftinction; of whom
fhe knew various anecdotes as far back as the
time of Charles II. Being fubject to fits of the
gout, which often confined her to her room, fhe
was fometimes difpofed to fee company. Hers

was

was fo amufing to me, that I was glad to pafs the evening with her as often as fhe defired it. Our fupper confifted only of half an anchovy a- piece, upon a flice of bread and butter, with half a pint of ale between us. But the enter- tainment was in her converfation.

The early hours I kept, and the little trouble I occafioned in the family, made her loth to part with me; and when I mentioned another lodging I had found, nearer the printing-houfe, at two fhillings a week, which fell in with my plan of faving, fhe perfuaded me to give it up, making herfelf an abatement of two fhillings: and thus I continued to lodge with her, during the remain- der of my abode in London, at eighteen-pence a week.

In a garret of the houfe there lived, in the moft retired manner, a lady feventy years of age, of whom I received the following account from my landlady. She was a Roman Catholic. In her early years fhe had been fent to the continent, and entered a convent with the defign of becoming a nun; but the climate not agreeing with her con- ftitution, fhe was obliged to return to England, where, as there were no monafteries, fhe made a vow to lead a monaftic life, in as rigid a man- ner as circumftances would permit. She accord- ingly difpofed of all her property to be applied to charitable ufes, referving to herfelf only twelve pounds a year; and of this fmall pittance fhe gave a part to the poor, living on water-gruel, and ne- ver making ufe of fire but to boil it. She had lived in this garret a great many years, without paying rent to the fucceffive Catholic inhabitants that had kept the houfe; who indeed confidered her abode with them as a bleffing. A prieft came every day to confefs her. I have afked her, faid my landlady, how, living as fhe did, fhe could find fo much employment for a confeffor? To
which

which she answered, that it was impossible to avoid vain thoughts.

I was once permitted to visit her. She was cheerful and polite, and her conversation agreeable. Her apartment was neat; but the whole furniture consisted of a mattress, a table, on which were a crucifix and a book, a chair, which she gave me to fit on, and over the mantlepiece a picture of St. Veronica displaying her handkerchief, on which was seen the miraculous impression of the face of Christ, which she explained to me with great gravity. Her countenance was pale, but she had never experienced sickness; and I may adduce her as another proof how little is sufficient to maintain life and health.

At the printing-house I contracted an intimacy with a sensible young man of the name of Wygate, who, as his parents were in good circumstances, had received a better education than is common with printers. He was a tolerable Latin scholar, spoke French fluently, and was fond of reading. I taught him, as well as a friend of his, to swim, by taking them twice only into the river; after which they stood in need of no farther assistance. We one day made a party to go by water to Chelsea, in order to see the College, and Don Saltero's curiosities. On our return, at the request of the company, whose curiosity Wygate had excited, I undressed myself, and leaped into the river. I swam from near Chelsea the whole way to Blackfriars Bridge, exhibiting, during my course, a variety of feats of activity and address, both upon the surface of the water as well as under it. This sight occasioned much astonishment and pleasure to those to whom it was new. In my youth I took great delight in this exercise. I knew, and could execute, all the evolutions and positions of

Thevenot;

Thevenot; and I added to them fome of my own invention, in which I endeavoured to unite gracefulnefs and utility. I took a pleafure in difplaying them all on this occafion, and was highly flattered with the admiration they excited.

Wygate, befides his being defirous of perfecting himfelf in this art, was the more attached to me from there being, in other refpects, a conformity in our taftes and ftudies. He at length propofed to me to make the tour of Europe with him, maintaining ourfelves at the fame time by working at our profeffion. I was on the point of confenting, when I mentioned it to my friend Mr. Denham, with whom I was glad to pafs an hour whenever I had leifure. He diffuaded me from the project, and advifed me to think of returning to Philadelphia, which he was about to do himfelf. I muft relate in this place a trait of this worthy man's character.

He had formerly been in bufinefs at Briftol, but failing, he compounded with his creditors, and departed for America, where, by affiduous application as a merchant, he acquired in a few years a very confiderable fortune. Returning to England in the fame veffel with myfelf, as I have related above, he invited all his old creditors to a feaft. When affembled, he thanked them for the readinefs with which they had received his fmall compofition; and, while they expected nothing more than a fimple entertainment, each found under his plate, when it came to be removed, a draft upon a banker for the refidue of his debt, with intereft.

He told me that it was his intention to carry back with him to Philadelphia a great quantity of goods, in order to open a ftore; and he offered to take me with him in the capacity of

F   clerk,

clerk, to keep his books, in which he would inftruct me, copy letters, and fuperintend the ftore. He added that, as foon as I had acquired a knowledge of mercantile tranfactions he would improve my fituation, by fending me with a cargo of corn and flour to the American iflands, and by procuring me other lucrative commif-fions; fo that, with good management and œconomy, I might in time begin bufinefs with advantage for myfelf.

I relifhed thefe propofals, London began to tire me; the agreeable hours I had paffed at Philadelphia prefented themfelves to my mind, and I wifhed to fee them revive. I confequently engaged myfelf to Mr. Denham, at a falary of fifty pounds a-year. This was indeed lefs than I earned as a compofitor, but then I had a much fairer profpect. I took leave therefore, as I believed for ever, of printing, and gave myfelf up entirely to my new occupation, fpending all my time either in going from houfe to houfe with Mr. Denham to purchafe goods, or in packing them up, or in expediting the workmen, &c. &c. When every thing however was on board, I had at laft a few days leifure.

During this interval, I was one day fent for by a gentleman, whom I knew only by name. It was Sir William Wyndham. I went to his houfe. He had by fome means heard of my performances between Chelfea and Blackfriars. and that I had taught the art of fwimming to Wygate and another young man in the courfe of a few hours. His two fons were on the point of fetting out on their travels; he was defirous that they fhould previoufly learn to fwim, and offered me a very liberal reward if I would undertake to inftruct them. They were not yet arrived in town, and the ftay I fhould make my-
feIf

felf was uncertain; I could not therefore accept his propofal. I was led however to fuppofe from this incident, that if I had wifhed to remain in London, and open a fwimming fchool, I fhould perhaps have gained a great deal of money. This idea ftruck me fo forcibly, that, had the offer been made fooner, I fhould have difmiffed the thought of returning as yet to America. Some years after, you and I had a more important bufinefs to fettle with one of the fons of Sir William Wyndham, then Lord Egremont. But let us not anticipate events.

I thus paffed about eighteen months in London, working almoft without intermiffion at my trade, avoiding all expence on my own account, except going now and then to the play, and purchafing a few books. But my friend Ralph kept me poor. He owed me about twenty-feven pounds, which was fo much money loft; and when confidered as taken from my little favings, was a very great fum. I had, notwithftanding this, a regard for him, as he poffeffed many amiable qualities. But tho' I had done nothing for myfelf in point of fortune, I had increafed my ftock of knowledge, either by the many excellent books I had read, or the converfation of learned and literary perfons with whom I was acquainted.

We failed from Gravefend the 23d of July 1726. For the incidents of my voyage I refer you to my Journal, where you will find all its circumftances minutely related. We landed at Philadelphia on the 11th of the following Octo-ber.

Keith had been deprived of his office of governor, and was fucceeded by Major Gordon. I met him walking in the ftreets as a private individual. He appeared a little afhamed at feeing me, but paffed on without faying any thing.

F 2

I fhould

I fhould have been equally afhamed myfelf at meeting Mifs Read, had not her family, juftly defpairing of my return after reading my letter, advifed her to give me up, and marry a potter, of the name of Rogers; to which fhe confented: but he never made her happy, and fhe foon feparated from him, refufing to cohabit with him or even bear his name, on account of a report which prevailed, of his having another wife. His fkill in his profeffion had feduced Mifs Read's parents; but he was as bad a fubjeét as he was excellent as a workman. He involved himfelf in debt, and fled, in the year 1727 or 1728, to the Weft Indies, where he died.

During my abfence Keimer had taken a more confiderable houfe, in which he kept a fhop, that was well fupplied with paper, and various other articles. He had procured fome new types, and a number of workmen; among whom, however, there was not one who was good for any thing; and he appeared not to want bufinefs.

Mr. Denham took a warehoufe in Water-ftreet, where we exhibited our commodities. I applied myfelf clofely, ftudied accounts, and became in a fhort time very expert in trade. We lodged and eat together. He was fincerely attached to me, and aéted towards me as if he had been my father. On my fide, I refpeéted and loved him. My fituation was happy; but it was a happinefs of no long duration.

Early in February 1727, when I entered into my twenty-fecond year, we were both taken ill. I was attacked with a pleurify, which had nearly carried me off; I fuffered terribly, and confidered it as all over with me. I felt indeed a fort of difappointment when I found myfelf likely to recover, and regretted that I had ftill to experience, fooner or later, the fame difagreeable fcene again.

I have

I have forgotten what was Mr. Denham's disorder; but it was a tedious one, and he at laft funk under it. He left me a fmall legacy in his will, as a teftimony of his friendfhip; and I was once more abandoned to myfelf in the wide world, the warehoufe being confided to the care of the teftamentary executor, who difmiffed me.

My brother-in-law, Holmes, who happened to be at Philadelphia, advifed me to return to my former profeffion; and Keimer offered me a very confiderable falary if I would undertake the management of his printing-office, that he might devote himfelf entirely to the fuperintendence of his fhop. His wife and relations in London had given me a bad character of him; and I was loth, for the prefent, to have any concern with him. I endeavoured to get employment as a clerk to a merchant; but not readily finding a fituation, I was induced to accept Keimer's propofal.

The following were the perfons I found in his printing-houfe.

Hugh Meredith, a Penfylvanian, about thirty five years of age. He had been brought up to hufbandry, was honeft, fenfible, had fome experience, and was fond of reading; but too much addicted to drinking.

Stephen Potts, a young ruftic, juft broke from fchool, and of ruftic education, with endowments rather above the common order, and a competent portion of underftanding and gaiety; but a little idle. Keimer had engaged thefe two at very low wages, which he had promifed to raife every three months a fhilling a week, provided their improvement in the typographic art fhould merit it. This future increafe of wages was the bait he made ufe of to enfnare them.

Meredith

Meredith was to work at the prefs, and Potts to
bind books, which he had engaged to teach
them, though he underftood neither himfelf.

John Savage, an Irifhman, who had been
brought up to no trade, and whofe fervice, for
a period of four years, Keimer had purchafed of
the captain of a fhip. He was alfo to be a prefl-
man.

George Webb, an Oxford fcholar, whofe time
he had in like manner bought for four years, in-
tending him for a compofitor. I fhall fpeak more
of him prefently.

Laftly, David Harry, a country lad, who was
apprenticed to him.

I foon perceived that Keimer's intention, in
engaging me at a price fo much above what he
was accuftomed to give, was, that I might form
all thefe raw journeymen and apprentices, who
fcarcely coft him any thing, and who, being in-
dentured, would, as foon as they fhould be fufficiently inftructed, enable him to do without me.
I neverthelefs adhered to my agreement. I put
the office in order, which was in the utmoft confufion, and brought his people, by degrees, to
pay attention to their work, and to execute it in
a more mafterly ftyle.

It was fingular to fee an Oxford fcholar in the
condition of a purchafed fervant. He was not
more than eighteen years of age ; and the following are the particulars he gave me of himfelf.
Born at Gloucefter, he had been educated at a
grammar fchool, and had diftinguifhed himfelf
among the fcholars by his fuperior ftyle of acting,
when they reprefented dramatic performances.
He was member of a literary club in the town ;
and fome pieces of his compofition, in profe as
well as in verfe, had been inferted in the Gloucefter papers. From hence he was fent to Oxford,

ford, where he remained about a year; but he
was not contented, and wished above all things
to see London, and become an actor.   At length,
having received fifteen guineas to pay his quarter's board, he decamped with the money from
Oxford, hid his gown in a hedge, and travelled
to London.   There, having no friend to direct
him, he fell into bad company, soon squandered
his fifteen guineas, could find no way of being
introduced to the actors, became contemptible,
pawned his clothes, and was in want of bread.
As he was walking along the streets, almost fa-
mished with hunger, and not knowing what to
do, a recruiting bill was put into his hand, which
offered an immediate treat and bounty-money to
whoever was disposed to serve in America.   He
instantly repaired to the house of rendezvous, in-
listed himself, was put on board a ship and conveyed to America, without ever writing a line
to inform his parents what was become of him.
His mental vivacity, and good natural disposition, made him an excellent companion; but he
was indolent, thoughtless, and to the last degree
imprudent.

John, the Irishman, soon ran away.   I began
to live very agreeably with the rest.   They respected me, and the more so as they found Keimer incapable of instructing them, and as they
learned something from me every day.   We never worked on a Saturday, it being Keimer's
sabbath; so that I had two days a week for reading.

I increased my acquaintance with persons of
knowledge and information in the town.   Keimer himself treated me with great civility and
apparent esteem; and I had nothing to give me
uneasiness but my debt to Vernon, which I was
unable to pay, my savings as yet being very little.

tle. He had the goodnefs, however, not to afk me for the money.

Our prefs was frequently in want of the neceffary quantity of letter; and there was no fuch trade as that of letter-founder in America. I had feen the practice of this art at the houfe of James, in London; but had at the time paid it very little attention. I however contrived to fabricate a mould. I made ufe of fuch letters as we had for punches, founded new letters of lead in matrices of clay, and thus fupplied, in a tolerable manner, the wants that were moft preffing.

I alfo, upon occafion, engraved various ornaments, made ink, gave an eye to the fhop; in fhort I was in every refpect the *factotum*. But ufeful as I made myfelf, I perceived that my fervices became every day of lefs importance, in proportion as the other men improved; and when Keimer paid me my fecond quarter's wages, he gave me to underftand that they were too heavy, and that he thought I ought to make an abatement. He became by degrees lefs civil, and affumed more the tone of mafter. He frequently found fault, was difficult to pleafe, and feemed always on the point of coming to an open quarrel with me.

I continued, however, to bear it patiently, conceiving that his ill-humour was partly occafioned by the derangement and embarraffment of his affairs. At laft a flight incident broke our connection. Hearing a noife in the neighbourhood, I put my head out at the window to fee what was the matter. Keimer being in the ftreet, obferved me, and in a loud and angry tone told me to mind my work; adding fome reproachful words, which piqued me the more as they were uttered in the ftreet; and the neighbours, whom the fame noife had attracted to the windows, were witneffes of the manner in which I was treated.

treated. He immediately came up to the print‑
ing room, and continued to exclaim againſt me.
The quarrel became warm on both ſides, and he
gave me notice to quit him at the expiration of
three months, as had been agreed between us;
regretting that he was obliged to give me ſo long
a term. I told him that his regret was ſuperflu‑
ous, as I was ready to quit him inſtantly; and
I took my hat and came out of the houſe, beg‑
ging Meredith to take care of ſome things which
I left, and bring them to my lodgings.

Meredith came to me in the evening. We
talked for ſome time upon the quarrel that had
taken place. He had conceived a great venera‑
tion for me, and was ſorry I ſhould quit the
houſe while he remained in it. He diſſuaded
me from returning to my native country, as I
began to think of doing. He reminded me that
Keimer owed more than he poſſeſſed; that his
creditors began to be alarmed; that he kept his
ſhop in a wretched ſtate, often ſelling things at
prime coſt for the ſake of ready money, and con‑
tinually giving credit without keeping any
accounts; that of conſequence he muſt very ſoon
fail, which would occaſion a vacancy from which
I might derive advantage. I objected my want
of money. Upon which he informed me that
his father had a very high opinion of me, and,
from a converſation that had paſſed between
them, he was ſure that he would advance what‑
ever might be neceſſary to eſtabliſh us, if I was
willing to enter into partnerſhip with him. " My
" time with Keimer," added he, "will be at an end
" next ſpring. In the mean time we may ſend
" to London for our preſs and types. I know
" that I am no workman; but if you agree to
" the propoſal, your ſkill in the buſineſs will be
" balanced by the capital I ſhall furniſh, and we
" will

" will fhare the profits equally." His propofal
was reafonable, and I fell in with it. His father,
who was then in the town, approved of it. He
knew that I had fome afcendancy over his fon,
as I had been able to prevail on him to abftain a
long time from drinking brandy; and he hoped
that, when more clofely connected with him, I
fhould cure him entirely of this unfortunate habit.

I gave the father a lift of what it would be
neceffary to import from London. He took it
to a merchant, and the order was given. We
agreed to keep the fecret till the arrival of the
materials, and I was in the mean time to procure
work, if poffible, in another printing-houfe; but
there was no place vacant, and I remained idle.
After fome days, Keimer having the expectation
of being employed to print fome New-Jerfey
money-bills, that would require types and engravings which I only could furnifh, and fearful
that Bradford, by engaging me, might deprive
him of this undertaking, fent me a very civil
meffage, telling me that old friends ought not to
be difunited on account of a few words, which
were the effect only of a momentary paffion, and
inviting me to return to him. Meredith perfuaded me to comply with the invitation, particularly as it would afford him more opportunities
of improving himfelf in the bufinefs by means of
my inftructions. I did fo; and we lived upon
better terms than before our feparation.

He obtained the New-Jerfey bufinefs; and, in
order to execute it, I conftructed a copper-plate
printing-prefs; the firft that had been feen in the
country. I engraved various ornaments and vig-
nettes for the bills; and we repaired to Burlington together, where I executed the whole to the
general fatisfaction; and he received a fum of
money

money for this work, which enabled him to keep his head above water for a confiderable time longer.

At Burlington I formed acquaintance with the principal perfonages of the province; many of whom were commiffioned by the affembly to fuperintend the prefs, and to fee that no more bills were printed than the law had prefcribed. Accordingly they were conftantly with us, each in his turn; and he that came commonly brought with him a friend or two to bear him company. My mind was more cultivated by reading than Keimer's; and it was for this reafon, probably, that they fet more value on my converfation. They took me to their houfes, introduced me to their friends, and treated me with the greateft civility; while Keimer, though mafter, faw himfelf a little neglected. He was, in fact, a ftrange animal, ignorant of the common modes of life, apt to oppofe with rudenefs generally received opinions, an enthufiaft in certain points of religion, difguftingly unclean in his perfon, and a little knavifh withall.

We remained there nearly three months; and at the expiration of this period I could include in the lift of my friends, Judge Allen, Samuel Buftil, fecretary of the province, Ifaac Pearfon, Jofeph Cooper, feveral of the Smiths, all members of the affembly, and Ifaac Deacon, infpector-general. The laft was a fhrewd and fubtle old man. He told me, that, when a boy, his firft employment had been that of carrying clay to brick-makers; that he did not learn to write till he was fomewhat advanced in life; that he was afterwards employed as an underling to a furveyor, who taught him his trade, and that by induftry he had at laft acquired a competent fortune. " I " forefee," faid he one day to me, " that you will
" foon

" foon fupplant this man," fpeaking of Keimer,
" and get a fortune in the bufinefs at Philadel-
" phia." He was wholly ignorant at the time of
my intention of eftablifhing myfelf there, or any
where elfe. Thefe friends were very ferviceable
to me in the end, as was I alfo, upon occafion, to
fome of them; and they have continued ever
fince their efteem for me.

Before I relate the particulars of my entrance
into bufinefs, it may be proper to inform you
what was at that time the ftate of my mind as to
moral principles, that you may fee the degree of
influence they had upon the fubfequent events of
my life.

My parents had given me betimes religious
impreffions; and I received from my infancy a
pious education in the principles of Calvinifm.
But fcarcely was I arrived at fifteen years of age,
when, after having doubted in turn of different
tenets, according as I found them combated in
the different books that I read, I began to doubt
of revelation itfelf. Some volumes againft deifm
fell into my hands. They were faid to be the
fubftance of fermons preached at Boyle's lecture.
It happened that they produced on me an effect
precifely the reverfe of what was intended by the
writers; for the arguments of the deifts, which
were cited in order to be refuted, appeared to
me much more forcible than the refutation itfelf.
In a word, I foon became a perfect deift. My
arguments perverted fome other young perfons;
particularly Collins and Ralph. But in the fequel,
when I recollected that they had both ufed me
extremely ill, without the fmalleft remorfe; when
I confidered the behaviour of Keith, another free-
thinker, and my own conduct towards Vernon
and Mifs Read, which at times gave me much
uneafinefs, I was led to fufpect that this doctrine,
though

though it might be true, was not very ufeful.
I began to entertain a lefs favourable opinion of
my London pamphlet, to which I had prefixed,
as a motto, the following lines of Dryden;

Whatever is, is right; though purblind man
Sees but part of the chain, the neareft link,
His eyes not carrying to the equal beam
That poifes all above.

and of which the object was to prove, from the
attributes of God, his goodnefs, wifdom, and
power, that there could be no fuch thing as evil
in the world; that vice and virtue did not in
reality exift, and were nothing more than vain
diftinctions. I no longer regarded it as fo blame-
lefs a work as I had formerly imagined; and I
fufpected that fome error muft have imperceptibly glided into my argument, by which all the
inferences I had drawn from it had been affected,
as frequently happens in metaphyfical reafonings.
In a word, I was at laft convinced that truth,
probity, and fincerity, in tranfactions between
man and man, were of the utmoft importance to
the happinefs of life; and I refolved from that
moment, and wrote the refolution in my journal,
to practife them as long as I lived.

Revelation indeed, as fuch, had no influence
on my mind; but I was of opinion that, though
certain actions could not be bad merely becaufe
revelation prohibited, or good becaufe it enjoined them, yet it was probable that thofe actions
were prohibited becaufe they were bad for us,
or enjoined becaufe advantageous in their nature,
all things confidered. This perfuafion, Divine
Providence, or fome guardian angel, and perhaps
a concurrence of favourable circumftances co-
operating, preferved me from all immorality, or
grofs and *voluntary* injuftice, to which my want
of religion was calculated to expofe me, in the
dangerous

dangerous period of youth, and in the hazard-
ous situations in which I sometimes found myself,
among strangers, and at a distance from the eye
and admonitions of my father. I may say *voluntary*, because the errors into which I had fallen,
had been in a manner the forced result either of
my own inexperience, or the dishonefty of others.
(Thus, before I entered on my new career, I had
imbibed solid principles, and a character of probity. ` I knew their value ; and I made a solemn
engagement with myself never to depart from
them.

I had not long returned from Burlington before our printing materials arrived from London.
I settled my accounts with Keimer, and quitted
him, with his own consent, before he had any
knowledge of our plan. We found a house to
let near the market. We took it ; and to render the rent less burthenfome (it was then twenty-four pounds a-year, but I have since known
it to let for seventy), we admitted Thomas Godfrey, a glazier, with his family, who eafed us of
a confiderable part of it ; and with him we agreed
to board.

We had no sooner unpacked our letters,
and put our press in order, than a person of
my acquaintance, George Houfe, brought us
a countryman, whom he had met in the streets
enquiring for a printer. Our money was almoft
exhausted by the number of things we had
been obliged to procure. The five shillings we
received from this countryman, the first fruit
of our earnings, coming so seasonably, gave me
more pleasure than any sum I have since gained;
and the recollection of the gratitude I felt on
this ocasion to George Houfe, has rendered
me often more difposed, than perhaps I should
otherwise have been, to encourage young begin-
ners in trade.

There

There are in every country morofe beings, who are always prognofticating ruin. There was one of this ftamp at Philadelphia. He was a man of fortune, declined in years, had an air of wifdom, and a very grave manner of fpeaking. His name was Samuel Mickle. I knew him not; but he ftopped one day at my door, and afked me if I was the young man who had lately opened a new printing-houfe. Upon my anfwering in the affirmative, he faid that he was very forry for me, as it was an extenfive undertaking, and the money that had been laid out upon it would be loft, Philadelphia being a place falling into decay; its inhabitants having all, or nearly all of them, been obliged to call together their creditors. That he knew, from undoubted fact, the circumftances which might lead us to fuppofe the contrary, fuch as new buildings, and the advanced price of rent, to be deceitful appearances, which in reality contributed to haften the general ruin; and he gave me fo long a detail of misfortunes, actually exifting, or which were foon to take place, that he left me almoft in a ftate of defpair. Had I known this man before I entered into trade, 1 fhould doubtlefs never have ventured. He continued however to live in this place of decay, and to declaim in the fame ftyle, refufing for many years to buy a houfe, becaufe all was going to wreck; and in the end I had the fatisfaction to fee him pay five times as much for one as it would have coft him had he purchafed it when he firft began his lamentations.

I ought to have related, that, during the autumn of the preceding year, I had united the majority of well-informed perfons of my acquaintance into a club, which we called by the name of the *Junto,* and the object of which was to improve our underftanding. We met every Friday evening.

ing. The regulations I drew up, obliged every
member to propofe, in his turn, one or more
queftions upon fome point of morality, politics or
philofophy, which were to be difcuffed by the
fociety; and to read, once in three months, an
effay of his own compofition, on whatever fubject
he pleafed./ Our debates were under the direction
of a prefident, and were to be dictated only by a
fincere defire of truth; the pleafure of difputing,
and the vanity of triumph having no fhare in the
bufinefs; and in order to prevent undue warmth,
every expreffion which implied obftinate adherence to an opinion, and all direct contradiction,
were prohibited, under fmall pecuniary penalties.

The firft members of our club were Jofeph
Breintal, whofe occupation was that of a fcrive-
ner. He was a middle-aged man, of a good natural difpofition, ftrongly attached to his friends,
a great lover of poetry, reading every thing that
came in his way, and writing tolerably well, ingenious in many little trifles, and of an agreeable
converfation.

Thomas Godfrey, a fkilful, though felf-taught
mathematician, and who was afterwards the inventor of what now goes by the name of Had-
ley's dial; but he had little knowledge out of
his own line, and was infupportable in company,
always requiring, like the majority of mathema-
ticians that have fallen in my way, an unufual
precifion in every thing that is faid, continually
contradicting, or making trifling diftinctions; a
fure way of defeating all the ends of converfation. He very foon left us.

Nicholas Scull, a furveyor, and who became
afterwards furveyor-general. He was fond of
books, and wrote verfes.

William Parfons, brought up to the trade of
a fhoe-maker, but who, having a tafte for reading,

ing, had acquired a profound knowledge of mathematics. He firſt ſtudied them with a view to aſtrology, and was afterwards the firſt to laugh at his folly. He alſo became ſurveyor-general.

William Mawgridge, a joiner, and very excellent mechanic; and in other reſpects a man of ſolid underſtanding.

Hugh Meredith, Stephen Potts, and George Webb, of whom I have already ſpoken.

Robert Grace, a young man of fortune; generous, animated, and witty; fond of epigrams, but more fond of his friends.

And laſtly, William Coleman, at that time a merchant's clerk, and nearly of my own age. He had a cooler and clearer head, a better heart, and more ſcrupulous morals, than almoſt any other perſon I have ever met with. He became a very reſpectable merchant, and one of our provincial judges. Our friendſhip ſubſiſted, without interruption, for more than forty years, till the period of his death; and the club continued to exiſt almoſt as long.

This was the beſt ſchool of politics and philoſophy that then exiſted in the province; for our queſtions, which were read a week previous to their difcuſſion, induced us to peruſe attentively ſuch books as were written upon the ſubjects propoſed, that we might be able to ſpeak upon them more pertinently. We thus acquired the habit of converſing more agreeably; every object being difcuſſed conformably to our regulations, and in a manner to prevent mutual difguſt. To this circumſtance may be attributed the long duration of the club; which I ſhall have frequent occaſion to mention as I proceed.

I have introduced it here, as being one of the means on which I had to count for ſucceſs in my buſineſs; every member exerting himſelf to pro-

G

cure work for us.   Breintnal, among others, obtained for us, on the part of the Quakers, the printing of forty sheets of their history; of which the rest was to be done by Keimer.   Our execution of this work was by no means masterly; as the price was very low.   It was in folio, upon *pro patria* paper, and in the *pica* letter, with heavy notes in the smallest type.   I composed a sheet a day, and Meredith put it to the press.   It was frequently eleven o'clock at night, sometimes later, before I had finished my distribution for the next day's task; for the little things which our friends occasionally sent us, kept us back in this work: but I was so determined to compose a sheet a day, that one evening, when my form was imposed, and my day's work, as I thought, at an end, an accident having broken this form, and deranged two complete folio pages, I immediately distributed, and composed them anew before I went to bed.

This unwearied industry, which was perceived by our neighbours, began to acquire us reputation and credit.   I learned, among other things, that our new printing-house being the subject of conversation at a club of merchants, who met every evening, it was the general opinion that it would fail; there being already two printing-houses in the town, Keimer's and Bradford's. But Dr. Bard, whom you and I had occasion to see, many years after, at his native town of St. Andrew's in Scotland, was of a different opinion. " The industry of this Franklin (said he) is superior to any thing of the kind I have ever witnessed.   I see him still at work when I return " from the club at night, and he is at it again in " the morning before his neighbours are out of " bed." This account struck the rest of the assembly, and shortly after one of its members came to
                                                    our

our houfe, and offered to fupply us with articles of ftationary; but we wifhed not as yet to embarrafs ourfelves with keeping a fhop. It is not for the fake of applaufe that I enter fo freely into the particulars of my induftry, but fuch of my defcendants as fhall read thefe memoirs may know the ufe of this virtue, by feeing in the recital of my life the effects it operated in my favour.

George Webb, having found a friend who lent him the neceffary fum to buy out his time of Keimer, came one day to offer himfelf to us as a journeyman. We could not employ him immediately; but I foolifhly told him, under the rofe, that I intended fhortly to publifh a new periodical paper, and that we fhould then have work for him. My hopes of fuccefs, which I imparted to him, were founded on the circumftance, that the only paper we had in Philadelphia at that time, and which Bradford printed, was a paltry thing, miferably conducted, in no refpect amufing, and which yet was profitable. I confequently fuppofed that a good work of this kind could not fail of fuccefs. Webb betrayed my fecret to Keimer, who, to prevent me, immediately publifhed the *profpectus* of a paper that he intended to inftitute himfelf, and in which Webb was to be engaged.

I was exafperated at this proceeding, and, with a view to counteract them, not being able at prefent to inftitute my own paper, I wrote fome humorous pieces in Bradford's, under the title of the Bufy Body*; and which was continued for feveral months by Breintnal. I hereby fixed the attention of the public upon Bradford's paper; and the *profpectus* of Keimer, which we turned

---

* A manufcript note in the file of the American Mercury, preferved in the Philadelphia library, fays, that Franklin wrote the firft five numbers, and part of the eight.

into

into ridicule, was treated with contempt. He began, notwithstanding, his paper; and after continuing it for nine months having at most not more than ninety subscribers, he offered it me for a mere trifle. I had for some time been ready for such an engagement; I therefore instantly took it upon myself, and in a few years it proved extremely profitable to me.

I perceive that I am apt to speak in the first person, though our partnership still continued. It is, perhaps, because, in fact, the whole business devolved upon me. Meredith was no compositor, and but an indifferent pressman; and it was rarely that he abstained from hard drinking. My friends were sorry to see me connected with him; but I contrived to derive from it the utmost advantage the case admitted.

Our first number produced no other effect than any other paper which had appeared in the province, as to type and printing; but some remarks, in my peculiar style of writing, upon the dispute which then prevailed between governor Burnet and the Massachusett assembly, struck some persons as above mediocrity, caused the paper and its editors to be talked of, and in a few weeks induced them to become our subscribers. Many others followed their example; and our subscription continued to increase. This was one of the first good effects of the pains I had taken to learn to put my ideas on paper. I derived this farther advantage from it, that the leading men of the place, seeing in the author of this publication a man so well able to use his pen, thought it right to patronise and encourage me.

The votes, laws, and other public pieces, were printed by Bradford. An address of the house of assembly to the governor had been executed by him in a very coarse and incorrect manner. We

We reprinted it with accuracy and neatnefs, and fent a copy to every member. They perceived the difference; and it fo ftrengthened the influence of our friends in the affembly, that we were nominated its printer for the following year.

Among thefe friends I ought not to forget one member in particular, Mr. Hamilton, whom I have mentioned in a former part of my narrative, and who was now returned from England. He warmly interefted himfelf for me on this occafion, as he did likewife on many others afterwards; having continued his kindnefs to me till his death.

About this period Mr. Vernon reminded me of the debt I owed him, but without preffing me for payment. I wrote a handfome letter on the occafion, begging him to wait a little longer, to which he confented; and as foon as I was able I paid him, principal and intereft, with many expreffions of gratitude; fo that this error of my life was in a manner atoned for.

But another trouble now happened to me, which I had not the fmalleft reafon to expect. Meredith's father, who, according to our agreement, was to defray the whole expence of our printing materials, had only paid a hundred pounds. Another hundred was ftill due, and the merchant being tired of waiting, commenced a fuit againft us. We bailed the action, but with the melancholy profpect, that, if the money was not forth-coming at the time fixed, the affair would come to iffue, judgment be put in execution, our delightful hopes be annihilated, and ourfelves entirely ruined; as the type and prefs muft be fold, perhaps at half their value, to pay the debt.

In this diftrefs, two real friends, whofe generous conduct I have never forgotten, and never fhall forget while I retain the remembrance of any

any thing, came to me feparately, without the knowledge of each other, and without my having applied to either of them. Each offered me whatever money might be neceffary, to take the bufinefs into my own hands, if the thing was practicable, as they did not like I fhould continue in partnerfhip with Meredith, who, they faid, was frequently feen drunk in the ftreets, and gambling at ale-houfes, which very much injured our credit. Thefe friends were William Coleman and Robert Grace. I told them, that while there remained any probability that the Merediths would fulfil their part of the compact, I could not propofe a feparation; as I conceived myfelf to be under obligations to them for what they had done already, and were ftill difpofed to do if they had the power: but in the end fhould they fail in their engagement, and our partnerfhip be diffolved, I fhould then think myfelf at liberty to accept the kindnefs of my friends.

Things remained for fome time in this ftate. At laft I faid one day to my partner, " Your father is perhaps diffatisfied with your having a fhare only in the bufinefs, and is unwilling to do for two, what he would do for you alone. Tell me frankly if that be the cafe, and I will refign the whole to you, and do for myfelf as well as I can."—" No (faid he) my father has really been difappointed in his hopes; he is not able to pay, and I wifh to put him to no farther inconvenience. I fee that I am not at all calculated for a printer; I was educated as a farmer, and it was abfurd in me to come here, at thirty years of age, and bind myfelf apprentice to a new trade. Many of my countrymen are going to fettle in North Carolina, where the foil is exceedingly favourable. I am tempted to go with them, and to refume my former occupation.
You

You will doubtlefs find friends who will affift you. If you will take upon yourfelf the debts of the partnerfhip, return my father the hundred pounds he has advanced, pay my little perfonal debts, and give me thirty pounds and a new faddle, I will renounce the partnerfhip, and confign over the whole ftock to you."

I accepted this propofal without hefitation. It was committed to paper, and figned and fealed without delay. I gave him what he demanded, and he departed foon after for Carolina, from whence he fent me, in the following year, two letters, containing the beft accounts that had yet been given of that country, as to climate, foil, agriculture, &c.; for he was well verfed in thefe matters. I publifhed them in my newfpaper, and they were received with great fatisfaction.

As foon as he was gone I applied to my two friends, and not wifhing to give a difobliging preference to either of them, I accepted from each half of what he offered me, and which it was neceffary I fhould have. I paid the partner-fhip debts, and continued the bufinefs on my own account; taking care to inform the public, by advertifement, of the partnerfhip being diffol-ved. This was, I think, in the year 1729, or thereabout.

Nearly at the fame period the people demanded a new emiffion of paper money; the exifting and only one that had taken place in the pro-vince, and which amounted to fifteen thoufand pounds, being foon to expire. The wealthy in-habitants, prejudiced againft every fort of paper currency, from the fear of its depreciation, of which there had been an inftance in the province of New-England, to the injury of its holders, ftrongly oppofed the meafure. We had difcuffed this affair in our junto, in which I was on the side of the new emiffion; convinced that the firft fmall fum, fabricated in 1723, had done much good in the province, by favouring commerce, induftry and population, fince all the houfes were now inhabited, and many others building; whereas I remembered to have feen, when I firft paraded the ftreets of Philadelphia eating my roll, the majority of thofe in Walnut-ftreet, Second-ftreet, Fourth-ftreet, as well as a great number in Chefnut and other ftreets, with papers on them fignifying that they were to be let; which made me think at the time that the inhabitants of the town were deferting it one after another.

Our debates made me fo fully mafter of the fubject, that I wrote and publifhed an anonymous pamphlet, entitled An Enquiry into the Nature and Neceffity of a Paper Currency. It was very well received by the lower and midling clafs of people; but it difpleafed the opulent, as it increafed the clamour in favour of the new emiffion. Having, however, no writer among them capable of anfwering it, their oppofition became lefs violent; and there being in the houfe of affembly a majority for the meafure, it paffed. The friends I had acquired in the houfe, perfuaded that I had done the country effential fervice on this occafion, rewarded me by giving me the printing of the bills. It was a lucrative employment, and proved a very feafonable help to me; another advantage which I derived from having habituated myfelf to write

Time and experience fo fully demonftrated the utility of paper currency, that it never after experienced any confiderable oppofition; fo that it foon amounted to 55,000l. and in the year 1739 to 80,000l. It has fince rifen, during the laft war, to 350,000l. trade, buildings and population having in the interval continually increafed:

but

but I am now convinced that there are limits beyond which paper money would be prejudicial.

I soon after obtained, by the influence of my friend Hamilton, the printing of the Newcaftle paper money, another profitable work, as I then thought it, little things appearing great to perfons of moderate fortune; and they were really great to me, as proving great encouragements. He alfo procured me the printing of the laws and votes of that government, which I retained as I continued in the bufinefs.

I now opened a fmall ftationer's fhop. I kept bonds and agreements of all kinds, drawn up in a more accurate form than had yet been feen in that part of the world; a work in which I was affifted by my friend Breintnal. I had alfo paper, parchment, pafteboard, books, &c. One Whitemafh, an excellent compofitor, whom I had known in London, came to offer himfelf. I engaged. him; and he continued conftantly and diligently to work with me. I alfo took an apprentice, the fon of Aquila Rofe.

I began to pay, by degrees, the debt I had contracted; and in order to infure my credit and character as a tradefman, I took care not only to be *really* induftrious and frugal, but alfo to avoid every appearance of the contrary. I was plainly dreffed, and never feen in any place of public amufement. I never went a fifhing or hunting. A book indeed enticed me fometimes from my work, but it was feldom, by ftealth, and occafioned no fcandal; and to fhow that I did not think myfelf above my profeffion, I conveyed home fometimes in a wheelbarrow the paper I purchafed at the warehoufes.

I thus obtained the reputation of being an induftrious young man, and very punctual in his payments. The merchants who imported articles

cles of stationary solicited my custom; others offered to furnish me with books, and my little trade went on prosperously.

Meanwhile the credit and business of Keimer diminishing every day, he was at last forced to sell his stock to satisfy his creditors; and he betook himself to Barbadoes, where he lived for some time in a very impoverished state. His apprentice, David Harry, whom I had instructed while I worked with Keimer, having bought his materials, succeeded him in the business. I was apprehensive, at first, of finding in Harry a powerful competitor, as he was allied to an opulent and respectable family; I therefore proposed a partnership, which, happily for me, he rejected with disdain. He was extremely proud, thought himself a fine gentleman, lived extravagantly, and pursued amusements which suffered him to be scarcely ever at home; of consequence he became in debt, neglected his business, and business neglected him. Finding in a short time nothing to do in the country, he followed Keimer to Barbadoes, carrying his printing materials with him. There the apprentice employed his old master as a journeyman. They were continually quarrelling; and Harry still getting in debt, was obliged at last to sell his press and types, and return to his old occupation of husbandry in Pennsylvania. The person who purchased them employed Keimer to manage the business; but he died a few years after.

I had now at Philadelphia no competitor but Bradford, who, being in easy circumstances, did not engage in the printing of books, except now and then as workmen chanced to offer themselves; and was not anxious to extend his trade. He had, however, one advantage over me, as he had the direction of the post office, and was of consequence

fequence fuppofed to have better opportunities of obtaining news. His paper was alfo fuppofed to be more advantageous to advertifing cuftomers; and in confequence of that fuppofition, his adver- tifements were much more numerous than mine: this was a fource of great profit to him, and dif- advantageous to me. It was to no purpofe that I really procured other papers, and diftributed my own, by means of the poft; the public took for granted my inability in this refpect; and I was indeed unable to conquer it in any other mode than by bribing the poft-boys, who ferved me only by ftealth, Bradford being fo illiberal as to forbid them. This treatment of his excited my refentment; and my difguft was fo rooted, that, when I afterwards fuccceded him in the poft-office, I took care to avoid copying his ex- ample.

I had hitherto continued to board with God- frey, who, with his wife and children, occupied part of my houfe, and half of the fhop for his bufinefs; at which indeed he worked very little, being always abforbed by mathematics. Mrs. Godfrey formed a wifh of marrying me to the daughter of one of her relations. She contrived various opportunities of bringing us together, till fhe faw that I was captivated; which was not difficult, the lady in queftion poffeffing great per- fonal merit. The parents encouraged my ad- dreffes, by inviting me continually to fupper, and leaving us together, till at laft it was time to come to an explanation. Mrs. Godfrey un- dertook to negociate our little treaty. I gave her to underftand, that I expected to receive with the young lady a fum of money that would enable me at leaft to difcharge the remainder of my debt for my printing materials. It was then, I be- lieve, not more than a hundred pounds. She

brought

brought me for anfwer, that they had no fuch fum at their difpofal. I obferved that it might eafily be obtained, by a mortgage on their houfe. The reply to this was, after a few days interval, that they did not approve of the match; that they had confulted Bradford; and found that the bufinefs of a printer was not lucrative; that my letters would foon be worn out, and muft be fupplied by new ones; that Keimer and Harry had failed, and that, probably, I fhould do fo too. Accordingly they forbade me the houfe, and the young lady was confined. I know not if they had really changed their minds, or if it was merely an artifice, fuppofing our affections to be too far engaged for us to defift, and that we fhould contrive to marry fecretly, which would leave them at liberty to give or not as they pleafed. But, fufpecting this motive, I never went again to their houfe.

Some time after Mrs. Godfrey informed me that they were very favourably difpofed towards me, and wifhed me to renew the acquaintance; but I declared a firm refolution never to have any thing more to do with the family. The Godfreys expreffed fome refentment at this; and as we could no longer agree, they changed their refidence, leaving me in poffeffion of the whole houfe. I then refolved to take no more lodgers. This affair having turned my thoughts to marriage, I looked around me, and made overtures of alliance in other quarters; but I foon found that the profeffion of a printer being generally looked upon as a poor trade, I could expect no money with a wife, at leaft if I wifhed her to poffefs any other charm. Meanwhile that paffion of youth, fo difficult to govern, had often drawn me into intrigues with defpicable women who fell in my way; which were not unaccompanied

with

with expence and inconvenience, befides the perpetual rifk of injuring my health, and catching
a difeafe which I dreaded above all things. But
I was fortunate enough to efcape this danger.

As a neighbour and old acquaintance, I had
kept up a friendly intimacy with the family of
Mifs Read. Her parents had retained an affection for me from the time of my lodging in their
houfe. I was often invited thither; they confulted me about their affairs, and I had been fometimes ferviceable to them. I was touched with
the unhappy fituation of their daughter, who
was almoft always melancholy, and continually
feeking folitude. I regarded my forgetfulnefs
and inconftancy, during my abode in London,
as the principal caufe of her misfortune; though
her mother had the candour to attribute the
fault to herfelf, rather than to me, becaufe, after
having prevented our marriage previoufly to my
departure, fhe had induced her to marry another
in my abfence.

Our mutual affection revived; but there ex-
ifted great obftacles to our union. Her marriage
was confidered, indeed, as not being valid, the
man having, it was faid, a former wife ftill living in England; but of this it was difficult to obtain a proof at fo great a diftance; and though
a report prevailed of his being dead, yet we had
no certainty of it; and fuppofing it to be true,
he had left many debts, for the payment of which
his fucceffor might be fued. We ventured neverthelefs, in fpite of all thefe difficulties; and I
married her on the firft of September 1730.
None of the inconveniences we had feared happened to us. She proved to me a good and faithful companion, and contributed effentially to the
fuccefs of my fhop. We profpered together, and
it was our mutual ftudy to render each other

happy,

happy. Thus I corrected, as well as I could, this great error of my youth.

Our club was not at that time eftablifhed at a tavern. We held our meeting at the houfe of Mr. Grace, who appropriated a room to the purpofe. Some member obferved one day, that as our books were frequently quoted in the courfe of our difcuffions, it would be convenient to have them collected in the room in which we affem-bled, in order to be confulted upon occafion; and that, by thus forming a common library of our individual collections, each would have the advantage of ufing the books of all the other members, which would nearly be the fame as if he poffeffed them all himfelf. The idea was ap-proved, and we accordingly brought fuch books as we thought we could fpare, which were placed at the end of the club-room. They amounted not to fo many as we expected; and though we made confiderable ufe of them, yet fome incon-veniences refulting, from want of care, it was agreed, after about a year, to deftroy the collecti-on; and each took away fuch books as belonged to him.

It was now that I firft ftarted the idea of efta-blifhing, by fubfcription, a public library. I drew up the propofals, had them ingroffed in form by Brockden the attorney, and my project fucceed-ed, as will be feen in the fequel * * * * *
* * * * * * * * * * *

[The life of Dr Franklin, as written by him-felf, fo far as it has yet been communicated to the world, breaks off in this place. We under-ftand that it was continued by him fomewhat farther, and we hope that the remainder will, at fome future period, be communicated to the pulic. We have no hefitation in fuppofing that
every

every reader will find himfelf greatly interefted
by the frank fimplicity and the philofophical difcernment by which thefe pages are fo eminently
chara&terifed.   We have therefore thought proper, in order as much as poffible to relieve his
regret, to fubjoin the following continuation, by
one of the Do&or's intimate friends.   It is ex-
tra&ed from an American periodical publication,
and was written by the late Dr. Stuber * of Philadelphia.]

THE promotion of literature had been little attended to in Penfylvania.   Moft of the inhabitants were too much immerfed in bufinefs to
think of fcientific purfuits ; and thofe few, whofe
inclinations led them to ftudy, found it difficult
to gratify them, from the want of fufficiently
large libraries.   In fuch circumftances, the efta-

* Dr. Stuber was born in Philadelphia, of German parents.   He was fent, at an early age, to the univerfity, where
his genius, diligence and amiable temper foon acquired him
the particular notice and favour of thofe under whofe immediate dire&ion he was placed.   After paffing through the
common courfe of ftudy, in a much fhorter time than ufual,
he left the univerfity, at the age of fixteen, with great reputation.   Not long after, he entered on the ftudy of Phyfic ;
and the zeal with which he purfued it, and the advances he
made, gave his friends reafon to form the moft flattering prof-
pe&s of his future eminence and ufefulnefs in the profeffion.
As Dr. Stuber's circumftances were very moderate, he did not
think this purfuit well calculated to anfwer them.   He therefore relinquifhed it, after he had obtained a degree in the profeffion, and qualified himfelf to pra&ife with credit and fuccefs ;
and immediately entered on the ftudy of Law.   In purfuit of
the laft mentioned obje&, he was prematurely arrefted, before
he had an opportunity of reaping the fruit of thofe talents
with which he was endowed, and of a youth fpent in the ardent and fuccefsful purfuit of ufeful and elegant literature.

blifhment

blifhment of a public library was an important event. This was firft fet on foot by Franklin, about the year 1731. Fifty perfons fubfcribed forty fhillings each, and agreed to pay ten fhillings annually. The number encreafed ; and in 1742, the company was incorporated by the name of " The Library Company of Philadelphia." Several other companies were formed in this city in imitation of it. Thefe were at length united with the library company of Philadelphia, which, thus received a confiderable acceffion of books and property. It now contains about eight thou-fand volumes on all fubjects, a philofophical apparatus, and a good beginning towards a collecti-tion of natural and artificial curiofities, befides landed property of confiderable value. The company have lately built an elegant houfe in Fifth-ftreet, in the front of which will be erected a marble ftatue of their founder, Benjamin Franklin.

    This inftitution was greatly encouraged by the friends of literature in America and in Great Britain. The Penn family diftinguifhed themfelves by their donations. Amongft the earlieft friends of this inftitution muft be mentioned the late Peter Collinfon, the friend and correfpondent of Dr. Franklin. He not only made confiderable prefents himfelf, and obtained others from his friends, but voluntarily undertook to manage the bufinefs of the company in London, recommending books, purchafing and fhipping them. His extenfive knowledge, and zeal for the promotion of fcience, enabled him to execute this important truft with the greateft advantage. He continued to perform thefe fervices for more than thirty years, and uniformly refufed to accept of any compenfation. During this time, he communi-cated to the directors every information relative

to

to improvements and difcoveries in the arts, agriculture, and philofophy.

The beneficial influence of this inftitution was foon evident. The cheapnefs of terms rendered it acceffible to every one. Its advantages were not confined to the opulent. The citizens in the middle and lower walks of life were equally partakers of them. Hence a degree of information was extended amongft all claffes of people, which is very unufual in other places. The example was foon followed. Libraries were eftablifhed in various places, and they are now become very numerous in the United States, and particularly in Pennfylvania. It is to be hoped that they will be ftill more widely extended, and that information will be every where increafed. This will be the beft fecurity for maintaining our liberties. A nation of well-informed men, who have been taught to know and prize the rights which God has given them, cannot be enflaved. It is in the regions of ignorance that tyranny reigns. It flies before the light of fcience. Let the citizens of America, then, encourage inftitutions calculated to diffufe knowledge amongft the people; and amongft thefe, public libraries are not the leaft important.

In 1732, Franklin began to publifh Poor Richard's Almanack. This was remarkable for the numerous and valuable concife maxims which it contained, all tending to exhort to induftry and frugality. It was continued for many years. In the almanack for the laft year, all the maxims were collected in an addrefs to the reader, entitled, The Way to Wealth. This has been tranflated into various languages, and inferted in different publications. It has alfo been printed on a large fheet, and may be feen framed in many houfes in this city. This addrefs contains, per-

H

haps, the beft practical fyftem of œconomy that ever has appeared. It is written in a manner intelligible to every one, and which cannot fail of convincing every reader of the juftice and propriety of the remarks and advice which it contains. The demand for this almanack was fo great, that ten thoufand have been fold in one year; which muft be confidered as a very large number, efpecially when we reflect, that this country was, at that time, but thinly peopled. It cannot be doubted that the falutary maxims contained in thefe almanacks muft have made a favourable impreffion upon many of the readers of them.

It was not long before Franklin entered upon his political career. In the year 1736, he was appointed clerk to the general affembly of Pennfylvania; and was re-elected by fucceeding affemblies for feveral years, until he was chofen a reprefentative for the city of Philadelphia.

Bradford was poffeffed of fome advantages over Franklin, by being poft-mafter, thereby having an opportunity of circulating his paper more extenfively, and thus rendering it a better vehicle for advertifements, &c. Franklin, in his turn, enjoyed thefe advantages, by being appointed poft-mafter of Philadelphia in 1737. Bradford, while in office, had acted ungeneroufly towards Franklin, preventing as much as poffible the circulation of his paper. He had now an opportunity of retaliating; but his noblenefs of foul prevented him from making ufe of it.

The police of Philadelphia had early appointed watchmen, whofe duty it was to guard the citizens againft the midnight robber, and to give an immediate alarm in cafe of fire. This duty is, perhaps, one of the moft important that can be committed to any fet of men. The regulations,

ons, however, were not sufficiently strict. Franklin saw the dangers arising from this cause, and suggested an alteration, so as to oblige the guardians of the night to be more watchful over the lives and property of the citizens. The propriety of this was immediately perceived, and a reform was effected.

There is nothing more dangerous to growing cities than <u>fires</u>. Other causes operate flowly, and almost imperceptibly; but these in a moment render abortive the labours of ages. On this account there should be, in all cities, ample provisions to prevent fires from spreading. Franklin early saw the necessity of these; and, about the year 1738, formed the first fire-company in this city. This example was soon followed by others; and there are now numerous fire-companies in the city and liberties. To these may be attributed in a great degree the activity in extinguishing fires, for which the citizens of Philadelphia are distinguished, and the inconsiderable damage which this city has sustained from this cause. Some time after, Franklin suggested the plan of an <u>association for insuring</u> houses from losses by fire, which was adopted; and the association continues to this day. The advantages experienced from it have been great.

From the first establishment of Pennsylvania, a spirit of dispute appears to have prevailed amongst its inhabitants. During the life-time of William Penn, the constitution had been three times altered. After this period, the history of Pennsylvania is little else than a recital of the quarrels between the proprietaries, or their governors, and the assembly. The <u>proprietaries</u> contended for the right of exempting their lands from taxes; to which the assembly would by no means consent. This subject of dispute interfered in al-

H 2

most

moſt every queſtion, and prevented the moſt ſa-
lutary laws, from being enacted. This at times
ſubjected the people to great inconveniences. In
the year 1744, during a war between France and
Great Britain, ſome French and Indians had
made inroads upon the frontier inhabitants of the
province, who were unprovided for ſuch an attack. It became neceſſary that the citizens
ſhould arm for their defence. Governor Thomas
recommended to the aſſembly, who were then
ſitting, to paſs a militia law. To this they
would agree only upon condition that he ſhould
give his aſſent to certain laws, which appeared
to them calculated to promote the intereſts of the
people. As he thought theſe laws would be injurious to the proprietaries, he refuſed his aſſent
to them; and the aſſembly broke up without paſ-
ſing a militia law. The ſituation of the province
was at this time truly alarming: expoſed to the
continual inroads of an enemy, and deſtitute of
every means of defence. At this criſis Franklin
ſtepped forth, and propoſed to a meeting of the
citizens of Philadelphia, a plan of a voluntary
aſſociation for the defence of the province. This
was approved of, and ſigned by twelve hundred
perſons immediately. Copies of it were circula-
ted throughout the province; and in a ſhort
time the number of ſigners amounted to ten
thouſand. Franklin was choſen colonel of the
Philadelphia regiment; but he did not think proper to accept of the honour.

Purſuits of a different nature now occupied the
greateſt part of his attention for ſome years. He
engaged in a courſe of electrical experiments,
with all the ardor and thirſt for diſcovery which
characterized the philoſophers of that day. Of
all the branches of experimental philoſophy electricity had been leaſt explored. The attractive
power of amber is mentioned by Theophraſtus
                                                    and

and Pliny, and, from them, by later naturalists.
In the year 1600, Gilbert, an English physician,
enlarged considerably the catalogue of substances
which have the property of attracting light bodies.
Boyle, Otto Guericke, a burgomaster of Magde-
burg, celebrated as the inventor of the air pump,
Dr. Wall, and Sir Isaac Newton added some facts.
Guericke first observed the repulsive power of
electricity, and the light and noise produced by
it. In 1709, Hawkesbee communicated some
important observations and experiments to the
world. For several years electricity was entirely
neglected, until Mr. Grey applied himself to it,
in 1728, with great assiduity. He, and his friend
Mr. Wheeler, made a great variety of experiments; in which they demonstrated, that electricity may be communicated from one body to
another, even without being in contact, and in
this way may be conducted to a great distance.
Mr. Grey afterwards found, that, by suspending
rods of iron by silk or hair lines, and bringing an
excited tube under them, sparks might be drawn,
and a light preceived at the extremities in the
dark.   M. Du Faye, intendant of the French
king's gardens, made a number of experiments,
which added not a little to the science. He made
the discovery of two kinds of electricity, which
he called *vitreous* and *resinous*; the former produced by rubbing glass, the latter from excited
sulphur, sealing-wax, &c. But this idea he afterwards gave up as erroneous. Between the years
1739 and 1742, Desaguliers made a number of
experiments, but added little of importance. He
first used the terms *conductors* and *electrics*, *per se*.
In 1742, several ingenious Germans engaged in
this subject. Of these the principal were, professor Boze of Wittemberg, professor Winkler of
Leipsic, Gordon, a Scotch Benedictine monk,

professor

profeſſor of philoſophy at Erfurt, and Dr. Ludolf
of Berlin. The reſult of their reſearches aſto-
niſhed the philoſophers of Europe. Their apparatus was large, and by means of it they were enabled to collect large quantities of electricity, and
thus to produce phenomena which had been
hitherto unobſerved. They killed ſmall birds,
and ſet ſpirits on fire. Their experiments excited the curioſity of other philoſophers. Collinſon, about the year 1745, ſent to the library company of Philadelphia an account of theſe experiments, together with a tube, and directions how
to uſe it. Franklin, with ſome of his friends,
immediately engaged in a courſe of experiments;
the reſult of which is well known. He was enabled to make a number of important diſcoveries,
and to propoſe theories to account for various
phenomena; which have been univerſally adopted, and which bid fair to endure for ages. His
obſervations he communicated, in a ſeries of
letters, to his friend Collinſon; the firſt of which
is dated March 28, 1747. In theſe he makes
known the power of points in drawing and
throwing off the electrical matter, which had hitherto eſcaped the notice of electricians. He
alſo made the grand diſcovery of a *plus* and *minus*,
or of a *poſitive* and *negative* ſtate of electricity.
We give him the honour of this, without heſi-
tation; although the Engliſh have claimed it for
their countryman Dr. Watſon. Watſon's paper
is dated January 21, 1748; Franklin's July 11,
1747; ſeveral months prior. Shortly after,
Franklin, from his principles of plus and minus
ſtate, explained, in a ſatisfactory manner, the
phenomena of the Leyden phial, firſt obſerved by
Mr. Cuneus, or by profeſſor Muſchenbroeck of
Leyden, which had much perplexed philoſophers.
He ſhewed clearly that the bottle, when charged,
                                        contained

contained no more electricity than before, but that as much was taken from one fide as was thrown on the other; and that, to difcharge it, nothing was neceffary but to make a communication between the two fides, by which the equilibrium might be reftored, and that then no figns of electricity would remain. He afterwards demonftrated, by experiments, that the electricity did not refide in the coating, as had been fuppofed, but in the pores of the glafs itfelf. After a phial was charged, he removed the coating, and found that upon applying a new coating the fhock might ftill be received. In the year 1749, he firft fuggefted his idea of explaining the phenomena of thunder-gufts, and of the aurora borealis, upon electrical principles. He points out many particulars in which lightning and electricity agree; and he adduces many facts, and reafoning from facts, in fupport of his pofitions. In the fame year he conceived the aftonifhingly bold and grand idea of afcertaining the truth of his doctrine, by actually drawing down the forked lightning, by means of fharp-pointed iron rods raifed into the region of the clouds. Even in this uncertain ftate, his paffion to be ufeful to mankind difplays itfelf in a powerful manner. Admitting the identity of electricity and lightning, and knowing the power of points in repelling bodies charged with electricity, and in conducting their fire filently and imperceptibly, he fuggefts the idea of fecuring houfes, fhips, &c. from being damaged by lightning, by erecting pointed iron rods, which fhould rife fome feet above the moft elevated part, and defcend fome feet into the ground or the water. The effect of thefe, he concluded, would be either to prevent a ftroke by repelling the cloud beyond the ftriking diftance, or by drawing off the electrical fire

which

which it contained; or, if they could not effect this, they would at leaft conduct the ftroke to the earth, without any injury to the building.

It was not until the fummer of 1752, that he was enabled to complete his grand and unparalleled difcovery by experiment. The plan which he had originally propofed, was, to erect on fome high tower, or other elevated place, a centry-box, from which fhould rife a pointed iron rod, infulated by being fixed in a cake of refin. Electrified clouds paffing over this, would, he conceived, impart to it a portion of their electricity, which would be rendered evident to the fenfes by fparks being emitted, when a key, a knuckle, or other conductor, was prefented to it. Philadelphia at this time afforded no opportunity of trying an experiment of this kind. Whilft Franklin was waiting for the erection of a fpire, it occurred to him, that he might have more ready accefs to the region of clouds by means of a common kite. He prepared one by attaching two crofs fticks to a filk handkerchief, which would not fuffer fo much from the rain as paper. To his upright ftick was affixed an iron point. The ftring was, as ufual, of hemp, except the lower end, which was filk. Where the hempen ftring terminated, a key was faftened. With this apparatus, on the appearance of a thunder-guft approaching, he went out into the commons, accompanied by his fon, to whom alone he communicated his intentions, well knowing the ridicule which, too generally for the intereft of fcience, awaits unfuccefsful experiments in philofophy. He placed himfelf under a fhed to avoid the rain. His kite was raifed. A thunder cloud paffed over it. No fign of electricity appeared. He almoft defpaired of fuccefs; when fuddenly he obferved the loofe fibres of his ftring to move

towards

towards an erect pofition. He now prefented his knuckle to the key, and received a ftrong fpark. How exquifite muft his fenfations have been at this moment! On this experiment depended the fate of his theory. If he fucceeded, his name would rank high amongft thofe who have improved fcience; if he failed, he muft inevitably be fubjected to the derifion of mankind, or, what is worfe, their pity, as a well-meaning man, but a weak, filly projector. The anxiety with which he looked for the refult of his experiment, may eafily be conceived. Doubts and defpair had begun to prevail, when the fact was afcertained in fo clear a manner, that even the moft incredulous could no longer withhold their affent. Repeated fparks were drawn from the key, a phial was charged, a fhock given, and all the experiments made, which are ufually performed with electricity.

About a month before this period, fome ingenious Frenchmen had completed the difcovery, in the manner originally propofed by Dr. Franklin. The letters which he fent to Mr. Collinfon, it is faid, were refufed a place amongft the papers of the Royal Society of London. However this may be, Collinfon publifhed them in a feparate volume, under the title of *New Experiments and Obfervations on Electricity, made at Philadelphia, in America.* They were read with avidity, and foon tranflated into different languages. A very incorrect French tranflation fell into the hands of the celebrated Buffon, who, notwithftanding the difadvantages under which the work laboured, was much pleafed with it, and repeated the experiments with fuccefs. He prevailed upon his friend, M. D'Alibard, to give to his countrymen a more correct tranflation of the work of the American electrician. This contributed much

towards

towards fpreading a knowledge of Franklin's principles in France. The King, Louis XV. hearing of thefe experiments, expreffed a wifh to be a fpectator of them. A courfe of experiments was given at the feat of the Duc D'Ayen, at St. Germain, by M. De Lor. The applaufes which the King beftowed upon Franklin, excited in Buffon, D'Alibard, and, De Lor, an earneft defire of afcertaining the truth of his theory of thunder-gufts. Buffon erected his apparatus on the tower of Montbar, M D'Alibard at Mary-la-ville, and De Lor at his houfe in the *Eftrapade* at Paris, fome of the higheft ground in that capital. D'Alibard's machine firft fhewed figns of electricity. On the 10th of May, 1752, a thundercloud paffed over it, in the abfence of M. D'Alibard; and a number of fparks were drawn from it by Coiffier, a joiner, with whom D'Alibard had left directions how to proceed, and by M. Raulet, the prior of Mary-la-ville. An account of this experiment was given to the Royal Academy of Sciences, in a memoir by M. D'Alibard, dated May 13th, 1752. On the 18th of May, M. De Lor proved equally fuccefsful with the apparatus erected at his own houfe. Thefe difcoveries foon excited the philofophers of other parts of Europe to repeat the experiment. Amongft thefe, none fignalized themfelves more than Father Beccaria cf Turin, to whofe obfervations fcience is much indebted. Even the cold regions of Ruffia were penetrated by the ardor for difcovery. Profeffor Richman bade fair to add much to the ftock of knowledge on this fubject, when an unfortunate flafh from his rod put a period to his exiftence. The friends of fcience will long remember with regret the amiable martyr to electricity.

By

By thefe experiments Franklin's theory was
eftablifhed in the moft firm manner. When the
truth of it could no longer be doubted, the vanity of men endeavoured to detract from its
merit. That an American, an inhabitant of the
obfcure city of Philadelphia, the name of which
was hardly known, fhould be able to make difcoveries, and to frame theories, which had efcaped the notice of the enlightened philofophers
of Europe, was too mortifying to be admitted.
He muft certainly have taken the idea from fome
one elfe. An American, a being of an inferior
order, make difcoveries! Impoffible. It was faid,
that the Abbé Nollet, in 1748, had fuggefted the
idea of the fimilarity of lightning and electricity,
in his *Leçons de Phyfique.* It is true, that the
Abbé mentions the idea, but he throws it out
as a bare conjecture, and propofes no mode of
afcertaining the truth of it. He himfelf acknow-
ledges, that Franklin firft entertained the bold
thought of bringing lightning from the heavens,
by means of pointed rods fixed in the air. The
fimilarity of electricity and lightning is fo ftrong,
that we need not be furprifed at notice being
taken of it, as foon as electrical phenomena became familiar. We find it mentioned by Dr.
Wall and Mr. Grey, while the fcience was in its
infancy. But the honour of forming a regular
theory of thunder-gufts, of fuggefting a mode of
determining the truth of it by experiments, and
of putting thefe experiments in practice, and
thus eftablifhing his theory upon a firm and folid
bafis, is inconteftibly due to Franklin. D'Alibard,
who made the firft experiments in France, fays,
that he only followed the track which Franklin
had pointed out.

It has been of late afferted, that the honour of
completing the experiment with the electrical
kite,

kite, does not belong to Franklin. Some late English paragraphs have attributed it to some Frenchman, whose name they do not mention; and the Abbé Bertholon gives it to M. De Romas, assessor to the presideal of Nerac; the English paragraphs probably refer to the same person. But a very slight attention will convince us of the injustice of this procedure: Dr. Franklin's experiment was made in June 1752; and his letter, giving an account of it, is dated October 19, 1752. M. De Romas made his first attempt on the 14th of May 1753, but was not successful until the 7th of June; a year after Franklin had completed the discovery, and when it was known to all the philosophers in Europe.

Besides these great principles, Franklin's letters on electricity contain a number of facts and hints, which have contributed greatly towards reducing this branch of knowledge to a science. His friend, Mr Kinnersley, communicated to him a discovery of the different kinds of electricity excited by rubbing glass and sulphur. This, we have said, was first observed by M. Du Faye; but it was for many years neglected. The philosophers were disposed to account for the phenomena, rather from a difference in the quantity of electricity collected; and even Du Faye himself seems at last to have adopted this doctrine. Franklin at first entertained the same idea; but upon repeating the experiments, he perceived that Mr. Kinnersley was right; and that the *vitreous* and *resinous* electricity of Du Faye were nothing more than the *positive* and *negative* states which he had before observed; that the glass globe charged *positively*, or increased the quantity of electricity on the prime conductor, whilst the globe of sulphur diminished its natural quantity, or charged *negatively*. These experiments and ob-

servations

fervations opened a new field for inveftigation,
upon which electricians entered with avidity;
and their labours have added much to the ftock
of our knowledge.

In September 1752, Franklin entered upon a
courfe of experiments, to determine the ftate of
electricity in the clouds. From a number of experiments he formed this conclufion : " that the
clouds of a thunder-guft are moft commonly in
a negative ftate of electricity, but fometimes in
a pofitive ftate ;" and from this it follows, as a
neceffary confequence, " that, for the moft part,
in thunder-ftrokes, it is the earth that ftrikes into
the clouds, and not the clouds that ftrike into the
earth." The letter containing thefe obfervations
is dated in September 1753; and yet the difcovery of afcending thunder has been faid to be of
a modern date, and has been attributed to the
Abbé Bertholon, who publifhed his memoir, on
the fubject in 1776.

Franklin's letters have been tranflated into
moft of the European languages, and into Latin.
In proportion as they have become known, his
principles have been adopted. Some oppofition
was made to his theories, particularly by the
Abbé Nollet, who was, however, but feebly fupported, whilft the firft philofophers of Europe
ftepped forth in defence of Franklin's principles ; amongft whom D'Alibard and Beccaria
were the moft diftinguifhed. The oppofition has
gradually ceafed, and the Franklinian fyftem is
now univerfally adopted, where fcience flou-
rifhes.

The important practical ufe which Franklin
made of his difcoveries, the fecuring of houfes
from injury by lightning, has been already mentioned. Pointed conductors are now very common in America; but prejudice has hitherto prevented

vented their general introduction into Europe,
notwithstanding the most undoubted proofs of
their utility have been given. But mankind can
with difficulty be brought to lay aside established
practices, or to adopt new ones. And perhaps
we have more reason to be surprised that a practice, however rational, which was proposed about
forty years ago, should in that time have been
adopted in so many places, than that it has not
universally prevailed. It is only by degrees that
the great body of mankind can be led into new
practices, however salutary their tendency. It is
now nearly eighty years since inoculation was introduced into Europe and America; and it is so
far from being general at present, that it will,
perhaps, require one or two centuries to render
it so.

In the year 1745, Franklin published an account of his new-invented Pennsylvania fire-
places, in which he minutely and accurately states
the advantages and disadvantages of different
kinds of fire-places; and endeavours to shew
that the one which he describes is to be preferred
to any other. This contrivance has given rise to
open stoves now in general use, which however
differ from it in construction, particularly in not
having an air-box at the back, through which a
constant supply of air, warmed in its passage, is
thrown into the room. The advantages of this
are, that as a stream of warm air is continually
flowing into the room, less fuel is necessary to
preserve a proper temperature, and the room
may be so tightened as that no air may enter
through cracks; the consequences of which are
colds, tooth-aches, &c.

Although philosophy was a principal object of
Franklin's pursuit for several years, he confined
himself not to this. In the year 1747, he became
a member

a member of the general affembly of Pennfylvania, as a burgefs for the city of Philadelphia.
Warm difputes at this time fubfifted between the
affembly and the proprietaries ; each contending
for what they conceived to be their juft rights.
Franklin, a friend to the rights of man from his
infancy, foon diftinguifhed himfelf as a fteady
opponent of the unjuft fchemes of the proprietaries. He was foon looked up to as the head of
the oppofition ; and to him have been attributed
many of the fpirited replies of the affembly, to
the meffages of the governors. His influence in
the body was very great. This arofe not from
any fuperior powers of eloquence ; he fpoke but
feldom, and he never was known to make any
thing like an elaborate harangue. His fpeeches
often confifted of a fingle fentence, or of a well-
told ftory, the moral of which was always ob-
vioufly to the point. He never attempted the
flowery fields of oratory. His manner was plain
and mild. His ftyle in fpeaking was, like that
of his writings, fimple, unadorned, and remarkably concife. With this plain manner, and his
penetrating and folid judgment, he was able to
confound the moft eloquent and fubtle of his
adverfaries, to confirm the opinions of his
friends, and to make converts of the unprejudiced who had oppofed him. With a fingle obfervation, he has rendered of no avail an elegant
and lengthy difcourfe, and determined the fate
of a queftion of importance.

But he was not contented with thus fupporting
the rights of the people. He wifhed to render
them permanently fecure, which can only be
done by making their value properly known ;
and this muft depend upon increafing and extending information to every clafs of men. We
have already feen that he was the founder of the
                                              public

public library, which contributed greatly towards improving the minds of the citizens. But
this was not sufficient. The schools then subsist-
ing were in general of little utility. The teachers
were men ill qualified for the important duty
which they had undertaken; and, after all, nothing more could be obtained than the rudiments
of a common English education. (Franklin drew
up a plan of an academy, to be erected in the city
of Philadelphia, suited to " the state of an infant
country ;" but in this, as in all his plans, he
confined not his views to the present time only.
He looked forward to the period when an institution on an enlarged plan would become neceffary.   With this view he confidered his academy
as " a foundation for pofterity to erect a feminary
of learning, more extenfive, and fuitable to future
circumftances."   In purfuance of this plan, the
conftitutions were drawn up and figned on the
13th of November 1749.   In thefe, twenty-four
of the moft refpectable citizens of Philadelphia
were named as truftees.   In the choice of thefe,
and in the formation of his plan, Franklin is faid
to have confulted chiefly with Thomas Hopkin-
fon, Efq; Rev. Richard Peters,   then fecretary
of the province, Tench Francis, Efq; attorney-
general, and Dr. Phineas Bond.

The following article fhews a fpirit of benevolence worthy of imitation ; and, for the honour
of our city, we hope that it continues to be in
force.

" In cafe of the difability of the *rector*, or any
mafter (eftablifhed on the foundation by receiving a certain falary), through ficknefs, or any
other natural infirmity, whereby he may be reduced to poverty, the truftees fhall have power
to contribute to his fupport, in proportion to
                                          his

his diftrefs and merit, and the ftock in their hands."

The laft claufe of the fundamental rules is ex-preffed in language fo tender and benevolent, fo truly parental, that it would do everlafting ho-nour to the hearts and heads of the founders.

" It is hoped and expected that the truftees will make it their pleafure, and in fome degree their bufinefs, to vifit the academy often ; to en-courage and countenance the youth, countenance and affift the mafters, and, by all means in their power, advance the ufefulnefs and reputation of the defign ; that they will look on the ftudents as, in fome meafure, their own children, treat them with familiarity and affection ; and when they have behaved well, gone through their ftu-dies, and are to enter the world, they fhall zea-loufly unite, and make all the intereft that can be made, to promote and eftablifh them, whe-ther in bufinefs, offices, marriages, or any other thing for their advantage. preferable to all other perfons whatfoever, even of equal merit."

The conftitutions being figned and made pub-lic, with the names of the gentlemen propofing themfelves as truftees and founders, the defign was fo well approved of by the public-fpirited ci-tizens of Philadelphia, that the fum of eight hun-dred pounds per annum, for five years, was in the courfe of a few weeks fubfcribed for carrying it into execution ; and in the beginning of Janu-ary following (viz. 1750) three of the fchools were opened, namely, the Latin and Greek fchools, the Mathematical, and the Englifh fchools. In purfuance of an article in the ori-ginal plan, a fchool for educating fixty boys and thirty girls (in the charter fince called the Chari-table School) was opened, and amidft all the difficulties with which the truftees have ftruggled

I   in

in refpect to their funds, has ftill been continued full for the fpace of forty years ; fo that allowing three years education for each boy and girl admitted into it, which is the general rule, at leaft twelve hundred children have received in it the chief part of their education, who might otherwife, in a great meafure, have been left without the means of inftruction. And many of thofe who have been thus educated, are now to be found among the moft ufeful and reputable citizens of this ftate.

The inftitution, thus fuccefsfully begun, continued daily to flourifh, to the great fatisfaction of Dr. Franklin ; who, notwithftanding the multiplicity of his other engagements and purfuits, at that bufy ftage of his life, was a conftant attendant at the monthly vifitations and examinations of the fchools, and made it his particular ftudy, by means of his extenfive correfpondence abroad, to advance the reputation of the feminary, and to draw ftudents and fcholars to it from different parts of America and the Weft Indies. Through the interpofition of his benevolent and learned friend, Peter Collinfon, of London, upon the application of the truftees, a charter of incorporation, dated July 13th, 1753, was obtained from the honourable proprietors of Pennfylvania, Thomas Penn and Richard Penn, Efqrs. accompanied with a liberal benefaction of five hundred pounds fterling ; and Dr. Franklin now began in good earneft to pleafe himfelf with the hopes of a fpeedy accomplifhment of his original defign, viz. the eftablifhment of a perfect inftitution, upon the plan of the European colleges and univerfities ; for which his academy was intended as a nurfery or foundation. To elucidate this fact, is a matter of confiderable importance in refpect to the memory and character of Dr. Franklin,

lin, as a philofopher, and as the friend and pa-
tron of learning and fcience; for, notwithftanding what is exprefsly declared by him in the pre-
amble to the conftitutions, viz. that the academy
was begun for " teaching the Latin and Greek
languages, with all ufeful branches of the arts and
fciences, fuitable to the ftate of an infant country,
and laying a foundation for pofterity to erect a
feminary of learning more extenfive, and fuitable
to their future circumftances ;" yet it has been
fuggefted of late, as upon Dr. Franklin's authority, that the Latin and Greek, or the dead languages, are an incumbrance upon a fcheme of
liberal education, and that the engrafting or
founding a college, or more extenfive feminary,
upon his academy, was without his approbation
or agency, and gave him difcontent. If the reverfe of this does not already appear, from what
has been quoted above, the following letters will
put the matter beyond difpute. They were written by him to a gentleman, who had at that time
publifhed the idea of a college, fuited to the
circumftances of a young country (meaning New-
York), a copy of which having been fent to Dr.
Franklin for his opinion, gave rife to that correfpondence which terminated about a year afterwards, in erecting the college upon the foundation of the academy, and eftablifhing that gentleman as the head of both, where he ftill continues, after a period of thirty-fix years, to prefide
with diftinguifhed reputation.

From thefe letters alfo, the ftate of the academy, at that time, will be feen.

Philad. April 19th, 1753.

SIR,

I received your favour of the 11th instant, with your new * piece on *Education*, which I shall carefully peruse, and give you my sentiments of it, as you desire, by next post.

I believe the young gentlemen, your pupils, may be entertained and instructed here, in mathematics and philosophy, to satisfaction. Mr. Alison † (who was educated at Glasgow) has been long accustomed to teach the latter, and Mr. Grew ‡ the former; and I think their pupils make great progress. Mr. Alison has the care of the Latin and Greek school, but as he has now three good assistants §, he can very well afford some hours every day for the instruction of those who are engaged in higher studies. The mathematical school is pretty well furnished with instruments. The English library is a good one; and we have belonging to it a middling apparatus for experimental philosophy, and purpose speedily to complete it. The Loganian library, one of the best collections in America, will shortly be opened; so that neither books nor instruments will be wanting; and as we are determined always to give good salaries, we have reason to believe we may have always an opportunity of choosing good masters; upon which, indeed, the success of the whole depends. We are obliged to you for your kind offers in this respect,

* A general idea of the college of Mirania.

† The Rev. and learned Mr. Francis Allison, afterwards D. D. and vice-provost of the college.

‡ Mr. Theophilus Grew, afterwards professor of mathematics in the college.

§ Those assistants were at that time Mr. Charles Thomson, late secretary of congress, Mr. Paul Jackson, and Mr. Jacob Duche.

and

and when you are settled in England, we may occasionally make use of your friendship and judgment.—

If it suits your conveniency to visit Philadelphia before your return to Europe, I shall be extremely glad to see and converse with you here, as well as to correspond with you after your settlement in England; for an acquaintance and communication with men of learning, virtue, and public spirit, is one of my greatest enjoyments.

I do not know whether you ever happened to see the first proposals I made for erecting this academy. I send them inclosed. They had (however imperfect) the desired success, being followed by a subscription of *four thousand pounds,* towards carrying them into execution. And as we are fond of receiving advice, and are daily improving by experience, I am in hopes we shall, in a few years, see a *perfect institution.*

I am very respectfully, &c.

B. FRANKLIN.

Mr. W. Smith, Long-Island.

Philad. May 3d, 1753.

SIR,

Mr. Peters has just now been with me, and we have compared notes on your new piece. We find nothing in the scheme of education, however excellent, but what is, in our opinion, very practicable. The great difficulty will be to find the Aratus *, and other suitable persons, to carry it

* The name given to the principal or head of the ideal college, the system of education in which hath nevertheless been nearly realized, or followed as a model, in the college and academy of Philadelphia, and some other American seminaries, for many years past.

into

into execution; but such may be had if proper encouragement be given. We have both received great pleasure in the perusal of it. For my part, I know not when I have read a piece that has more affected me—so noble and just are the sentiments, so warm and animated the language; yet as censure from your friends may be of more use, as well as more agreeable to you than praise, I ought to mention, that I wish you had omitted not only the quotation from the Review *, which you are now justly dissatisfied with, but those expressions of resentment against your adversaries, in pages 65 and 79. In such cases, the noblest victory is obtained by neglect, and by shining on.

Mr. Allen has been out of town these ten days; but before he went he directed me to procure him six copies of your piece. Mr. Peters has taken ten. He purposed to have written to you; but omits it, as he expects so soon to have the pleasure of seeing you here. He desires me to present his affectionate compliments to you, and to assure you that you will be very welcome to him. I shall only say, that you may depend on my doing all in my power to make your visit to Philadelphia agreeable to you.

I am, &c.

B. FRANKLIN

Mr. Smith.

Philad. Nov. 27th, 1753.

DEAR SIR,

Having written you fully, *via* Bristol, I have now little to add. Matters relating to the academy

---

* The quotation alluded to (from the London Monthly Review for 1749), was judged to reflect too severely on the discipline

my remain in *ſtatu quo*. The truſtees would be glad to ſee a rector eſtabliſhed there, but they dread entering into new engagements till they are got out of debt; and I have not yet got them wholly over to my opinion, that a good profeſſor, or teacher of the higher branches of learning, would draw ſo many ſcholars as to pay great part, if not the whole of his ſalary. Thus, unleſs the proprietors (of the province) ſhall think fit to put the finiſhing hand to our inſtitution, it muſt, I fear, wait ſome few years longer before it can arrive at that ſtate of perfection, which to me it ſeems now capable of; and all the pleaſure I promiſed myſelf in ſeeing you ſettled among us, vaniſhes into ſmoke.

But good Mr. Collinſon writes me word, that no endeavours of his ſhall be wanting; and he hopes, with the archbiſhop's aſſiſtance, to be able to prevail with our proprietors *. I pray God grant them ſucceſs.

My ſon preſents his affectionate regards, with, dear Sir,

Yours, &c.

B. FRANKLIN.

P. S. I have not been favoured with a line from you ſince your arrival in England.

Philad. April 18*th*, 1754.

DEAR SIR,

I have had but one letter from you ſince your arrival in England, which was a ſhort one, *via*

---

diſcipline and government of the Engliſh univerſities of Oxford and Cambridge, and was expunged from the following editions of this work.

* Upon the application of archbiſhop Herring and P. Collinſon, Eſq; at Dr. Franklin's requeſt, (aided by the letters of Mr Allen and Mr. Peters) the hon. Thomas Penn, Eſq; ſubſcribed an annual ſum, and afterwards gave at leaſt 5000 l. to the founding or engrafting the college upon the academy.

Boſton,

Bofton, dated October 18th, acquainting me that you had written largely by Capt. Davis.—Davis was loft, and with him your letters, to my great difappointment.—Mefnard and Gibbon have fince arrived here, and I hear nothing from you. —My comfort is, an imagination that you only omit writing becaufe you are coming, and purpofe to tell me every thing *viva voce*. So not knowing whether this letter will reach you, and hoping either to fee or hear from you by the Myrtilla, Capt. Budden's fhip, which is daily expected, I only add, that I am, with great efteem and affection,

Yours, &c.

B. FRANKLIN.

Mr. Smith.

About a month after the date of this laft letter, the gentleman to whom it was addreffed arrived in Philadelphia, and was immediately placed at the head of the feminary; whereby Dr. Franklin and the other truftees were enabled to profecute their plan, for perfecting the inftitution, and opening the college upon the large and liberal foundation on which it now ftands; for which purpofe they obtained their additional charter, dated May 27th, 1755.

Thus far we thought it proper to exhibit in one view Dr. Franklin's fervices in the foundation and eftablifhment of this feminary. He foon afterward embarked for England, in the public fervice of his country; and having been generally employed abroad, in the like fervice, for the greateft part of the remainder of his life (as will appear in our fubfequent account of the fame), he had but few opportunities of taking any fur-

ther

ther active part in the affairs of the feminary, until his final return in the year 1785, when he found its charters violated, and his ancient colleagues, the original founders, deprived of their trust, by an act of the legislature; and although his own name had been inserted among the new trustees, yet he declined to take his feat among them, or have any concern in the management of their affairs, till the institution was restored by law to its original owners. He then assembled his old colleagues at his own house, and being chosen their president, all their future meetings were, at his request, held there, till within a few months of his death, when with reluctance, and at their desire, left he might be too much injured by his attention to their business, he suffered them to meet at the college.

Franklin not only gave birth to many useful institutions himself, but he was also instrumental in promoting those which had originated with other men. About the year 1752, an eminent physician of this city, Dr. Bond, considering the deplorable state of the poor, when visited with disease, conceived the idea of establishing an hospital. Notwithstanding very great exertions on his part, he was able to interest few people so far in his benevolent plan, as to obtain subscriptions from them. Unwilling that his scheme should prove abortive, he sought the aid of Franklin, who readily engaged in the business, both by using his influence with his friends, and by stating the advantageous influence of the proposed institution in his paper. These efforts were attended with success. Considerable sums were subscribed; but they were still short of what was necessary. Franklin now made another exertion. He applied to the assembly; and, after some opposition, obtained leave to bring in a bill, specifying, that

as

as foon as two thoufand pounds were fubfcribed,
the fame fum fhould be drawn from the treafury
by the fpeaker's warrant, to be applied to the
purpofes of the inftitution. The oppofition, as
the fum was granted upon a contingency which
they fuppofed would never take place, were
filent, and the bill paffed. The friends of the
plan now redoubled their efforts, to obtain fubfcriptions to the amount ftated in the bill, and
were foon fuccefsful. This was the foundation
of the Pennfylvania Hofpital, which, with the
Bettering-houfe and Difpenfary, bears ample teftimony of the humanity of the citizens of Philadelphia.

Dr. Franklin had conducted himfelf fo well in
the office of poft-mafter, and had fhown himfelf
to be fo well acquainted with the bufinefs of that
department, that it was thought expedient to
raife him to a more dignified ftation. In 1753
he was appointed deputy poft-mafter-general for
the Britifh colonies. The profits arifing from
the poftage of letters formed no inconfiderable
part of the revenue, which the crown of Great-
Britain derived from thefe colonies. In the
hands of Franklin, it is faid, that the poft-office
in America yielded annually thrice as much as
that of Ireland.

The American colonies were much expofed to
depredations on their frontiers, by the Indians;
and more particularly whenever a war took place
between France and England. The colonies, in-
dividually, were either too weak to take efficient
meafures for their own defence, or they were
unwilling to take upon themfelves the whole
burden of erecting forts and maintaining garri-
fons, whilft their neighbours, who partook
equally with themfelves of the advantages, contributed nothing to the expence. Sometimes
also

alfo the difputes, which fubfifted between the
governors and affemblies, prevented the adoption of means of defence; as we have feen was
the cafe in Pennfylvania in 1745. To devife a
plan of union between the colonies, to regulate
this and other matters, appeared a defirable object.   To accomplifh this, in the year 1754, commiffioners from New-Hampfhire, Maffachufetts,
Rhode-Ifland, New-Jerfey, Pennfylvania, and
Maryland, met at Albany.   Dr. Franklin attended here, as a commiffioner from Pennfylvania,
and produced a plan, which, from the place of
meeting, has been ufually termed " The Albany
Plan of Union." This propofed, that application fhould be made for an act of parliament, to
eftablifh in the colonies a general government, to
be adminiftered by a prefident-general, appointed
by the crown, and by a grand council, confifting of members chofen by the reprefentatives of
the different colonies; their number to be in
direct proportion to the fums paid by each colony
into the general treafury, with this reftriction,
that no colony fhould have more than feven, nor
lefs than two reprefentatives. The whole executive authority was committed to the prefident-
general. The power of legiflation was lodged
in the grand council and prefident-general joint-
ly; his confent being made neceffary to paffing a
bill into a law. The power vefted in the prefident and council were, to declare war and peace,
and to conclude treaties with the Indian nations;
to regulate trade with, and to make purchafes of
vacant lands from them, either in the name of
the crown, or of the union; to fettle new colonies, to make laws for governing thefe until
they fhould be erected into feparate governments,
and to raife troops, build forts, fit out armed
veffels, and ufe other means for the general defence:

fence : and, to effect thefe things, a power was given to make laws, laying fuch duties, impofts, or taxes, as they fhould find neceffary, and as would be leaft burthenfome to the people. All laws were to be fent to England for the king's approbation ; and unlefs difapproved of within three years, were to remain in force. All offi- cers in the land or fea fervice were to be nomi- nated by the prefident-general, and approved of by the general council ; civil officers were to be nominated by the council, and approved by the prefident. Such are the outlines of the plan pro- pofed, for the confideration of the congrefs, by Dr. Franklin. After feveral days difcuffion, it was unanimoufly agreed to by the commiffioners, a copy tranfmitted to each affembly, and one to the king's council. The fate of it was fingular. It was difapproved of by the miniftry of Great Britain, becaufe it gave too much power to the reprefentatives of the people ; and it was re- jected by every affembly, as giving to the prefi- dent-general, the reprefentative of the crown, an influence greater than appeared to them pro- per, in a plan of government intended for free- men. Perhaps this rejection, on both fides, is the ftrongeft proof that could be adduced of the excellence of it, as fuited to the fituation of America and Great-Britain at that time. It ap- pears to have fteered exactly in the middle, be- tween the oppofite interefts of both.

Whether the adoption of this plan would have prevented the feparation of America from Great Britain, is a queftion which might afford much room for fpeculation. It may be faid, that, by enabling the colonies to defend themfelves, it would have removed the pretext upon which the ftamp-act, tea-act, and other acts of the Britifh parliament, were paffed ; which excited a fpirit

of

of oppofition, and laid the foundation for the feparation of the two countries. But, on the other hand, it muft be admitted, that the reftriction laid by Great-Britain upon our commerce, obliging us to fell our produce to her citizens only, and to take from them various articles, of which, as our manufactures were difcouraged, we ftood in need, at a price greater than that for which they could have been obtained from other nations, muft inevitably produce diffatiffaction, even though no duties were impofed by the parliament; a circumftance which might ftill have taken place. Befides, as the prefident-general was to be appointed by the crown, he muft, of neceffity, be devoted to its views, and would, therefore, refufe his affent to any laws, however falutary to the community, which had the moft remote tendency to injure the interefts of his fovereign. Even fhould they receive his affent, the approbation of the king was to be neceffary; who would indubitably, in every inftance, prefer the advantage of his home dominions to that of his colonies. Hence would enfue perpetual difagreements between the council and the prefident-general, and thus, between the people of America and the crown of Great-Britain:——While the colonies continued weak, they would be obliged to fubmit, and as foon as they acquired ftrength they would become more urgent in their demands, until, at length, they would fhake off the yoke, and declare themfelves independent.

Whilft the French were in poffeffion of Canada, their trade with the natives extended very far; even to the back of the Britifh fettlements. They were difpofed, from time to time, to eftablifh pofts within the territory, which the Englifh claimed as their own. Independent of the injury to the fur-trade, which was confiderable, the

the colonies fuffered this further inconvenience,
that the Indians were frequently inftigated to
commit depredations on their frontiers. In the
year 1753, encroachments were made upon the
boundaries of Virginia. Remonftrances had no
effect. In the enfuing year, a body of men was
fent out under the command of Mr. Wafhington,
who, though a very young man, had, by his
conduct in the preceding year, fhewn himfelf
worthy of fuch an important truft. Whilft
marching to take poffeffion of the poft at the
junction of the Allegany and Monongahela, he
was informed that the French had already erected a fort there. A detachment of their men
marched againft him. He fortified himfelf as
ftrongly as time and circumftances would admit.
A fuperiority of numbers foon obliged him to
furrender *Fort Neceffity*. He obtained honourable
terms for himfelf and men, and returned to Virginia. The government of Great-Britain now
thought it neceffary to interfere. In the year
1755, General Braddock, with fome regiments
of regular troops, and provincial levies, was fent
to difpoffefs the French of the pofts upon which
they had feized. After the men were all ready,
a difficulty occurred, which had nearly prevented the expedition. This was the want of waggons. Franklin now ftepped forward, and with
the affiftance of his fon, in a little time procured
a hundred and fifty. Braddock unfortunately
fell into an ambufcade, and perifhed, with a
number of his men. Wafhington, who had accompanied him as an aid-de-camp, and had
warned him, in vain, of his danger, now difplayed great military talents in effecting a retreat
of the remains of the army, and in forming a
junction with the rear, under colonel Dunbar,
upon whom the chief command now devolved.
                                              With

With some difficulty they brought their little body to a place of safety; but they found it necessary to destroy their waggons and baggage, to prevent them from falling into the hands of the enemy. For the waggons which he had furnished, Franklin had given bonds to a large amount. The owners declared their intentions of obliging him to make a restitution of their property. Had they put their threats in execution, ruin must inevitably have been the consequence. Governor Shirley, finding that he had incurred these debts for the service of government, made arrangements to have them discharged, and released Franklin from his disagreeable situation.

The alarm spread through the colonies, after the defeat of Braddock, was very great. Preparations to arm were every where made. In Pennsylvania, the prevalence of the quaker interest prevented the adoption of any system of defence, which would compel the citizens to bear arms. Franklin introduced into the assembly a bill for organizing a militia, by which every man was allowed to take arms or not, as to him should appear fit. The quakers, being thus left at liberty, suffered the bill to pass; for although their principles would not suffer them to fight, they had no objections to their neighbours fighting for them. In consequence of this act a very respectable militia was formed. The sense of impending danger infused a military spirit in all, whose religious tenets were not opposed to war. Franklin was appointed colonel of a regiment in Philadelphia, which consisted of 1200 men.

The north-western frontier being invaded by the enemy, it became necessary to adopt measures for its defence. Franklin was directed by the governor to take charge of this business. A

power

power of raifing men, and of appointing officers to command them, was vefted in him. He foon levied a body of troops, with which he repaired to the place at which their prefence was neceffary. Here he built a fort, and placed the garrifon in fuch a pofture of defence, as would enable them to withftand the inroads, to which the inhabitants had previoufly been expofed. He remained here for fome time, in order the more completely to difcharge the truft committed to him. Some bufinefs of importance at length rendered his prefence neceffary in the affembly, and he returned to Philadelphia.

The defence of her colonies was a great expence to Great Britain. The moft effectual mode of leffening this was, to put arms into the hands of the inhabitants, and to teach them their ufe. But England wifhed not that the Americans fhould become acquainted with their own ftrength. She was apprehenfive, that, as foon as this period arrived, they would no longer fubmit to that monopoly of their trade, which to them was highly injurious, but extremely advantageous to the mother country. In comparifon with the profits of this, the expence of maintaining armies and fleets to defend them was trifling. She fought to keep them dependent upon her for her protection, the beft plan which could be devifed for retaining them in peaceable fubjection. The leaft appearance of a military fpirit was therefore to be guarded againft, and, although a war then raged, the act organizing a militia was difapproved of by the miniftry. The regiments which had been formed under it were difbanded, and the defence of the province entrufted to regular troops.

The difputes between the proprietaries and the people continued in full force, although a war

was

was raging on the frontiers. Not even the fenfe
of danger was fufficient to reconcile, for ever fo
fhort a time, their jarring interefts. The affembly ftill infifted upon the juftice of taxing the
proprietary eftates, but the governors conftantly
refufed to give their affent to this meafure, without which no bill could pafs into a law. Enraged
at the obftinacy, and what they conceived to be
unjuft proceedings of their opponents, the affembly at length determined to apply to the mother
country for relief. A petition was addreffed to
the king, in council, ftating the inconveniencies
under which the inhabitants laboured, from the
attention of the proprietaries to their private interefts, to the negleft of the general welfare of
the community, and praying for redrefs. Franklin was appointed to prefent this addrefs, as agent
for the province of Pennfylvania, and departed
from America in June 1757. In conformity to
the inftruftions which he had received from the
legiflature, he held a conference with the proprietaries, who then refided in England, and endeavoured to prevail upon them to give up the long-
contefted point. Finding that they would hear-
ken to no terms of accommodation, he laid his
petition before the council. During this time
governor Denny affented to a law impofing a tax,
in which no difcrimination was made in favour
of the eftates of the Penn family. They, alarmed
at this intelligence, and Franklin's exertions, ufed
their utmoft endeavours to prevent the royal
fanftion being given to this law, which they reprefented as highly iniquitous, defigned to throw
the burthen of fupporting government upon them,
and calculated to produce the moft ruinous confequences to them and their pofterity. The caufe
was amply difcuffed before the privy council.
The Penns found here fome ftrennous advocates;

nor were there wanting fome who warmly ef-
poufed the fide of the people. After fome time
fpent in debate, a propofal was made, that Franklin fhould folemnly engage, that the affeffment
of the tax fhould be fo made, as that the proprietary eftates fhould pay no more than a due proportion. This he agreed to perform, the Penn
family withdrew their oppofition, and tranquility
was thus once more reftored to the province.

The mode in which this difpute was terminated is a ftriking proof of the high opinion entertained of Franklin's integrity and honour, even
by thofe who confidered him as inimical to their
views. Nor was their confidence ill founded.
The affeffment was made upon the ftricteft principles of equity; and the proprietary eftates bore
only a proportionable fhare of the expences of
fupporting government.

After the completion of this important bufinefs, Franklin remained at the court of Great
Britain, as agent for the province of Pennfylvania. The extenfive knowledge which he poffeffed of the fituation of the colonies, and the regard
which he always manifefted for their interefts,
occafioned his appointment to the fame office by
the colonies of Maffachuffetts, Maryland, and
Georgia. His conduct, in this fituation, was
fuch as rendered him ftill more dear to his countrymen.

He had now an opportunity of indulging in
the fociety of thofe friends, whom his merits had
procured him while at a diftance. The regard
which they had entertained for him was rather
increafed by a perfonal acquaintance. The oppofition which had been made to his difcoveries in
philofophy gradually ceafed, and the rewards of
literary merit were abundantly conferred upon
him. The royal fociety of London, which had

at

at firft refufed his performances admiffion into
its tranfactions, now thought it an honour to
rank him amongft its fellows. Other focieties
of Europe were equally ambitious of calling him
a member. The univerfity of St. Andrews, in
Scotland, conferred upon him the degree of Doctor of Laws. Its example was followed by the
univerfities of Edinburgh and of Oxford. His
correfpondence was fought for by the moft eminent philofophers of Europe. His letters to thefe
abound with true fcience, delivered in the moft
fimple unadorned manner.

The province of Canada was at this time in
the poffeffion of the French, who had originally
fettled it. The trade with the Indians, for which
its fituation was very convenient, was exceedingly lucrative. The French traders here found
a market for their commodities, and received in
return large quantities of rich furs, which they
difpofed of at a high price in Europe. Whilft
the poffeffion of this country was highly advantageous to France, it was a grievous inconvenience to the inhabitants of the Britifh colonies.
The Indians were almoft generally defirous to cultivate the friendfhip of the French, by whom
they were abundantly fupplied with arms and
ammunition. Whenever a war happened, the
Indians were ready to fall upon the frontiers:
and this they frequently did, even when Great
Britain and France were at peace. From thefe
confiderations, it appeared to be the intereft of
Great Britain to gain the poffeffion of Canada.
But the importance of fuch an acquifition was not
well underftood in England. Franklin about
this time publifhed his Canada pamphlet, in which
he, in a very forcible manner, pointed out the
advantages which would refult from the conqueft
of this province.

An expedition againſt it was planned, and the command given to General Wolfe. His ſucceſs is well known. At the treaty in 1762, France ceded Canada to Great Britain, and by her ceſſion of Louiſiana, at the ſame time, relinquiſhed all her poſſeſſions on the continent of America.

Although Dr. Franklin was now principally occupied with political purſuits, he found time for philoſophical ſtudies. He extended his electrical reſearches, and made a variety of experiments, particularly on the tourmalin. The ſingular properties which this ſtone poſſeſſes of being electrified on one ſide poſitively and on the other negatively, by heat alone, without friction, had been but lately obſerved.

Some experiments on the cold produced by evaporation, made by Dr. Cullen, had been communicated to Dr. Franklin, by Profeſſor Simpſon of Glaſgow. Theſe he repeated, and found, that, by the evaporation of ether in the exhauſted receiver of an air-pump, ſo great a degree of cold was produced in a ſummer's day, that water was converted into ice. This diſcovery he applied to the ſolution of a number of phenomena, particularly a ſingular fact, which philoſophers had endeavoured in vain to account for, viz. that the temperature of the human body, when in health, never exceeds 96 degrees of Fahrenheit's thermometer, although the atmoſphere which ſurrounds it may be heated to a much greater degree. This he attributed to the increaſed perſpiration, and conſequent evaporation, produced by the heat.

In a letter to Mr. Small of London, dated in May 1760, Dr. Franklin makes a number of obſervations, tending to ſhew that, in North America, north-eaſt ſtorms begin in the ſouth-weſt parts. It appears, from actual obſervation, that a north-caſt ſtorm, which extended a conſidera-

ble

ble diftance, commenced at Philadelphia nearly four hours before it was felt at Bofton. He endeavoured to account for this, by fuppofing that, from heat, fome rarefaction takes place about the gulph of Mexico, that the air further north being cooler rufhes in, and is fucceeded by the cooler and denfer air ftill further north, and that thus a continued current is at length produced.

The tone produced by rubbing the brim of a drinking glafs with a wet finger had been generally known. A Mr. Pockrich, an Irifhman, by placing on a table a number of glaffes of different fizes, and tuning them by partly filling them with water, endeavoured to form an inftrument capable of playing tunes. He was prevented by an untimely end, from bringing his invention to any degree of perfection. After his death fome improvements were made upon his plan. The fweetnefs of the tones induced Dr. Franklin to make a variety of experiments ; and he at length formed that elegant inftrument, which he has called the *Armonica.*

In the fummer of 1762 he returned to America. On his paffage he obferved the fingular effect produced by the agitation of a veffel, containing oil floating on water. The furface of the oil remains fmooth and undifturbed, whilft the water is agitated with the utmoft commotion. No fatisfactory explanation of this appearance has, we believe, ever been given.

Dr. Franklin received the thanks of the affembly of Pennfylvania, " as well for the faithful difcharge of his duty to that province in particular, as for the many and important fervices done to America in general, during his refidence in Great Britain." A compenfation of 5000l. Pennfylvania currency was alfo decreed him for his fervices during fix years.

During

During his abfence he had been annually elected member of the affembly. On his return to
Pennfylvania he again took his feat in this body,
and continued a fteady defender of the liberties
of the people.

In December 1762, a circumftance which cauf-
ed great alarm in the province took place. A
number of Indians had refided in the county of
Lancafter, and conducted themfelves uniformly
as friends to the white inhabitants. Repeated depredations on the frontiers had exafperated the
inhabitants to fuch a degree, that they determined on revenge upon every Indian. A number
of perfons, to the amount of about 120, principally inhabitants of Donnegal and Peckftang or
Paxton townfhips, in the county of York, affembled; and, mounted on horfeback, proceeded to
the fettlement of thefe harmlefs and defencelefs
Indians, whofe number had now been reduced to
about twenty. The Indians received intelligence
of the attack which was intended againft them,
but difbelieved it. Confidering the white people
as their friends, they apprehended no danger from
them. When the party arrived at the Indian fettlement, they found only fome women and children, and a few old men, the reft being abfent
at work. They murdered all whom they found,
and amongft others the chief Shahaes, who had
been always diftinguifhed for his friendfhip to the
whites. This bloody deed excited much indignation in the well-difpofed part of the community.

The remainder of thefe unfortunate Indians,
who, by abfence, had efcaped the maffacre, were
conducted to Lancafter, and lodged in the gaol
as a place of fecurity. The governor iffued a proclamation expreffing the ftrongeft difapprobation
of the action, offering a reward for the difcovery

of

of the perpetrators of the deed, and prohibiting all injuries to the peaceable Indians in future. But, notwithftanding this, a party of the fame men fhortly after marched to Lancafter, broke open the gaol, and inhumanly butchered the innocent Indians who had been placed there for fecurity. Another proclamation was iffued, but it had no effect. A detachment marched down to Philadelphia, for the exprefs purpofe of murdering fome friendly Indians, who had been removed to the city for fafety. A number of the citizens armed in their defence. The Quakers, whofe principles are oppofed to fighting, even in their own defence, were moft active upon this occafion. The rioters came to Germantown. The governor fled for fafety to the houfe of Dr. Franklin, who, with fome others, advanced to meet the Paxton boys, as they were called, and had influence enough to prevail upon them to relinquifh their undertaking, and return to their homes.

The difputes between the proprietaries and the affembly, which, for a time, had fubfided, were again revived. The proprietaries were diffatisfied with the conceffions made in favour of the people, and made great ftruggles to recover the privilege of exempting their eftates from taxation, which they had been induced to give up.

In 1763 the affembly paffed a militia bill, to which the governor refufed to give his affent, unlefs the affembly would agree to certain amendments which he propofed. Thefe confifted in increafing the fines, and, in fome cafes, fubftituting death for fines. He wifhed too that the officers fhould be appointed altogether by himfelf, and not be nominated by the people, as the bill had propofed. Thefe amendments the affembly confidered as inconfiftent with the fpirit of liberty. They

They would not adopt them; the governor was obftinate, and the bill was loft.

Thefe, and various other circumftances, encreafed the uneafinefs which fubfifted between the proprietaries and the affembly, to fuch a degree, that, in 1764, a petition to the king was agreed to by the houfe, praying an alteration from a *proprietary to a regal* government. Great oppofition was made to this meafure, not only in the houfe, but in the public prints. A fpeech of Mr. Dickenfon, on the fubject, was publifhed, with a preface by Dr. Smith, in which great pains were taken to fhew the impropriety and impolicy of this proceeding. A fpeech of Mr. Galloway, in reply to Mr. Dickenfon, was publifhed, accompanied with a preface by Dr. Franklin; in which he ably oppofed the principles laid down in the preface to Mr Dickenfon's fpeech. This application to the throne produced no effect. The proprietary government was ftill continued.

At the election for a new affembly, in the fall of 1764, the friends of the proprietaries made great exertions to exclude thofe of the adverfe party; and they obtained a fmall majority in the city of Philadelphia. Franklin now loft his feat in the houfe, which he had held for fourteen years. On the meeting of the affembly, it appeared that there was ftill a decided majority of Franklin's friends. He was immediately appointed provincial agent, to the great chagrin of his enemies, who made a folemn proteft againft his appointment; which was refufed admiffion upon the minutes, as being unprecedented. It was, however, publifhed in the papers, and produced a fpirited reply from him, juft before his departure for England.

The difturbances produced in America by Mr. Grenville's ftamp-act, and the oppofition made to

it,

it, are well known. Under the marquis of Rockingham's adminiſtration, it appeared expedient to endeavour to calm the minds of the coloniſts; and the repeal of the odious tax was contemplated. Amongſt other means of collecting information on the diſpoſition of the people to ſubmit to it, Dr. Franklin was called to the bar of the houſe of commons. The examination which he here underwent was publiſhed, and contains a ſtriking proof of the extent and accuracy of his information, and the facility with which he communicated his ſentiments. He repreſented facts in ſo ſtrong a point of view, that the inexpediency of the act muſt have appeared clear to every unprejudiced mind. The act, after ſome oppoſition, was repealed, about a year after it was enacted, and before it had ever been carried into execution.

In the year 1766, he made a viſit to Holland and Germany, and received the greateſt marks of attention from men of ſcience. In his paſſage through Holland, he learned from the watermen the effect which a diminution of the quantity of water in canals has, in impeding the progreſs of boats. Upon his return to England, he was led to make a number of experiments; all of which tended to confirm the obſervation. Theſe, with an explanation of the phenomenon, he communicated in a letter to his friend, Sir John Pringle, which is contained in the volume of his philoſophical pieces.

In the following year he travelled into France, where he met with a no leſs favourable reception than he had experienced in Germany. He was introduced to a number of literary characters, and to the king, Louis XV.

Several letters written by Hutchinſon, Oliver, and others, to perſons in eminent ſtations in Great-Britain, came into the hands of Dr. Franklin.

lin. Thefe contained the moft violent invectives againft the leading characters of the ftate of Maffachufetts, and ftrenuoufly advifed the profecution of vigorous meafures, to compel the people to obedience to the meafures of the miniftry. Thefe he tranfmitted to the legiflature, by whom they were publifhed. Attefted copies of them were fent to Great-Britain, with an addrefs, praying the king to difcharge from office perfons who had rendered themfelves fo obnoxious to the people, and who had fhewn themfelves fo unfriendly to their interefts. The publication of thefe letters produced a duel between Mr. Whately and Mr. Temple; each of whom was fufpected for having been inftrumental in procuring them. To prevent any further difputes on this fubject Dr. Franklin, in one of the papers, declared that he had fent them to America, but would give no information concerning the manner in which he had obtained them; nor was this ever difcovered.

Shortly after, the petition of the Maffachufett's affembly was taken up for examination, before the privy council. Dr. Franklin attended as agent for the affembly; and here a torrent of the moft violent and unwarranted abufe was poured upon him by the folicitor general Wedderburne, who was engaged as council for Oliver and Hutchinfon. The petition was declared to be fcandalous and vexatious, and the prayer of it refufed.

Although the parliament of Great-Britain had repealed the ftamp-act, it was only upon the principle of expediency. They ftill infifted upon their right to tax the colonies; and, at the fame time that the ftamp-act was repealed, an act was paffed, declaring the right of parliament to bind the colonies in all cafes whatfoever. This language was ufed even by the moft ftrenuous oppofers of the ftamp-act; and, amongft others,

by

by Mr. Pitt. This right was never recognized by the colonists; but, as they flattered themselves that it would not be exercised, they were not very active in remonstrating against it. Had this pretended right been suffered to remain dormant, the colonists would cheerfully have furnished their quota of supplies, in the mode to which they had been accustomed; that is, by acts of their own assemblies, in consequence of requisitions from the secretary of state. If this practice had been pursued, such was the disposition of the colonies towards the mother country, that, notwithstanding the disadvantages under which they laboured, from restraints upon their trade, calculated solely for the benefit of the commercial and manufacturing interests of Great-Britain, a separation of the two countries might have been a far distant event. The Americans, from their earliest infancy, were taught to venerate a people from whom they were descended; whose language, laws, and manners, were the same as their own. They looked up to them as models of perfection; and, in their prejudiced minds, the most enlightened nations of Europe were considered as almost barbarians, in comparison with Englishmen. The name of an Englishman conveyed to an American the idea of every thing good and great. Such sentiments instilled into them in early life, what but a repetition of unjust treatment could have induced them to entertain the most distant thought of separation! The duties on glass, paper, leather, painters' colours, tea, &c.; the disfranchisement of some of the colonies; the obstruction to the measures of the legislature in others, by the king's governors; the contemptuous treatment of their humble remonstrances, stating their grievances and praying a redress of them, and

other

other violent and oppreffive meafures, at length excited an ardent fpirit of oppofition. Inftead of endeavouring to allay this by a more lenient conduct, the miniftry feemed refolutely bent upon reducing the colonies to the moft flavifh obedience to their decrees. But this tended only to aggravate. Vain were all the efforts made ufe of to prevail upon them to lay afide their defigns, to convince them of the impoffibility of carrying them into effect, and of the mifchievous confequences which muft enfue from a continuance of the attempt. They perfevered, with a degree of inflexibility fcarcely paralleled.

The advantages which Great-Britain derived from her colonies were fo great, that nothing but a degree of infatuation, little fhort of madnefs, could have produced a continuance of meafures calculated to keep up a fpirit of uneafinefs, which might occafion the flighteft wifh for a feparation. When we confider the great improvements in the fcience of government, the general diffufion of the principles of liberty amongft the people of Europe, the effects which thefe have already produced in France, and the probable confequences which will refult from them elfewhere, all of which are the offspring of the American revolution, it cannot but appear ftrange, that events of fo great moment to the happinefs of mankind, fhould have been ultimately occafioned by the wickednefs or ignorance of a Britifh miniftry.

Dr. Franklin left nothing untried to prevail upon the miniftry to confent to a change of meafures. In private converfations, and in letters to perfons in government, he continually expatiated upon the impolicy and injuftice of their conduct towards America; and ftated, that, notwithftanding the attachment of the colonifts to the

mother

mother country, a repetition of ill treatment muſt ultimately alienate their affections. They liſtened not to his advice. They blindly perſevered in their own ſchemes, and left to the coloniſts no alternative, but oppoſition or unconditional ſubmiſſion. The latter accorded not with the principles of freedom, which they had been taught to revere. To the former they were compelled, though reluctantly, to have recourſe.

Dr. Franklin, finding all efforts to reſtore harmony between Great-Britain and her colonies uſeleſs, returned to America in the year 1775; juſt after the commencement of hoſtilities. The day after his return he was elected by the legiſlature of Pennſylvania a delegate to congreſs. Not long after his election a committee was appointed, conſiſting of Mr. Lynch, Mr. Harriſon, and himſelf, to viſit the camp at Cambridge, and, in conjunction with the commander in chief, to endeavour to convince the troops, whoſe term of enliſtment was about to expire, of the neceſſity of their continuing in the field, and perſevering in the cauſe of their country.

In the fall of the ſame year he viſited Canada, to endeavour to unite them in the common cauſe of liberty; but they could not be prevailed upon to oppoſe the meaſures of the Britiſh government. M. Le Roy, in a letter annexed to Abbé Fauchet's eulogium of Dr. Franklin, ſtates that the ill ſucceſs of this negociation was occaſioned, in a great degree, by religious animoſities, which ſubſiſted between the Canadians and their neighbours, ſome of whom had at different times burnt their chapels.

When Lord Howe came to America, in 1776, veſted with power to treat with the coloniſts, a correſpondence took place between him and Dr. Franklin, on the ſubject of a reconciliation.

Dr.

Dr. Franklin was afterwards appointed, together with John Adams and Edward Rutledge, to wait upon the commiſſioners, in order to learn the extent of their power. Theſe were found to be only to grant pardons upon ſubmiſſion. Theſe were terms which would not be accepted ; and the object of the commiſſioners could not be obtained.

The momentous queſtion of independence was ſhortly after brought into view, at a time when the fleets and armies, which were ſent to enforce obedience, were truly formidable. With an army, numerous indeed, but ignorant of diſcipline, and entirely unſkilled in the art of war, without money, without a fleet, without allies, and with nothing but the love of liberty to ſupport them, the coloniſts determined to ſeparate from a country, from which they had experienced a repetition of injury and inſult. In this queſtion, Dr. Franklin was decidedly in favour of the meaſure propoſed, and had great influence in bringing over others to his ſentiments.

The public mind had been pretty fully prepared for this event, by Mr. Paine's celebrated pamphlet, *Common Senſe.* There is good reaſon to believe that Dr. Franklin had no inconſiderable ſhare, at leaſt, in furniſhing materials for this work.

In the convention which aſſembled at Philadelphia in 1776, for the purpoſe of eſtabliſhing a new form of government for the ſtate of Pennſylvania, Dr. Franklin was choſen preſident. The late conſtitution of this ſtate, which was the reſult of their deliberations, may be conſidered as a digeſt of his principles of government. The ſingle legiſlature, and the plural executive, ſeem to have been his favourite tenets.

In

In the latter end of 1776, Dr. Franklin was appointed to affift in the negociations which had been fet on foot by Silas Deane at the court of France. A conviction of the advantages of a commercial intercourfe with America, and a defire of weakening the Britifh empire by difmembering it, firft induced the French court to liften to propofals of an alliance. But they fhewed rather a reluctance to the meafure, which, by Dr. Franklin's addrefs, and particularly by the fuccefs of the American arms againft general Burgoyne, was at length overcome; and in February 1778, a treaty of alliance, offenfive and defenfive, was concluded; in confequence of which France became involved in the war with Great-Britain.

Perhaps no perfon could have been found, more capable of rendering effential fervices to the United States at the court of France, than Dr. Franklin. He was well known as a philofopher, and his character was held in the higheft eftimation. He was received with the greateft marks of refpect by all the literary characters; and this refpect was extended amongft all claffes of men. His perfonal influence was hence very confiderable. To the effects of this were added thofe of various performances which he publifhed, tending to eftablifh the credit and character of the United States. To his exertions in this way, may, in no fmall degree, be afcribed the fuccefs of the loans negotiated in Holland and France, which greatly contributed to bringing the war to a happy conclufion.

The repeated ill fuccefs of their arms, and more particularly the capture of Cornwallis and his army, at length convinced the Britifh nation of the impoffibility of reducing the Americans to fubjection. The trading intereft particularly became

clamorous

clamorous for peace. The miniftry were unable longer to oppofe their wifhes. Provifional articles of peace were agreed to, and figned at Paris on the 30th of November, 1782, by Dr. Franklin, Mr. Adams, Mr. Jay, and Mr. Laurens, on the part of the United States; and by Mr. Ofwald on the part of Great-Britain. Thefe formed the bafis of the definitive treaty, which was concluded the 3d of September 1783, and figned by Dr. Franklin, Mr. Adams, and Mr. Jay, on the one part, and by Mr. David Hartley on the other.

On the 3d of April 1783, a treaty of amity and commerce, between the United States and Sweden, was concluded at Paris, by Dr. Franklin and the Count Von Krutz.

A fimilar treaty with Pruffia was concluded in 1785, not long before Dr. Franklin's departure from Europe.

Dr. Franklin did not fuffer his political purfuits to engrofs his whole attention. Some of his performances made their appearance in Paris. The object of thefe was generally the promotion of induftry and œconomy.

In the year 1784, when animal magnetifm made great noife in the world, particularly at Paris, it was thought a matter of fuch importance, that the king appointed commiffioners to examine into the foundation of this pretended fcience. Dr. Franklin was one of the number. After a fair and diligent examination, in the courfe of which Mefmer repeated a number of experiments, fome of which were tried upon themfelves, they determined that it was a mere trick, intended to impofe upon the ignorant and credulous —Mefmer was thus interrupted in his career to wealth and fame, and a moft infolent attempt to impofe upon the human underftanding baffled.

The

The important ends of Dr. Franklin's miffion being completed by the eftablifhment of American independence, and the infirmities of age and difeafe coming upon him, he became defirous of returning to his native country. Upon application to congrefs to be recalled, Mr. Jefferfon was appointed to fucceed him, in 1785. Sometime in September of the fame year, Dr. Franklin arrived in Philadelphia. He was fhortly after chofen member of the fupreme executive council for the city; and foon after was elected prefident of the fame.

When a convention was called to meet in Philadelphia, in 1787, for the purpofe of giving more energy to the government of the union, by revifing and amending the articles of confederation, Dr. Franklin was appointed a delegate from the State of Pennfylvania. He figned the conftitution which they propofed for the union, and gave it the moft unequivocal marks of his approbation.

A fociety for political enquiries, of which Dr. Franklin was prefident, was eftablifhed about this period. The meetings were held at his houfe. Two or three effays read in this fociety were publifhed. It did not long continue.

In the year 1787, two focieties were eftablifhed in Philadelphia, founded in the principles of the moft liberal and refined humanity—*The Philadelphia Society for alleviating the miferies of public prifons ;* and the *Pennfylvania Society for promocing the abolition of flavery, the relief of free negroes unlawfully held in bondage, and the improvement of the condition of the African race.* Of each of thefe Dr. Franklin was prefident. The labours of thefe bodies have been crowned with great fuccefs; and they continue to profecute, with unwearied diligence, the laudable defigns for which they were eftablifhed.

I.   Dr.

Dr. Franklin's increasing infirmities prevented his regular attendance at the council-chamber; and, in 1788, he retired wholly from public life.

His constitution had been a remarkably good one. He had been little subject to disease, except an attack of the gout occasionally, until about the year 1781, when he was first attacked with symptoms of the calculous complaint, which continued during his life. During the intervals of pain from this grievous disease, he spent many chearful hours, conversing in the most agreeable and instructive manner. His faculties were entirely unimpaired, even to the hour of his death.

His name, as president of the Abolition Society, was signed to the memorial presented to the House of Representatives of the United States, on the 12th of February 1789, praying them to exert the full extent of power vested in them by the constitution, in discouraging the traffic of the human species. This was his last public act. In the debates to which this memorial gave rise, several attempts were made to justify the trade. In the Federal Gazette of March 25th there appeared an essay, signed Historicus, written by Dr. Franklin, in which he communicated a speech, said to have been delivered in the Divan of Algiers in 1687, in opposition to the prayer of the petition of a sect called *Erika*, or purists, for the abolition of piracy and slavery. This pretended African speech was an excellent parody of one delivered by Mr. Jackson of Georgia. All the arguments urged in favour of negro slavery, are applied with equal force to justify the plundering and enslaving of Europeans. It affords, at the same time, a demonstration of the futility of the arguments in defence of the slave trade, and of the strength of mind and ingenuity of the author, at his advanced period of life. It furnished too

a no

a no lefs convincing proof of his power of imitating the ftyle of other times and nations, than
his celebrated parable againft perfecution.   And
as the latter led many perfons to fearch the fcrip-
tures with a view to find it, fo the former cau-
fed many perfons to fearch the book-ftores and
libraries, for the work from which it was faid to
be extracted *.

(In the beginning of April following, he was
attacked with a fever and complaint of his breaft,
which terminated his exiftence.) The following
account of his laft illnefs was written by his friend
and Phyfician, Dr. Jones.

" The ftone, with which he had been afflicted
for feveral years, had for the laft twelve months
confined him chiefly to his bed; and during the
extreme painful paroxyfms, he was obliged to
take large dofes of laudanum to mitigate his tor-
tures—ftill, in the intervals of pain, he not only
amufed himfelf with reading and converfing cheerfully with his family, and a few friends who vi-
fited him, but was often employed in doing bufinefs of a public as well as private nature, with
various perfons who waited on him for that purpofe; and in every inftance difplayed, not only
that readinefs and difpofition of doing good,
which was the diftinguifhing characteriftic of his
life, but the fulleft and cleareft poffeffion of his
uncommon mental abilities; and not unfrequent-
ly indulged himfelf in thofe *jeux d'efprit* and entertaining anecdotes, which were the delight of
all who heard him.

" About fixteen days before his death, he was
feized with a feverifh indifpofition, without any
particular fymptoms attending it, till the third or
fourth day, when he complained of a pain in the
left breaft, which increafed till it became extreme-

* This fpeech will be found among the Effays.

ly acute, attended with a cough and laborious breathing. During this ftate, when the feverity of his pains fometimes drew forth a groan of complaint, he would obferve—that he was afraid he did not bear them as he ought—acknowledged his grateful fenfe of the many bleffings he had received from that Supreme Being, who had raifed him from fmall and low beginnings to fuch high rank and confideration among men—and made no doubt but his prefent afflictions were kindly intended to wean him from a world, in which he was no longer fit to act the part affigned him. In this frame of body and mind he continued till five days before his death, when his pain and difficulty of breathing entirely left him, and his family were flattering themfelves with the hopes of his recovery, when an impofthumation, which had formed itfelf in his lungs, fuddenly burft, and difcharged a great quantity of matter, which he continued to throw up while he had fufficient ftrength to do it, but, as that failed, the organs of refpiration became gradually oppreffed—a calm lethargic ftate fucceeded——and, on the 17th of April 1790, about eleven o'clock at night, he quietly expired, clofing a long and ufeful life of eighty-four years and three months.

" It may not be amifs to add to the above account, that Dr. Franklin, in the year 1735, had a fevere pleurify, which terminated in an abfcefs of the left lobe of his lungs, and he was then almoft fuffocated with the quantity and fuddennefs of the difcharge. A fecond attack of a fimilar nature happened fome years after this, from which he foon recovered, and did not appear to fuffer any inconvenience in his refpiration from thefe difeafes."

The

The following epitaph on himfelf, was written by him many years previous to his death:

THE BODY
of
BENJAMIN FRANKLIN, Printer,
(Like the cover of an old book,
Its contents torn out,
And ftript of its lettering and gilding)
Lies here, food for worms;
Yet the work itfelf fhall not be loft,
For it will (as he believed) appear once more,
In a new
And more beautiful edition,
Corrected and amended
by
The Author.

EXTRACTS *from the laft Will and Teftament of*
Dr. FRANKLIN.

WITH regard to my books, thofe I had in
France, and thofe I left in Philadelphia, being
now affembled together here, and a catalogue
made of them, it is my intention to difpofe of
the fame as follows:

My hiftory of the Academy of Sciences, in fixty or feventy volumes quarto, I give to the philofophical fociety of Philadelphia, of which I have
the honour to be prefident. My collection in folio of *Les Arts & les Metiers*, I give to the American philofophical fociety, eftablifhed in New
England, of which I am a member. My quarto
edition of the fame *Arts & Metiers*, I give to the
library company of Philadelphia. Such and fo
many of my books as I fhall mark, in the faid
catalogue, with the name of my grandfon Benjamin Franklin Bache, I do hereby give to him:
and fuch and fo many of my books, as I fhall
mark

mark in the said catalogue with the name of my grandson William Bache, I do hereby give to him : and such as shall be marked with the name of Jonathan Williams, I hereby give to my cousin of that name. The residue and remainder of all my books, manuscripts and papers, I do give to my grandson William Temple Franklin. My share in the library company of Philadelphia I give to my grandson Benjamin Franklin Bache, confiding that he will permit his brothers and sisters to share in the use of it.

I was born in Boston, New England, and owe my first instructions in literature to the free grammar-schools established there. I therefore give one hundred pounds sterling to my executors, to be by them, the survivors or survivor of them, paid over to the managers of the free schools in my native town of Boston, to be by them, or the person or persons who shall have the superintendence and management of the said schools, put out to interest, and so continued at interest for ever ; which interest annually shall be laid out in silver medals, and given as honorary rewards annually by the directors of the said free schools, for the encouragement of scholarship in the said schools, belonging to the said town, in such manner as to the discretion of the select men of the said town shall seem meet.

Out of the salary that may remain due to me, as president of the state, I give the sum of two thousand pounds to my executors, to be by them, the survivors or survivor of them, paid over to such person or persons as the legislature of this state, by an act of assembly, shall appoint to receive the same, in trust, to be employed for making the Schuylkil navigable.

During the number of years I was in business as a stationer, printer, and post-master, a great
many

many small sums became due to me, for books, advertisements, postage of letters, and other matters, which were not collected, when, in 1757, I was sent by the assembly to England as their agent—and, by subsequent appointments, continued there till 1775—when, on my return, I was immediately engaged in the affairs of congress, and sent to France in 1776, where I remained nine years, not returning till 1785; and the said debts not being demanded in such a length of time, are become in a manner obsolete, yet are nevertheless justly due.—These, as they are stated in my great folio leger, E, I bequeath to the contributors of the Pennsylvania hospital; hoping that those debtors, and the descendants of such as are deceased, who now, as I find, make some difficulty of satisfying such antiquated demands as just debts, may however be induced to pay or give them as charity to that excellent institution. I am sensible that much must inevitably be lost; but I hope something considerable may be recovered. It is possible too that some of the parties charged may have existing old unsettled accounts against me: in which case the managers of the said hospital will allow and deduct the amount, or pay the balance, if they find it against me.

I request my friends Henry Hill, Esq. John Jay, Esq. Francis Hopkinson, Esq. and Mr. Edward Duffield, of Bonfield, in Philadelphia county, to be the executors of this my last will and testament, and I hereby nominate and appoint them for that purpose.

I would have my body buried with as little expence or ceremony as may be.

Philadelphia, July 17, 1788.

CODICIL.

CODICIL.

I Benjamin Franklin, in the foregoing or annexed laft will and teftament, having further confidered the fame, do think proper to make and
publifh the following codicil, or addition thereto:

It having long been a fixed political opinion of
mine, that in a democratical ftate there ought to
be no offices of profit, for the reafons I had given
in an article of my drawing in our conftitution,
it was my intention, when I accepted the office
of prefident, to devote the appointed falary to
fome public ufe: Accordingly I had already, before I made my laft will, in July laft, given large
fums of it to colleges, fchools, building of churches,
&c.; and in that will I bequeathed two thoufand pounds more to the ftate, for the purpofe of
making the Skuylkil navigable; but underftanding fince, that fuch a fum will do but little towards accomplifhing fuch a work, and that the
project is not likely to be undertaken for many
years to come—and having entertained another
idea, which I hope may be more extenfively ufeful, I do hereby revoke and annul the bequeft,
and direct that the certificates I have for what remains due to me of that falary, be fold towards
raifing the fum of two thoufand pounds fterling,
to be difpofed of as I am now about to order.

It has been an opinion, that he who receives
an eftate from his anceftors, is under fome obligation to tranfmit the fame to pofterity. This
obligation lies not on me, who never inherited
a fhilling from any anceftor or relation. I fhall,
however, if it is not diminifhed by fome accident
before my death, leave a confiderable eftate among
my defcendants and relations. The above obfervation is made merely as fome apology to my
family, for my making bequefts that do not appear

pear to have any immediate relation to their advantage.

I was born in Bofton, New-England, and owe my firft inftructions in literature to the free grammar-fchools eftablifhed there. I have therefore confidered thofe fchools in my will.

But I am alfo under obligations to the ftate of Maffachufetts, for having, unafked, appointed me formerly their agent, with a handfome falary, which continued fome years: and although I accidentally loft in their fervice, by tranfmitting governor Hutchinfon's letters, much more than the amount of what they gave me, I do not think that ought in the leaft to diminifh my gratitude. I have confidered that, among artifans, good apprentices are moft likely to make good citizens; and having myfelf been bred to a manual art, printing, in my native town, and afterwards affifted to fet up my bufinefs in Philadelphia by kind loans of money from two friends there, which was the foundation of my fortune, and of all the utility in life that may be afcribed to me—I wifh to be ufeful even after my death, if poffible, in forming and advancing other young men, that may be ferviceable to their country in both thefe towns.

To this end I devote two thoufand pounds fterling, which I give, one thoufand thereof to the inhabitants of the town of Bofton, in Maffachufetts, and the other thoufand to the inhabitants of the city of Philadelphia, in truft, to and for the ufes, intents, and purpofes, herein after mentioned and declared.

The faid fum of one thoufand pounds fterling, if accepted by the inhabitants of the town of Bofton, fhall be managed under the direction of the felect men, united with the minifters of the oldeft epifcopalian, congregational, and prefby-

terian

terian churches in that town, who are to let out
the fame upon intereft at five per cent. per annum,
to fuch young married artificers, under the age
of twenty-five years, as have ferved an apprenticefhip in the faid town, and faithfully fulfilled
the duties required in their indentures, fo as to
obtain a good moral character from at leaft two
refpectable citizens, who are willing to become
fureties in a bond, with the applicants, for the
repayment of the money fo lent, with intereft,
according to the terms herein after prefcribed;
all which bonds are to be taken for Spanifh milled
dollars, or the value thereof in current gold coin:
and the manager fhall keep a bound book, or
books, wherein fhall be entered the names of thofe
who fhall apply for, and receive the benefit of
this inftitution, and of their fureties, together
with the fums lent, the dates, and other neceffary an¹ proper records, refpecting the bufinefs and
concerns of this inftitution: and as thefe loans
are intended to affift young married artificers in
fetting up their bufinefs, they are to be proportioned by the difcretion of the managers, fo as not
to exceed fixty pounds fterling to one perfon,
nor to be lefs than fifteen pounds.

And if the number of appliers fo entitled fhould
be fo large as that the fum will not fuffice to
afford to each as much as might otherwife not be
improper, the proportion to each fhall be diminifhed, fo as to afford to every one fome affiftance. Thefe aids may therefore be fmall at firft,
but as the capital increafes by the accumulated
intereft, they will be more ample. And in order
to ferve as many as poffible in their turn, as well
as to make the repayment of the principal borrowed more eafy, each borrower fhall be obliged
to pay with the yearly intereft one tenth part of
the principal; which fums of principal and inte-

reft

rest so paid in, shall be again let out to fresh bor-
rowers. And it is presumed, that there will be
always found in Boston virtuous and benevolent
citizens, willing to bestow a part of their time in
doing good to the rising generation, by superin-
tending and managing this institution gratis; it
is hoped that no part of the money will at any
time lie dead, or be diverted to other purposes,
but be continually augmenting by the interest,
in which there may in time be more than the occasion in Boston shall require: and then some
may be spared to the neighbouring or other towns
in the said state of Massachusetts, which may desire to have it, such towns engaging to pay
punctually the interest, and the proportions of
the principal annually to the inhabitants of the
town of Boston. If this plan is executed, and
succeeds, as projected, without interruption for
one hundred years, the sum will be then one hundred and thirty-one thousand pounds; of which
I would have the managers of the donation to the
town of Boston then lay out, at their discretion,
one hundred thousand pounds in public works,
which may be judged of most general utility to
the inhabitants; such as fortifications, bridges,
aqueducts, public buildings, baths, pavements,
or whatever may make living in the town more
convenient to its people, and render it more
agreeable to strangers resorting thither for health,
or a temporary residence. The remaining thirty-
one thousand pounds I would have continued to
be let out to interest, in the manner above directed, for one hundred years; as I hope it will have
been found that the institution has had a good
effect on the conduct of youth, and been of service to many worthy characters and useful citizens. At the end of this second term, if no unfortunate accident has prevented the operation,

the

the fum will be four millions and fixty-one
thoufand pounds fterling; of which I leave one
million and fixty-one thoufand pounds to the
difpofition and management of the inhabitants
of the town of Bofton, and the three millions
to the difpofition of the government of the ftate;
not prefuming to carry my views farther.

All the directions herein given refpecting the
difpofition and management of the donation to
the inhabitants of Bofton, I would have obferved
refpecting that to the inhabitants of Philadelphia;
only, as Philadelphia is incorporated, I requeft
the corporation of that city to undertake the
management, agreeable to the faid directions:
and I do hereby veft them with full and ample
powers for that purpofe. And having confidered
that the covering its ground-plat with buildings
and pavements, which carry off moft rain, and
prevent its foaking into the earth and renewing
and purifying the fprings whence the water of
the wells muft gradually grow worfe, and in time
be unfit for ufe, as I find has happened in all old
cities; I recommend, that, at the end of the firft
hundred years, if not done before, the corporation
of the city employ a part of the hundred thoufand
pounds in bringing by pipes the water of Wiffa-
hickoncreek into the town, fo as to fupply the
inhabitants, which I apprehend may be done
without great difficulty, the level of that creek
being much above that of the city, and may be
made higher by a dam. I alfo recommend
making the Skuylkil completely navigable. At
the end of the fecond hundred years, I would
have the difpofition of the four millions and
fixty-one thoufand pounds divided between the
inhabitants of the city of Philadelphia and the
government of Pennfylvania, in the fame manner
as herein directed with refpect to that of the
                                    inhabitants

inhabitants of Bofton and the government of Maffachufetts. It is my defire that this inftitution fhould take place, and begin to operate within one year after my deceafe; for which purpofe due notice fhould be publicly given previous to the expiration of that year, that thofe for whofe benefit this eftablifhment is intended may make their refpective applications : and I hereby direct my executors, the furvivors and furvivor of them, within fix months after my deceafe to pay over the faid fum of two thoufand pounds fter-ling to fuch perfons as fhall be duly appointed by the felect men of Bofton and the corporation of Philadelphia, to receive and take charge of their refpective fums of one thoufand pounds each for the purpofes aforefaid. Confidering the accidents to which all human affairs and projects are fubject in fuch a length of time, I have perhaps too much flattered myfelf with a vain fancy, that thefe difpofitions, if carried into exe-cution, will be continued without interruption, and have the effects propofed : I hope however, that, if the inhabitants of the two cities fhould not think fit to undertake the execution, they will at leaft accept the offer of thefe donations, as a mark of my good will, token of my gratitude, and teftimony of my defire to be ufeful to them even after my departure. I wifh, indeed, that they may both undertake to endeavour the execution of my project, becaufe I think, that, though unforefeen difficulties may arife, ex-pedients will be found to remove them, and the fcheme be found practicable. If one of them accepts the money with the conditions, and the other refufes, my will then is, that both fums be given to the inhabitants of the city accepting; the whole to be applied to the fame purpofes, and under the fame regulations directed for the fepa-rate

rate parts; and if both refufe, the money remain of courfe in the mafs of my eftate, and
it is to be difpofed of therewith, according to
my will made the feventeenth day of July
1788.

My fine crab-tree walking-ftick, with a gold
head curioufly wrought in the form of the cap
of Liberty, I gave to my friend and the friend
of mankind, General Wafhington. If it were
a fceptre, he has merited it, and would become
it.

E S S A Y S

HUMOROUS, MORAL, and LITERARY, &c.

ON EARLY MARRIAGES.

TO JOHN ALLEYNE, ESQ.

DEAR JACK,

YOU defire, you fay, my impartial thoughts on the fubject of an early marriage, by way of anfwer to the numberlefs objections that have been made by numerous perfons to your own. You may remember, when you confulted me on the occafion, that I thought youth on both fides to be no objection. Indeed, from the marriages that have fallen under my obfervation, I am rather inclined to think, that early ones ftand the beft chance of happinefs. The temper and habits of the young are not yet become fo ftiff and uncomplying, as when more advanced in life; they form more eafily to each other, and hence many occafions of difguft are removed. And if youth has lefs of that prudence which is neceffary to manage a family, yet the parents and elder friends of young married perfons are generally at hand to afford their advice, which amply fupplies that defect; and by early marriage, youth is fooner formed to regular

lar and ufeful life ; and poffibly fome of thofe
accidents or connections, that might have injured the conftitution, or reputation, or both,
are thereby happily prevented. Particular circumftances of particular perfons, may poffibly
fometimes make it prudent to delay entering
into that ftate ; but in general, when nature has
rendered our bodies fit for it, the prefumption is
in nature's favour, that fhe has not judged amifs
in making us defire it.   Late marriages are often
attended, too, with this further inconvenience,
that there is not the fame chance that the parents
fhall live to fee their offspring educated. " Late
children," fays the Spanifh proverb, " are early
" orphans."   A melancholy reflection to thofe
whofe cafe it may be ! With us, in America, marriages are generally in the morning of life ; our
children are therefore educated and fettled in the
world by noon ; and thus, our bufinefs being
done, we have an afternoon and evening of
cheerful leifure to ourfelves, fuch as our friend
at prefent enjoys. By thefe early marriages we
are bleffed with more children ; and from the
mode among us, founded by nature, of every
mother fuckling and nurfing her own child, more
of them are raifed.   Thence the fwift progrefs
of population among us, unparalleled in Europe.
In fine, I am glad you are married, and congra-
tulate you moft cordially upon it. You are now
in the way of becoming a ufeful citizen ; and
you have efcaped the unnatural ftate of celibacy
for life—the fate of many here, who never intended it, but who having too long poftponed
the change of their condition, find, at length,
that it is too late to think of it, and fo live all
their lives in a fituation that greatly leffens a
man's value. An odd volume of a fet of books,
bears not the value of its proportion to the fet :

what

what think you of the odd half of a pair of
fciffars ? it can't well cut any thing ; it may poffibly ferve to fcrape a trencher.

Pray make my compliments and beft wifhes
acceptable to your bride. I am old and heavy,
or I fhould ere this have prefented them in perfon. I fhall make but fmall ufe of the old man's
privilege, that of giving advice to younger
friends. Treat your wife always with refpect ;
it will procure refpect to you, not only from
her, but from all that obferve it. Never ufe a
flighting expreffion to her, even in jeft ; for
flights in jeft, after frequent bandyings, are apt
to end in angry earneft. Be ftudious in your
profeffion, and you will be learned. Be induftrious and frugal, and you will be rich. Be
fober and temperate, and you will be healthy.
Be in general virtuous, and you will be happy.
At leaft, you will, by fuch conduct, ftand the
beft chance for fuch confequences. I pray God
to blefs you both ! being ever your affectionate
friend,

B. FRANKLIN.

ON THE DEATH OF HIS BROTHER,
Mr. JOHN FRANKLIN.

TO MISS HUBBARD.

I CONDOLE with you. We have loſt a
moſt dear and valuable relation. But it is the
will of God and nature, that theſe mortal bodies
be laid aſide, when the ſoul is to enter into real
life. This is rather an embryo ſtate, a prepara-
tion for living. A man is not completely born
until he be dead. Why then ſhould we grieve
that a new child is born among the immortals,
a new member added to their happy ſociety?
We are ſpirits. That bodies ſhould be lent us,
while they can afford us pleaſure, aſſiſt us in acquiring knowledge, or doing good to our fellow-
creatures, is a kind and benevolent act of God.
When they become unfit for theſe purpoſes, and
afford us pain inſtead of pleaſure, inſtead of an
aid become an incumbrance, and anſwer none of
the intentions for which they were given, it is
equally kind and benevolent that a way is provided by which we may get rid of them. Death
is that way. We ourſelves, in ſome caſes, prudently chooſe a partial death. A mangled painful limb, which cannot be reſtored, we willingly
cut off. He who plucks out a tooth, parts with
it freely, ſince the pain goes with it: and he
who quits the whole body, parts at once with
all pains, and poſſibilities of pains and diſeaſes,
it was liable to, or capable of making him ſuffer.

Our

Our friend and we were invited abroad on a party of pleafure, which is to laft for ever. His chair was ready firft; and he is gone before us. We could not all conveniently ftart together: and why fhould you and I be grieved at this, fince we are foon to follow, and know where to find him?

Adieu,

B. FRANKLIN.

TO THE LATE

DOCTOR MATHER OF BOSTON.

REV. SIR,

I RECEIVED your kind letter, with your excellent advice to the people of the United States, which I read with great pleasure, and hope it will be duly regarded. Such writings, though they may be lightly passed over by many readers, yet, if they make a deep impression on one active mind in a hundred, the effects may be considerable.

Permit me to mention one little instance, which, though it relates to myself, will not be quite uninteresting to you. When I was a boy, I met with a book entitled "Essays to do good," which I think was written by your father. It had been so little regarded by a former possessor, that several leaves of it were torn out; but the remainder gave me such a turn of thinking, as to have an influence on my conduct through life: for I have always set a greater value on the character of a doer of good, than any other kind of reputation; and if I have been, as you seem to think, a useful citizen, the public owes the advantage of it to that book.

You mention your being in your seventy-eighth year. I am in my seventy-ninth. We are grown old together. It is now more than sixty years since I left Boston; but I remember well both your father and grandfather, having heard them both in the pulpit, and seen them in their houses. The last time I saw your father

was

was in the beginning of 1724, when I visited him after my first trip to Pennsylvania. He received me in his library; and on my taking leave, shewed me a shorter way out of the house, through a narrow passage, which was crossed by a beam overhead. We were still talking as I withdrew, he accompanying me behind, and I turning partly towards him, when he said hastily, " Stoop, Stoop!" I did not understand him till I felt my head hit against the beam. He was a man who never missed any occasion of giving instruction; and upon this he said to me : " You are young, and have " the world before you : stoop as you go through " it, and you will miss many hard thumps." This advice, thus beat into my heart, has frequently been of use to me; and I often think of it, when I see pride mortified, and misfortunes brought upon people by their carrying their heads too high.

I long much to see again my native place; and once hoped to lay my bones there. I left it in 1723. I visited it in 1733, 1743, 1753, and 1763; and in 1773 I was in England. In 1775 I had a sight of it, but could not enter, it being in possession of the enemy. I did hope to have been there in 1783, but could not obtain my dismission from this employment here; and now I fear I shall never have that happiness. My best wishes however attend my dear country, " esto perpetua." It is now blessed with an excellent constitution : may it last for ever !

This powerful monarchy continues its friendship for the United States. It is a friendship of the utmost importance to our security, and should be carefully cultivated. Britain has not yet well digested the loss of its dominion over us ; and has still at times some flattering hopes

of

of recovering it. Accidents may increafe thofe hopes, and encourage dangerous attempts. A breach between us and France would infallibly bring the Englifh again upon our backs: and yet we have fome wild beafts among our countrymen, who are endeavouring to weaken that connection.

Let us preferve our reputation, by performing our engagements; our credit, by fulfilling our contracts; and our friends, by gratitude and kindnefs: for we know not how foon we may have occafion for all of them.

With great and fincere efteem,

I have the honour to be,

Reverend Sir,

Your moft obedient and

moft humble fervant,

PASSY, May 12,   B. FRANKLIN.
     1784.

THE

THE WHISTLE:

A TRUE STORY.

WRITTEN TO HIS NEPHEW.

WHEN I was a child, at feven years old, my friends, on a holiday, filled my pocket with coppers. I went directly to a fhop where they fold toys for children; and being charmed with the found of a *whiftle*, that I met by the way in the hands of another boy, I voluntarily offered him all my money for one. I then came home, and went whiftling all over the houfe, much pleafed with my *whiftle*, but difturbing all the family. My brothers, and fifters, and coufins, underftanding the bargain I had made, told me I had given four times as much for it as it was worth. This put me in mind what good things I might have bought with the reft of the money; and they laughed at me fo much for my folly, that I cried with vexation; and the reflection gave me more chagrin than the *whiftle* gave me pleafure.

This however was afterwards of ufe to me, the impreffion continuing on my mind; fo that often, when I was tempted to buy fome unneceffary thing, I faid to myfelf *Don't give too much for the whiftle*; and fo I faved my money.

As I grew up, came into the world, and obferved the actions of men, I thought I met with many, very many, who *gave too much for the whiftle.*

When I faw any one too ambitious of court favours, facrificing his time in attendance on
levees,

levees, his repofe, his liberty, his virtue, and perhaps his friends, to attain it, I have faid to myfelf, *This man gives too much for his whiftle.*

When I faw another fond of popularity, conftantly employing himfelf in political buftles, neglecting his own affairs, and ruining them by that neglect: *He pays, indeed fays I, too much for his whiftle.*

If I knew a mifer, who gave up every kind of comfortable living, all the pleafure of doing good to others, all the efteem of his fellow-citizens, and the joys of benevolent friendfhip, for the fake of accumulating wealth; *Poor man, fays I, you do indeed pay too much for your whiftle.*

When I meet a man of pleafure, facrificing every laudable improvement of the mind, or of his fortune, to mere corporeal fenfations; *Miftaken man, fays I, you are providing pain for yourfelf, inftead of pleafure: you give too much for your whiftle.*

If I fee one fond of fine clothes, fine furniture, fine equipages, all above his fortune, for which he contracts debts, and ends his career in prifon; *Alas, fays I, he has paid dear, very dear, for his whiftle.*

When I fee a beautiful, fweet-tempered girl married to an ill-natured brute of a hufband: *What a pity it is, fays I, that fhe has paid fo much for a whiftle!*

In fhort, I conceived that great part of the miferies of mankind were brought upon them by the falfe eftimates they had made of the value of things, and by their giving too much for their *whiftles.*

A PETI-

A PETITION

I ADDRESS myself to all the friends of youth, and conjure them to direct their compassionate regard to my unhappy fate, in order to remove the prejudices of which I am the victim. There are twin sisters of us: and the two eyes of man do not more resemble, nor are capable of being upon better terms with each other, than my sister and myself, were it not for the partiality of our parents, who make the most injurious distinctions between us. From my infancy, I have been led to consider my sister as a being of a more elevated rank. I was suffered to grow up without the least instruction, while nothing was spared in her education. She had masters to teach her writing, drawing, music, and other accomplishments; but if by chance I touched a pencil, a pen, or a needle, I was bitterly rebuked: and more than once I have been beaten for being aukward, and wanting a graceful manner. It is true, my sister associated me with her upon some occasions; but she always made a point of taking the lead, calling upon me only from necessity, or to figure by her side.

But conceive not, Sirs, that my complaints are instigated merely by vanity— No; my uneasiness is occasioned by an object much more serious. It is the practice in our family, that the whole business of providing for its subsistence falls upon my sister and myself. It

any

any indifpofition fhould attack my fifter—and I
mention it in confidence, upon this occafion,
that fhe is fubject to the gout, the rheumatifm,
and cramp, without making mention of other
accidents—what would be the fate of our poor
family? Muft not the regret of our parents be
exceffive, at having placed fo great a difference
between fifters who are fo perfectly equal? Alas!
we muft perifh from diftrefs: for it would not
be in my power to fcrawl a fuppliant petition
for relief, having been obliged to employ the
hand of another in tranfcribing the requeft which
I have now the honour to prefer to you.

Condefcend, Sirs, to make my parents fenfible
of the injuftice of an exclufive tendernefs, and
of the neceffity of diftributing their care and affection among all their children equally.

　　　　I am, with a profound refpect,

　　　　　　SIRS,

　　　　Your obedient fervant,

　　　　　　　　THE LEFT HAND.

THE

THE

HANDSOME AND DEFORMED LEG.

THERE are two forts of people in the world, who, with equal degrees of health and wealth, and the other comforts of life, become, the one happy, and the other miferable. This arifes very much from the different views in which they confider things, perfons, and events; and the effect of thofe different views upon their own minds.

In whatever fituation men can be placed, they may find conveniencies and inconveniencies: in whatever company, they may find perfons and converfation more or lefs pleafing: at whatever table, they may meet with meats and drinks of better and worfe tafte, difhes better and worfe dreffed: in whatever climate, they will find good and bad weather: under whatever government, they may find good and bad laws, and good and bad adminiftration of thofe laws: in whatever poem, or work of genius, they may fee faults and beauties: in almoft every face, and every perfon they may difcover fine features and defects, good and bad qualities.

Under thefe circumftances, the two forts of people above mentioned fix their attention, thofe who are difpofed to be happy, on the conveniences of things, the pleafant parts of converfation, the well dreffed difhes, the goodnefs of the wines, the fine weather, &c. and enjoy all with chearfullnefs. Thofe who are to be unhappy, think and fpeak only of the contraries. Hence they are continually difcontented themfelves, and, by their remarks, four the pleafures of fociety; offend

perfonally

personally many people, and make themselves every where disagreeable. If this turn of mind was founded in nature, such unhappy persons would be the more to be pitied. But as the disposition to criticise, and to be disgusted, is, perhaps, taken up originally by imitation, and is, unawares, grown into a habit, which, though at present strong, may nevertheless be cured, when those who have it are convinced of its bad effects on their felicity; I hope this little admonition may be of service to them, and put them on changing a habit, which, though in the exercise it is chiefly an act of imagination, yet has serious consequences in life, as it, brings on real griefs and misfortunes. For as many are offended by, and nobody loves, this sort of people; no one shews them more than the most common civility and respect, and scarcely that; and this frequently puts them out of humour, and draws them into disputes and contentions. If they aim at obtaining some advantage in rank or fortune, nobody wishes them success, or will stir a step, or speak a word to favour their pretensions. If they incur public censure or disgrace, no one will defend or excuse, and many join to aggravate their misconduct, and render them completely odious. If these people will not change this bad habit, and condescend to be pleased with what is pleasing, without fretting themselves and others about the contraries, it is good for others to avoid an acquaintance with them; which is always disagreeable, and sometimes very inconvenient, especially when one finds oneself entangled in their quarrels.

An old philosophical friend of mine was grown, from experience, very cautious in this particular, and carefully avoided any intimacy with such people. He had, like other philosophers, a thermometer

mometer to fhew him the heat of the weather;
and a barometer, to mark when it was likely to
prove good or bad; but there being no inftrument invented to difcover, at firft fight, this unpleafing difpofition in a perfon, he, for that purpofe, made ufe of his legs; one of which was remarkably handfome, the other, by fome accident,
crooked and deformed. If a ftranger, at the firft
interview, regarded his ugly leg more than his
handfome one, he doubted him. If he fpoke of
it, and took no notice of the handfome leg, that
was fufficient to determine my philofopher to have
no further acquaintance with him. Every body
has not this two legged inftrument; but every
one, with a little attention, may obferve figns of
that carping, fault-finding difpofition, and take
the fame refolution of avoiding the acquaintance
of thofe infected with it. I therefore advife thofe
critical, querulous, difcontented, unhappy people, that if they wifh to be refpected and beloved
by others, and happy in themfelves, they fhould
leave off looking at the ugly leg.

CONVERSATION

OF A

COMPANY OF EPHEMERÆ;

WITH THE SOLILOQUY OF ONE ADVANCED IN AGE.

TO MADAME BRILLIANT.

YOU may remember, my dear friend, that when we lately fpent that happy day, in the delightful garden and fweet fociety of the *Moulin Joly*, I ftopt a little in one of our walks, and ftaid fome time behind the company. We had been fhewn numberlefs fkeletons of a kind of little fly, called an Ephemera, whofe fucceffive generations, we were told, were bred and expired within the day. I happened to fee a living company of them on a leaf, who appeared to be engaged in converfation. You know I underftand all the inferior animal tongues: my too great application to the ftudy of them, is the beft excufe I can give for the little progrefs I have made in your charming language. I liftened through curiofity to the difcourfe of thefe little creatures; but as they, in their national vivacity, fpoke three or four together, I could make but little of their converfation. I found, however, by fome expreffions that I heard now and then, they were difputing warmly on the merit of two foreign muficians, one a *coufin*, the

the other a *mufcheto*; in which difpute they fpent
their time, feemingly as regardlefs of the fhort-
nefs of life as if they had been fure of living a
month. Happy people! thought I, you live certainly under a wife, juft, and mild government,
fince you have no public grievances to complain
of, nor any fubject of contention, but the per-
fections or imperfections of foreign mufic. I
turned my head from them to an old grey-headed
one, who was fingle on another leaf, and talking
to himfelf. Being amufed with his foliloquy, I
put it down in writing, in hopes it will likewife
amufe her to whom I am fo much indebted for
the moft pleafing of all amufements, her delicious company, and heavenly harmony.

" It was," fays he, " the opinion of learned
" philofophers of our race, who lived and flou-
" rifhed long before my time, that this vaft
" world the *Moulin Joly* could not itfelf fubfift
" more than eighteen hours : and I think there
" was fome foundation for that opinion ; fince,
" by the apparent motion of the great luminary,
" that gives life to all nature, and which in my
" time has evidently declined towards the ocean
" at the end of our earth, it muft then finifh its
" courfe, be extinguifhed in the waters that fur-
" round us, and leave the world in cold and
" darknefs, neceffarily producing univerfal death
" and deftruction. I have lived feven of thofe
" hours ; a great age, being no lefs than 420 mi-
" nutes of time. How very few of us continue
" fo long ? I have feen generations born, flourifh,
" and expire. My prefent friends are the chil-
" dren and grand-children of the friends of my
" youth, who are now, alas, no more! And I
" muft foon follow them ; for, by the courfe of
" nature, though ftill in health, I cannot expect
" to live above feven or eight minutes longer.
" What

" What now avails all my toil and labour, in
" amaffing honey-dew on this leaf, which I can-
" not live to enjoy! What the political ftruggles
" I have been engaged in, for the good of my
" compatriot inhabitants of this bufh, or my phi-
" lofophical ftudies, for the benefit of our race
" in general! for in politics (what can laws do
" without morals?) our prefent race of ephemeræ
" will in a courfe of minutes become corrupt,
" like thofe of other and older bufhes, and con-
" fequently as wretched: And in philofophy how
" fmall our progrefs! Alas! art is long, and life
" is fhort! My friend would comfort me with
" the idea of a name, they fay, I fhall leave be-
" hind me; and they tell me I have lived long
" enough to nature and to glory. But what
" will fame be to an ephemera who no longer
" exifts? and what will become of all hiftory in
" the eighteenth hour, when the world itfelf,
" even the whole *Moulin Joly*, fhall come to its
" end, and be buried in univerfal ruin?"——

To me, after all my eager purfuits, no folid
pleafures now remain, but the reflection of a long
life fpent in meaning well, the fenfible converfation of a few good lady ephemeræ, and now and
then a kind fmile and a tune from the ever amiable Brilliant.

B. FRANKLIN.

MORALS of CHESS.

PLAYING at chefs is the moft ancient and moft univerfal game known among men; for its original is beyond the memory of hiftory, and it has, for numberlefs ages, been the amufement of all the civilized nations of Afia, the Perfians, the Indians, and the Chinefe. Europe has had it above a thoufand years; the Spaniards have fpread it over their part of America, and it begins lately to make its appearance in thefe States. It is fo interefting in itfelf, as not to need the view of gain to induce engaging in it; and thence it is never played for money. Thofe therefore, who have leifure for fuch diverfions, cannot find one that is more innocent; and the following piece, written with a view to correct (among a few young friends) fome little improprieties in the practice of it, fhews, at the fame time, that it may, in its effects on the mind, be not merely innocent, but advantageous, to the vanquifhed as well as the victor.

THE game of chefs is not merely an idle amufement. Several very valuable qualities of the mind, ufeful in the courfe of human life, are to be acquired or ftrengthened by it, fo as to become habits, ready on all occafions. For life is a kind of chefs, in which we have often points to gain, and competitors or adverfaries to contend with, and in which there is a vaft variety of good and ill events, that are, in fome degree, the effects of prudence or the want of it. By playing at chefs, then, we may learn,

I. *Forefight*, which looks a little into futurity, and confiders the confequences that may attend

N   an

an action : for it is continually occurring to the player, " If I move this piece, what will be the " advantage of my new fituation ? what ufe " can my adverfary make of it to annoy me ? " What other moves can I make to fupport it, " and to defend myfelf from his attacks ?"

II. *Circumfpection*, which furveys the whole chefs-board, or fcene of action, the relations of the feveral pieces and fituations, the dangers they are refpectively expofed to, the feveral poffibilities of their aiding each other, the probabilities that the adverfary may take this or that move, and attack this or the other piece, and what different means can be ufed to avoid his ftroke, or turn its confequences againft him.

III. *Caution*, not to make our moves too haftily. This habit is beft acquired by obferving ftrictly the laws of the game, fuch as, " If you touch " a piece, you muft move it fomewhere, if you " fet it down, you muft let it ftand :" and it is therefore beft that thefe rules fhould be obferved, as the game thereby becomes more the image of human life, and particularly of war ; in which, if you have incautioufly put yourfelf into a bad and dangerous pofition, you cannot obtain your enemy's leave to withdraw your troops, and place them more fecurely, but you muft abide all the confequences of your rafhnefs.

And, laftly, we learn by chefs the habit of *not being difcouraged by prefent bad appearances in the ftate of our affairs*, the habit *of hoping for a favourable change*, and that of *perfevering in the fearch of refources*. The game is fo full of events there is fuch a variety of turns in it, the fortune of it is fo fubject to fudden viciffitudes, and one fo frequently, after long contemplation, difcovers the means of extricating onefelf from a fuppofed infurmountable difficulty, that one is encouraged

to

to continue the conteft to the laft, in hopes of
victory by our own fkill, or at leaft of giving a
ftale mate, by the negligence of our adverfary.
And whoever confiders, what in chefs he often
fees inftances of, that particular pieces of fuccefs
are apt to produce prefumption, and its confe-
quent inattention, by which the lofs may be
recovered, will learn not to be too much difcouraged by the prefent fuccefs of his adverfary, nor
to defpair of final good fortune, upon every
check he receives in the purfuit of it.

That we may, therefore, be induced more
frequently to choofe this beneficial amufement,
in preference to others, which are not attended
with the fame advantages, every circumftance
which may increafe the pleafure of it fhould be
regarded; and every action or word that is
unfair, difrefpectful, or that in any way may give
uneafinefs, fhould be avoided, as contrary to the
immediate intention of both the players, which
is to pafs the time agreeably.

Therefore, firft, if it is agreed to play according
to the ftrict rules; then thofe rules are to be
exactly obferved by both parties, and fhould
not be infifted on for one fide, while deviated
from by the other—for this is not equitable.

Secondly, If it is agreed not to obferve the
rules exactly, but one party demands indulgen-
cies, he fhould then be as willing to allow them
to the other.

Thirdly, No falfe move fhould ever be made
to extricate yourfelf out of a difficulty, or to gain
an advantage. There can be no pleafure in playing with a perfon once detected in fuch unfair
practice.

Fourthly, If your adverfary is long in playing,
you ought not to hurry him, or exprefs any uneafinefs at his delay. You fhould not fing, nor

N 2 whiftle,

whiftle, nor look at your watch, nor take up a
book to read, nor make a tapping with your feet
on the floor, or with your fingers on the table,
nor do any thing that may difturb his attention.
For all thefe things difpleafe; and they do not
fhew your fkill in playing, but your craftinefs or
your rudenefs.

Fifthly, You ought not to endeavour to amufe
and deceive your adverfary, by pretending to
have made bad moves, and faying that you have
now loft the game, in order to make him fecure
and carelefs, and inattentive to your fchemes:
for this is fraud and deceit, not fkill in the game.

Sixthly, You muft not, when you have gained
a victory, ufe any triumphing or infulting expreffion, nor fhow too much pleafure; but endeavour to confole your adverfary, and make
him lefs diffatisfied with himfelf, by every kind
of civil expreffion that may be ufed with truth,
fuch as, " You underftand the game better than
" I, but you are a little inattentive;" or, " you
" play too faft;" or, " you had the beft of the
" game, but fomething happened to divert your
" thoughts, and that turned it in my favour."

Seventhly, If you are a fpectator while others
play, obferve the moft perfect filence. For if
you give advice, you offend both parties; him
againft whom you give it, becaufe it may caufe
the lofs of his game; him in whofe favour you
give it, becaufe, though it be good, and he follows it, he lofes the pleafure he might have had,
if you had permitted him to think until it had
occurred to himfelf. Even after a move, or
moves, you muft not, by replacing the pieces,
fhow how it might have been placed better: for
that difpleafes, and may occafion difputes and
doubts about their true fituation. All talking to
the players leffens or diverts their attention, and

is

is therefore unpleafing. Nor fhould you give the leaft hint to either party, by any kind of noife or motion. If you do, you are unworthy to be a fpectator. If you have a mind to exercife or fhew your judgment, do it in playing your own game, when you have an opportunity, not in criticifing, or meddling with, or counfelling the play of others.

Laftly, If the game is not to be played rigor-oufly, according to the rules above mentioned, then moderate your defire of victory over your adverfary, and be pleafed with one over your-felf. Snatch not eagerly at every advantage of-fered by his unfkilfulnefs or inattention; but point out to him kindly, that by fuch a move he places or leaves a piece in danger and unfup-ported; that by another he will put his king in a perilous fituation, &c. By this generous civi-lity (fo oppofite to the unfairnefs above forbid-den) you may, indeed, happen to lofe the game to your opponent, but you will win what is bet-ter, his efteem, his refpect, and his affection; together with the filent approbation and good-will of impartial fpectators.

THE

ART OF PROCURING PLEASANT DREAMS,

INSCRIBED TO MISS ***,

BEING WRITTEN AT HER REQUEST.

As a great part of our life is fpent in fleep, during which we have fometimes pleafing, and
fometimes painful dreams, it becomes of fome
confequence to obtain the one kind, and avoid
the other ; for, whether real or imaginary, pain
is pain, and pleafure is pleafure. If we can fleep
without dreaming, it is well that painful dreams
are avoided. If, while we fleep, we can have
any pleafing dreams, it is, as the French fay, *tant
gagné*, fo much added to the pleafure of life.

To this end it is, in the firft place, neceffary
to be careful in preferving health, by due exercife, and great temperance ; for, in ficknefs, the
imagination is difturbed ; and difagreeable, fometimes terrible, ideas are apt to prefent themfelves.
Exercife fhould precede meals, not immediately
follow them : the firft promotes, the latter, unlefs moderate, obftructs digeftion. If, after exercife, we feed fparingly, the digeftion will be
eafy and good, the body lightfome, the temper
cheerful, and all the animal functions performed
agreeably. Sleep, when it follows, will be natural and undifturbed. While indolence, with
full feeding, occafion night-mares and horrors in-
expreffible : we fall from precipices, are affaulted
by wild beafts, murderers, and demons, and experience

rience every variety of diftrefs. Obferve, however, that the quantities of food and exercife are relative things: thofe who move much may, and indeed ought, to eat more; thofe who ufe little exercife, fhould eat little. In general, mankind, fince the improvement of cookery, eat about twice as much as nature requires. Suppers are not bad, if we have not dined; but reftlefs nights naturally follow hearty fuppers, after full dinners. Indeed, as there is a difference in conftitutions, fome reft well after thefe meals; it cofts them only a frightful dream, and an apoplexy, after which they fleep till doomfday. Nothing is more common in the newfpapers, than inftances of people, who, after eating a hearty fupper, are found dead a-bed in the morning.

Another means of preferving health, to be attended to, is the having a conftant fupply of frefh air in your bed-chamber. It has been a great miftake, the fleeping in rooms exactly clofed, and in beds furrounded by curtains. No outward air, that may come in to you, is fo unwholfome as the unchanged air, often breathed, of a clofe chamber. As boiling water does not grow hotter by longer boiling, if the particles that receive greater heat can efcape; fo living bodies do not putrify, if the particles, as faft as they become putrid, can be thrown off. Nature expels them by the pores of the fkin and lungs, and in a free open air, they are carried off; but, in a clofe room, we receive them again, though they become more and more corrupt. A number of perfons crowded into a fmall room, thus fpoil the air in a few minutes, and even render it mortal, as in the Black Hole at Calcutta. A fingle perfon is faid to fpoil only a gallon of air per minute, and therefore requires a longer time to fpoil a chamberfull; but it is done, however, in proportion,

portion, and many putrid diforders hence have their origin. It is recorded of Methufalem, who, being the longeft liver, may be fuppofed to have beft preferved his health, that he flept always in the open air; for, when he had lived five hundred years, an angel faid to him: " Arife, Me-" thufalem; and build thee an houfe, for thou " fhalt live yet five hundred years longer." But Methufalem anfwered and faid: " If I am to live " but five hundred years longer, it is not worth " while to build me an houfe—I will fleep in the " air as I have been ufed to do." Phyficians, af-ter having for ages contended that the fick fhould not be indulged with frefh air, have at length difcovered that it may do them good. It is there-fore to be hoped that they may in time difcover likewife, that it is not hurtful to thofe who are in health; and that we may be then cured of the *acrophobia* that at prefent diftreffes weak minds, and make them choofe to be ftifled and poifoned, rather than leave open the window of a bed-cham-ber, or put down the glafs of a coach.

Confined air, when faturated with perfpirable matter *, will not receive more: and that matter muft remain in our bodies, and occafion difeafes: but it gives fome previous notice of its being about to be hurtful, by producing certain uneafi-neffes, flight indeed at firft, fuch as, with regard to the lungs, is a trifling fenfation, and to the pores of the fkin a kind of reftleffnefs which is difficult to defcribe, and few that feel it know the caufe of it. But we may recollect, that fome-times, on waking in the night, we have, if warmly covered, found it difficult to get afleep again. We

* What phyficians call the perfpirable matter is, that va-pour which paffes off from our bodies, from the lungs, and through the pores of the fkin. The quantity of this is faid to be five-eights of what we eat.

turn

turn often without finding repose in any position.
This fidgettiness, to use a vulgar expression for
want of a better, is occasioned wholly by an uneasiness in the skin, owing to the retension of the
perspirable matter—the bed-clothes having received their quantity, and, being saturated, refusing
to take any more. To become sensible of this by
an experiment, let a person keep his position in
the bed, but throw off the bed-clothes, and suffer
fresh air to approach the part uncovered of his
body; he will then feel that part suddenly refresh-
ed; for the air will immediately relieve the skin,
by receiving, licking up, and carrying off, the
load of perspirable matter that incommoded it.
For every portion of cool air that approaches the
warm skin, in receiving its part of that vapour,
receives therewith a degree of heat, that rarifies
and renders it higher, when it will be pushed
away, with its burthen, by cooler, and therefore
heavier fresh air; which, for a moment, supplies
its place, and then, being likewise changed, and
warmed, gives way to a succeeding quantity.
This is the order of nature, to prevent animals
being infected by their own perspiration. He
will now be sensible of the difference between the
part exposed to the air, and that which, remaining sunk in the bed, denies the air access: for
this part now manifests its uneasiness more dif-
tinctly by the comparison, and the seat of the uneasiness is more plainly perceived, than when the
whole surface of the body was affected by it.

Here, then, is one great and general cause of
unpleasing dreams. For when the body is uneafy, the mind will be disturbed by it, and disagreeable ideas of various kinds will, in sleep, be the
natural consequences. The remedies, preventa-
tive, and curative, follow:

1, By

1. By eating moderately (as before advifed for health's fake) lefs perfpirable matter is produced in a given time; hence the bed-clothes receive it longer before they are faturated; and we may, therefore, fleep longer, before we are made uneafy by their refufing to receive any more.

2. By ufing thinner and more porous bed-clothes, which will fuffer the perfpirable matter more eafily to pafs through them, we are lefs incommoded, fuch being longer tolerable.

3. When you are awakened by this uneafinefs, and find you cannot eafily fleep again, get out of bed, beat up and turn your pillow, fhake the bed-clothes well, with at leaft twenty fhakes, then throw the bed open, and leave it to cool; in the meanwhile, continuing undreft, walk about your chamber, till your fkin has had time to difcharge its load, which it will do fooner as the air may be drier and colder. When you begin to feel the cold air unpleafant, then return to your bed; and you will foon fall afleep, and your fleep will be fweet and pleafant. All the fcenes prefented to your fancy, will be of the pleafing kind. I am often as agreeably entertained with them, as by the fcenery of an opera. If you happen to be too indolent to get out of bed, you may, inftead of it, lift up your bed-clothes with one arm and leg, fo as to draw in a good deal of frefh air, and, by letting them fall, force it out again. This, repeated twenty times, will fo clear them of the perfpirable matter they have imbibed, as to permit your fleeping well for fome time afterwards. But this latter method is not equal to the former.

Thofe who do not love trouble, and can afford to have two beds, will find great luxury in rifing, when they wake in a hot bed, and going into the cool one. Such fhifting of beds would alfo be of great fervice to perfons ill of a fever, as it

refrefhes

refreshes and frequently procures sleep. A very large bed, that will admit a removal so distant from the first situation as to be cool and sweet, may in a degree answer the same end.

One or two observations more will conclude this little piece. Care must be taken, when you lie down, to dispose your pillow so as to suit your manner of placing your head, and to be perfectly easy; then place your limbs so as not to bear inconveniently hard upon one another, as, for instance. the joints of your ancles: for though a bad position may at first give but little pain, and be hardly noticed, yet a continuance will render it less tolerable, and the uneasiness may come on while you are asleep, and disturb your imagination.

These are the rules of the art. But though they will generally prove effectual in producing the end intended, there is a case in which the most punctual observance of them will be totally fruitless. I need not mention the case to you, my dear friend: but my account of the art would be imperfect without it. The case is, when the person who desires to have pleasant dreams has not taken care to preserve, what is necessary above all things,

A GOOD CONSCIENCE.

ADVICE TO A YOUNG TRADESMAN.

WRITTEN ANNO 1748.

TO MY FRIEND A. B.

As you have defired it of me, I write the following hints, which have been of fervice to me, and may, if obferved, be fo to you.

REMEMBER that *time* is money. He that can earn ten fhillings a day by his labour, and goes abroad, or fits idle one half of that day, though he fpends but fixpence during his diverfion or idlenefs, ought not to reckon *that* the only expence; he has really fpent, or rather thrown away, five fhillings befides.

Remember that *credit* is money. If a man lets his money lie in my hands after it is due, he gives me the intereft, or fo much as I can make of it during that time. This amounts to a confiderable fum where a man has good and large credit, and makes good ufe of it.

Remember that money is of a prolific generating nature. Money can beget money, and its offspring can beget more, and fo on. Five fhillings turned is fix; turned again, it is feven and three-pence; and fo on till it becomes an hundred pounds. The more there is of it, the more it produces every turning, fo that the profits rife quicker and quicker. He that kills a breeding fow, deftroys all her offspring to the thoufandth generation. He that murders a crown, deftroys all that it might have produced, even fcores of pounds.

Remember

Remember that fix pounds a year is but a groat a day. For this little fum (which may be daily wafted either in time or expence, unperceived), a man of credit may, on his own fecurity, have the conftant poffeffion and ufe of an hundred pounds. So much in ftock, brifkly turned by an induftrious man, produces great advantage.

Remember this faying, "The good paymafter is lord of another man's purfe." He that is known to pay punctually and exactly to the time he promifes, may at any time, and on any occafion, raife all the money his friends can fpare. This is fometimes of great ufe. After induftry and frugality, nothing contributes more to the raifing of a young man in the world, than punctuality and juftice in all his dealings : therefore never keep borrowed money an hour beyond the time you promifed, left a difappointment fhut up your friend's purfe for ever.

The moft trifling actions that affect a man's credit are to be regarded. The found of your hammer at five in the morning, or nine at night, heard by a creditor, makes him eafy fix months longer : but if he fees you at a billiard table, or hears your voice at a tavern, when you fhould be at work, he fends for his money the next day; demands it before he can receive it in a lump.

It fhews, befides, that you are mindful of what you owe; it makes you appear a careful, as well as an honeft man, and that ftill increafes your credit.

Beware of thinking all your own that you poffefs, and of living accordingly. It is a miftake that many people who have credit fall into. To prevent this, keep an exact account, for fome time, both of your expences and your income.

come. If you take the pains at firſt to mention particulars, it will have this good effect; you will diſcover how wonderfully ſmall trifling expences mount up to large ſums, and will diſcern what might have been, and may for the future be ſaved, without occaſioning any great inconvenience.

In ſhort, the way to wealth, if you deſire it, is as plain as the way to market. It depends chiefly on two words, *induſtry* and *frugality*; that is, waſte neither *time* nor *money*, but make the beſt uſe of both. Without induſtry and frugality nothing will do, and with them every thing. He that gets all he can honeſtly, and ſaves all he gets (neceſſary expences excepted), will certainly become *rich*—if that Being who governs the world, to whom all ſhould look for a bleſſing on their honeſt endeavours, doth not, in his wiſe providence, otherwiſe determine.

AN OLD TRADESMAN.

NECESSARY HINTS TO THOSE THAT WOULD
BE RICH.

WRITTEN ANNO 1736.

THE ufe of money is all the advantage there is in having money.

For fix pounds a year you may have the ufe of one hundred pounds, provided you are a man of known prudence and honefty.

He that fpends a groat a day idly, fpends idly above fix pounds a year, which is the price for the ufe of one hundred pounds.

He that waftes idly a groat's worth of his time per day, one day with another, waftes the privilege of ufing one hundred pounds each day.

He that idly lofes five fhillings worth of time, lofes five fhillings, and might as prudently throw five fhillings into the fea.

He that lofes five fhillings, not only lofes that fum, but all the advantage that might be made by turning it in dealing, which, by the time that a young man becomes old, will amount to a confiderable fum of money.

Again : he that fells upon credit, afks a price for what he fells equivalent to the principal and intereft of his money for the time he is to be kept out of it; therefore, he that buys upon credit, pays intereft for what he buys; and he that pays ready money, might let that money out to ufe : fo that he that poffeffes any thing he has bought, pays intereft for the ufe of it.

Yet,

Yet, in buying goods, it is beſt to pay ready money, becauſe, he that ſells upon credit, expects to loſe five per cent. by bad debts ; therefore he charges, on all he ſells upon credit, an advance that ſhall make up that deficiency.

Thoſe who pay for what they buy upon credit, pay their ſhare of this advance.

He that pays ready money, eſcapes, or may eſcape, that charge.

> A penny ſav'd is two-pence clear ;
> A pin a day 's a groat a year.

THE WAY TO MAKE MONEY PLENTY IN
EVERY MAN'S POCKET.

At this time, when the general complaint is that—" money is fcarce," it will be an act of kindnefs to inform the moneylefs how they may reinforce their pockets. I will acquaint them with the true fecret of money-catching—the certain way to fill empty purfes—and how to keep them always full. Two fimple rules, well obferved, will do the bufinefs.

Firft, let honefty and induftry be thy conftant companions; and,

Secondly, fpend one penny lefs than thy clear gains.

Then fhall thy hide-bound pocket foon begin to thrive, and will never again cry with the empty belly-ach: neither will creditors infult thee, nor want opprefs, nor hunger bite, nor nakednefs freeze thee. The whole hemifphere will fhine brighter, and pleafure fpring up in every corner of thy heart. Now, therefore, embrace thefe rules and be happy. Banifh the bleak winds of forrow from thy mind, and live independent. Then fhalt thou be a man, and not hide thy face at the approach of the rich, nor fuffer the pain of feeling little when the fons of fortune walk at thy right hand: for independency, whether with little or much, is good fortune, and placeth thee on even ground with the proudeft of the golden fleece. Oh, then, be wife, and let induftry walk with thee in the morning, and attend thee until thou reacheft the evening hour for reft. Let honefty be as the breath of thy foul, and ne-

O ver

ver forget to have a penny, when all thy expences are enumerated and paid: then fhalt thou
reach the point of happinefs, and independence
fhall be thy fhield and buckler, thy helmet and
crown; then fhall thy foul walk upright, nor
ftoop to the filken wretch becaufe he hath riches,
nor pocket an abufe becaufe the hand which offers
it wears a ring fet with diamonds.

AN ŒCONOMICAL PROJECT.

[*A Tranflation of this letter appeared in one of the Daily Papers of Paris about the Year 1784. The following is the Original Piece, with fome Additions and Corrections made in it by the Author.*]

TO THE AUTHORS OF THE JOURNAL.

MESSIEURS,

YOU often entertain us with accounts of new difcoveries. Permit me to communicate to the public, through your paper, one that has lately been made by myfelf, and which I conceive may be of great utility.

I was the other evening in a grand company, where the new lamp of Meffrs. Quinquet and Lange was introduced, and much admired for its fplendor; but a general enquiry was made, whether the oil it confumed was not in proportion to the light it afforded, in which cafe there would be no faving in the ufe of it. No one prefent could fatisfy us in that point, which all agreed ought to be known, it being a very defirable thing to leffen, if poffible, the expence of lighting our apartments, when every other article of family expence was fo much augmented.

I was pleafed to fee this general concern for œconomy; for I love œconomy exceedingly.

I went home, and to bed, three or four hours after midnight, with my head full of the fubject. An accidental fudden noife waked me about fix in the morning, when I was furprized to find my room filled with light; and I imagined at firft, that a number of thofe lamps had been brought into it: but, rubbing my eyes, I perceived the light came in at the windows. I got up and look-ed out to fee what might be the occafion of it, when I faw the fun juft rifing above the horizon, from whence he poured his rays plentifully into my chamber, my domeftic having negligently omitted the preceding evening to clofe the fhut-ters.

I looked at my watch, which goes very well, and found that it was but fix o'clock; and ftill thinking it fomething extraordinary that the fun fhould rife fo early, I looked into the almanack, where I found it to be the hour given for his ri-fing on that day. I looked forward too, and found he was to rife ftill earlier every day till to-wards the end of June; and that at no time in the year he retarded his rifing fo long as till eight o'clock. Your readers, who with me have never feen any figns of funfhine before noon, and fel-dom regard the aftronomical part of the almanack, will be as much aftonifhed as I was, when they hear of his rifing fo early; and efpecially when I affure them, *that he gives light as foon as he rifes.* I am convinced of this. I am certain of my fact. One cannot be more certain of any fact. I faw it with my own eyes. And having repeated this obfervation the three following mornings, I found always precifely the fame refult.

Yet fo it happens, that when I fpeak of this difcovery to others, I can eafily perceive by their countenances, though they forbear expreffing it in words, that they do not quite believe me. One, indeed, who is a learned natural philofopher, has affured me, that I muft certainly be miftaken as to the circumftance of the light coming into my room; for it being well known, as he fays, that there

there could be no light abroad at that hour, it follows that none could enter from without; and that of confequence, my windows being accidentally left open, inftead of letting in the light, had only ferved to let out the darknefs: and he ufed many ingenious arguments to fhew me how I might, by that means, have been deceived. I own that he puzzled me a little, but he did not fatisfy me; and the fubfequent obfervations I made, as above mentioned, confirmed me in my firft opinion.

This event has given rife, in my mind, to feveral ferious and important reflections. I confidered that, if I had not been awakened fo early in the morning, I fhould have flept fix hours longer by the light of the fun, and in exchange have lived fix hours the following night by candlelight; and the latter being a much more expenfive light than the former, my love of œconomy induced me to mufter up what little arithmetic I was mafter of, and to make fome calculations, which I fhall give you, after obferving, that utility is, in my opinion, the teft of value in matters of invention, and that a difcovery which can be applied to no ufe, or is not good for fomething, is good for nothing.

I took for the bafis of my calculation the fuppofition that there are 100,000 families in Paris, and that thefe families confume in the night half a pound of bougies, or candles, per hour. I think this is a moderate allowance, taking one family with another; for though I believe fome confume lefs, I know that many confume a great deal more. Then eftimating feven hours per day, as the medium quantity between the time of the fun's rifing and ours, he rifing during the fix following months from fix to eight hours before noon, and there being feven hours of courfe per

night

night in which we burn candles, the account will stand thus—

In the fix months between the twentieth of March and the twentieth of September, there are

Nights - - - -	183
Hours of each night in which we burn candles - - -	7

Multiplication gives for the total number of hours - - -	1,281
Thefe 1,281 hours multiplied by 100,000, the number of inhabitants, give - - - -	128,100,000
One hundred twenty-eight millions and one hundred thoufand hours, fpent at Paris by candlelight, which, at half a pound of wax and tallow per hour, gives the weight of - - -	64,050,000
Sixty-four millions and fifty thoufand of pounds, which, eftimating the whole at the medium price of thirty fols the pound, makes the fum of ninety-fix millions and feventy-five thoufand livres tournois - - -	96,075,000

An immenfe fum! that the city of Paris might fave every year, by the œconomy of ufing funfhine inftead of candles.

If it fhould be faid, that people are apt to be obftinately attached to old cuftoms, and that it will be difficult to induce them to rife before noon, confequently my difcovery can be of little ufe; I anfwer, *Nil defperandum.* I believe all who have common fenfe, as foon as they have learnt from this paper that it is day-light when the fun rifes, will contrive to rife with him; and,

to

to compel the reft, I would propofe the following regulations.

Firft. Let a tax be laid of a louis per window, on every window that is provided with fhutters to keep out the light of the fun.

Second. Let the fame falutary operation of police be made ufe of to prevent our burning candles, that inclined us laft winter to be more œconomical in burning wood; that is, let guards be placed in the fhops of the wax and tallow-chandlers, and no family be permitted to be fupplied with more than one pound of candles per week.

Third. Let guards alfo be pofted to ftop all the coaches, &c. that would pafs the ftreets after funfet, except thofe of phyficians, furgeons, and midwives.

Fourth. Every morning, as foon as the fun rifes, let all the bells in every church be fet ringing: and if that is not fufficient, let cannon be fired in every ftreet, to wake the fluggards effectually, and make them open their eyes to fee their true intereft.

All the difficulty will be in the firft two or three days; after which the reformation will be as natural and eafy as the prefent irregularity: for, *ce n'eft que le premier pas qui coute.* Oblige a man to rife at four in the morning, and it is more than probable he fhall go willingly to bed at eight in the evening; and, having had eight hours fleep, he will rife more willingly at four the morning following. But this fum of ninety-fix millions and feventy-five thoufand livres is not the whole of what may be faved by my œconomical project. You may obferve, that I have calculated upon only one half of the year, and much may be faved in the other, though the days are fhorter. Befides, the immenfe ftock of wax and tallow left unconfumed during the fummer, will probably

bly make candles much cheaper for the enfuing winter, and continue cheaper as long as the propofed reformation fhall be fupported.

For the great benefit of this difcovery, thus freely communicated and beftowed by me on the public, I demand neither place, penfion, exclufive privilege, or any other reward whatever. I expect only to have the honour of it. And yet I know there are little envious minds who will, as ufual, deny me this, and fay that my invention was known to the ancients, and perhaps they may bring paffages out of the old books in proof of it. I will not difpute with thefe people that the ancients knew not the fun would rife at certain hours; they poffibly had, as we have, almanacks that predicted it: but it does not follow from thence that they knew *he gave light as foon as he rofe.* This is what I claim as my difcovery. If the ancient knew it, it muft have been long fince forgotten, for it certainly was unknown to the moderns, at leaft to the Parifians; which to prove, I need ufe but one plain fimple argument. They are as well inftructed, judicious, and prudent a people as exift any where in the world, all profeffing, like myfelf, to be lovers of œconomy; and, from the many heavy taxes required from them by the neceffities of the ftate, have furely reafon to be œconomical. I fay it is impoffible that fo fenfible a people, under fuch circumftances, fhould have lived fo long by the fmoky, unwholfome, and enormoufly expenfive light of candles, if they had really known that they might have had as much pure light of the fun for nothing.

I am, &c.

A s ABONNE.

ON

ON MODERN INNOVATIONS IN THE ENGLISH LANGUAGE AND IN PRINTING.

TO NOAH WEBSTER, JUN. ESQ. AT HARTFORD.

Philadelphia, Dec. 26, 1789.

DEAR SIR,

I RECEIVED, fome time fince, your *Differtations on the Englifh Language.* It is an excellent work, and will be greatly ufeful in turning the thoughts of our countrymen to correct writing. Pleafe to accept my thanks for it, as well as for the great honour you have done me in its dedication. I ought to have made this acknowledgement fooner, but much indifpofition prevented me.

I cannot but applaud your zeal for preferving the purity of our language both in its expreffion and pronunciation, and in correcting the popular errors feveral of our ftates are continually falling into with refpect to both. Give me leave to mention fome of them, though poffibly they may already have occurred to you. I wifh, however, that in fome future publication of yours, you would fet a difcountenancing mark upon them. The firft I remember, is the word *improved.* When I left New-England in the year 1723, this word had never been ufed among us, as far as I know, but in the fenfe of *ameliorated,* or *made better,* except once in a very old book of Dr. Mather's, entitled *Remarkable Providences.* As that man wrote a very obfcure hand, I remember that when I read that word in his book, ufed inftead of the word *employed,* I conjectured that it was an error

of

of the printer, who had miftaken a fhort *l* in the writing for an *r*, and a *y* with too fhort a tail for a *v*, whereby *employed* was converted into *improved:* but when I returned to Bofton in 1733, I found this change had obtained favour, and was then become common; for I met with it often in perufing the newfpapers, where it frequently made an appearance rather ridiculous. Such, for inftance, as the advertifement of a country houfe to be fold, which had been many years *improved* as a tavern; and in the character of a deceafed country gentleman, that he had been, for more than thirty years, *improved* as a juftice of the peace. This ufe of the word *improve* is peculiar to New-England, and not to be met with among any other fpeakers of Englifh, either on this or the other fide of the water.

During my late abfence in France, I find that feveral other new words have been introduced into our parliamentary language. For example, I find a verb formed from the fubftantive *notice. I fhould not have* noticed *this, were it not that the gentleman,* &c. Alfo another verb, from the fubftantive *advocate; The gentleman who* advocates, *or who has* advocated *that motion,* &c. Another from the fubftantive *progrefs*, the moft aukward and abominable of the three: *The committee having* progreffed, *refolved to adjourn.* The word *oppofed*, though not a new word, I find ufed in a new manner, as, *The gentlemen who are* oppofed *to this meafure, to which I have alfo myfelf always been* oppofed. If you fhould happen to be of my opinion with refpect to thefe innovations, you will ufe your authority in reprobating them.

The Latin language, long the vehicle ufed in diftributing knowledge among the different nations of Europe, is daily more and more neglected; and one of the modern tongues, viz. French,

feems,

feems, in point of univerfality, to have fupplied its place. It is fpoken in all the courts of Europe; and moft of the literati, thofe even who do not fpeak it, have acquired knowledge of it, to enable them eafily to read the books that are written in it. This gives a confiderable advantage to that nation. It enables its authors to inculcate and fpread through other nations, fuch fentiments and opinions, on important points, as are moft conducive to its interefts, or which may contribute to its reputation, by promoting the common interefts of mankind. It is, perhaps, owing to its being written in French, that Voltaire's Treatife on Toleration has had fo fudden and fo great an effect on the bigotry of Europe, as almoft entirely to difarm it. The general ufe of the French language has likewife a very advantageous effect on the profits of the bookfelling branch of commerce, it being well known, that the more copies can be fold that are ftruck off from one compofition of types, the profits increafe in a much greater proportion than they do in making a greater number of pieces in any other kind of manufacture. And at prefent there is no capital town in Europe without a French bookfeller's fhop correfponding with Paris. Our Englifh bids fair to obtain the fecond place. The great body of excellent printed fermons in our language, and the freedom of our writings on political fubjects, have induced a great number of divines of different fects and nations, as well as gentlemen concerned in public affairs, to ftudy it, fo far at leaft as to read it. And if we were to endeavour the facilitating its progrefs, the ftudy of our tongue might become much more general. Thofe who have employed fome part of their time in learning a new language, muft have frequently obferved, that while their ac-

quaintance

quaintance with it was imperfect, difficulties, fmall in themfelves, operated as great ones in ob-ftructing their progrefs. A book, for example, ill printed, or a pronunciation in fpeaking not well articulated, would render a fentence unin-telligible, which from a clear print, or a diftinct fpeaker, would have been immediately compre-hended. If, therefore, we would have the be-nefit of feeing our language more generally known among mankind, we fhould endeavour to remove all the difficulties, however fmall, that difcou-rage the learning of it. But I am forry to ob-ferve that, of late years, thofe difficulties, inftead of being diminifhed, have been augmented.

In examining the Englifh books that were print-ed between the reftoration and the acceffion of George the Second, we may obferve, that all fub-ftantives were begun with a capital, in which we imitated our mother tongue, the German. This was more particularly ufeful to thofe who were not well acquainted with the Englifh, there be-ing fuch a prodigious number of our words that are both verbs and fubftantives, and fpelt in the fame manner, though often accented differently in pronunciation. This method has, by the fan-cy of printers, of late years been entirely laid afide; from an idea, that fuppreffing the capi-tals fhews the character to greater advantage; thofe letters, prominent above the line, difturb-ing its even, regular appearance. The effect of this change is fo confiderable, that a learned man of France, who ufed to read our books, though not perfectly acquainted with our language, in converfation with me on the fubject of our au-thors, attributed the greater obfcurity he found in our modern books, compared with thofe of the period above mentioned, to a change of ftyle for the worfe in our writers; of which

mistake

miftake I convinced him, by marking for him each fubftantive with a capital, in a paragraph, which he then eafily underftood, though before he could not comprehend it. This fhews the inconvenience of that pretended improvement.

From the fame fondnefs for an uniform and even appearance of characters in the line, the printers have of late banifhed alfo the Italic types, in which words of importance to be attended to in the fenfe of the fentence, and words on which an emphafis fhould be put in reading, ufed to be printed. And lately another fancy has induced other printers to ufe the round *s* inftead of the long one, which formerly ferved well to diftinguifh a word readily by its varied appearance. Certainly the omitting this prominent letter makes a line appear more even, but renders it lefs immediately legible; as the paring of all men's nofes might fmooth and level their faces, would render their phyfiognomies lefs diftinguifhable. Add to all thefe improvements backwards, another modern fancy, that *grey* printing is more beautiful than black. Hence the Englifh new books are printed in fo dim a character as to be read with difficulty by old eyes, unlefs in a very ftrong light and with good glaffes. Whoever compares a volume of the Gentleman's Magazine, printed between the years 1731 and 1740, with one of thofe printed in the laft ten years, will be convinced of the much greater degree of perfpicuity given by black than by the grey. Lord Chefterfield pleafantly remarked this difference to Faulkner, the printer of the Dublin Journal, who was vainly making encomiums on his own paper, as the moft complete of any in the world. " But " Mr. Faulkner," fays my lord, " don't you think " it might be ftill farther improved, by ufing paper " and ink not quite fo near of a colour ?"—For all
thefe

thefe reafons I cannot but wifh that our American printers would, in their editions, avoid thefe fancied improvements, and thereby render their works more agreeable to foreigners in Europe, to the great advantage of our bookfelling commerce.

Farther, to be more fenfible of the advantage of clear and diftinct printing, let us confider the affiftance it affords in reading well aloud to an auditory. In fo doing the eye generally flides forward three or four words before the voice. If the fight clearly diftinguifhes what the coming words are, it gives time to order the modulation of the voice to exprefs them properly. But if they are obfcurely printed, or difguifed by omitting the capitals and long ſ's, or otherwife, the reader is apt to modulate wrong; and finding he has done fo, he is obliged to go back and begin the fentence again; which leffens the pleafure of the hearers. This leads me to mention an old error in our mode of printing. We are fenfible that when a queftion is met with in the reading, there is a proper variation to be ufed in the management of the voice. We have, therefore, a point, called an interrogation, affixed to the queftion, in order to diftinguifh it. But this is abfurdly placed at its end, fo that the reader does not difcover it till he finds that he has wrongly modulated his voice, and is therefore obliged to begin again the fentence. To prevent this, the Spanifh printers, more fenfibly, place an interrogation at the beginning as well as at the end of the queftion. We have another error of the fame kind in printing plays, where fomething often occurs that is marked as fpoken *afide*. But the word *afide* is placed at the end of the fpeech, when it ought to precede it, as a direction to the reader, that he may govern his voice accordingly. The practice of our ladies in meeting five or fix together,

ther, to form little bufy parties. where each is
employed in fome ufeful work, while one reads
to them, is fo commendable in itfelf, that it de-
ferves the attention of authors and printers to
make it as pleafing as poffible, both to the reader
and hearers.

My beft wifhes attend you, being with fincere
efteem,

Sir,

Your moft obedient and

very humble fervant,

B. FRANKLIN.

AN ACCOUNT OF THE HIGHEST COURT OF JUDI-
CATURE IN PENNSYLVANIA, VIZ.

THE COURT OF THE PRESS.

POWER OF THIS COURT.

IT may receive and promulgate accufations of
all kinds, againft all perfons and characters among
the citizens of the ftate, and even againft all
inferior courts; and may judge, fentence, and
condemn to infamy, not only private individuals,
but public bodies, &c. with or without enquiry
or hearing, at the court's difcretion.

*In whofe favour, or for whofe emolument this court
is eftablifhed.*

In favour of about one citizen in five hundred
who by education, or practice in fcribbling,
has acquired a tolerable ftyle as to grammar and
conftruction, fo as to bear printing; or who is
poffeffed of a prefs and a few types. This five
hundredth part of the citizens have the privilege
of accufing and abufing the other four hundred
and ninety-nine parts, at their pleafure; or they
may hire out their pen and prefs to others, for
that purpofe.

Practice of this court.

It is not governed by any of the rules of the
common courts of law. The accufed is allowed
no grand jury to judge of the truth of the accu-
fation before it is publicly made; nor is the name
of the accufer made known to him; nor has he

an

an opportunity of confronting the witneffes againft him, for they are kept in the dark, as in the Spanifh court of inquifition. Nor is there any petty jury of his peers fworn to try the truth of the charges. The proceedings are alfo fometimes fo rapid, that an honeft good citizen may find himfelf fuddenly and unexpectedly accufed, and in the fame morning judged and condemned, and fentence pronounced againft him that he is a rogue and a villain. Yet if an officer of this court receives the flighteft check for mifconduct in this his office, he claims immediately the rights of a free citizen by the conftitution, and demands to know his accufer, to confront the witneffes, and to have a fair trial by a jury of his peers.

The foundation of its authority.

It is faid to be founded on an article in the ftate conftitution, which eftablifhed the liberty of the prefs———a liberty which every Pennfylvanian would fight and die for, though few of us, I believe, have diftinct ideas of its nature and extent. It feems, indeed, fomewhat like the liberty of the prefs, that felons have, by the common law of England before conviction; that is, to be either preffed to death or hanged. If, by the liberty of the prefs, were underftood merely the liberty of difcuffing the propriety of public meafures and political opinions, let us have as much of it as you pleafe; but if it means the liberty of affronting, calumniating, and defaming one another, I, for my part, own myfelf willing to part with my fhare of it, whenever our legiflators fhall pleafe fo to alter the law; and fhall cheerfully confent to exchange my liberty of abufing others, for the privilege of not being abufed myfelf.

P   By

By whom this court is commissioned or constituted.

It is not by any commission from the supreme executive council, who might previously judge of the abilities, integrity, knowledge, &c. of the person to be appointed to this great trust, of deciding upon the characters and good fame of the citizens: for this court is above that council, and may accuse, judge, and condemn it at pleasure. Nor is it hereditary, as is the court of dernier resort in the peerage of England. But any man who can procure pen, ink, and paper, with a press, a few types, and a huge pair of blacking balls, may commissionate himself, and his court is immediately established in the plenary possession and exercise of its rights. For if you make the least complaint of the judge's conduct, he daubs his blacking balls in your face wherever he meets you: and besides tearing your private character to splinters, marks you out for the odium of the public, as an enemy to the liberty of the press.

Of the natural support of this court.

Its support is founded in the depravity of such minds as have not been mended by religion, nor improved by good education.

> There is a lust in man no charm can tame,
> Of loudly publishing his neighbour's shame:

Hence,

> On eagles' wings, immortal scandals fly,
> While virtuous actions are but born and die.
> DRYDEN.

Whoever feels pain in hearing a good character of his neighbour, will feel a pleasure in the reverse. And of those who, despairing to rise
to

to diftinction by their virtues, are happy if others can be depreffed to a level with themfelves, there are a number fufficient in every great town to maintain one of thefe courts by their fubfcription. A fhrewd obferver once faid, that in walking the ftreets of a flippery morning, one might fee where the good-natured people lived, by the afhes thrown on the ice before the doors : probably he would have formed a different conjecture of the temper of thofe whom he might find engaged in fuch fubfcriptions.

Of the checks proper to be eftablifhed againft the abufes of power in thofe courts.

Hitherto there are none. But fince fo much has been written and publifhed on the federal conftitution ; and the neceffity of checks, in all other parts of good government, has been fo clearly and learnedly explained, I find myfelf fo far enlightened as to fufpect fome check may be proper in this part alfo : but I have been at a lofs to imagine any that may not be conftrued an infringement of the facred liberty of the prefs. At length, however, I think I have found one, that, inftead of diminifhing general liberty, fhall augment it ; which is, by reftoring to the people a fpecies of liberty of which they have been deprived by our laws, I mean the liberty of the cudgel ! In the rude ftate of fociety prior to the exiftence of laws, if one man gave another ill-language, the affronted perfon might return it by a box on the ear ; and if repeated, by a good drubbing ; and this without offending againft any law : but now the right of making fuch returns is denied, and they are punifhed as breaches of the peace, while the right of abufing feems to remain in full force ; the laws made againft it being rendered ineffectual by the liberty of the prefs.

My

My propofal then is, to leave the liberty of the prefs untouched, to be exercifed in its full extent, force, and vigour, but to permit the liberty of the cudgel to go with it, *pari paſſu*. Thus, my fellow citizens, if an impudent writer attacks your reputation—dearer perhaps to you than your life, and puts his name to the charge you may go to him as openly, and break his head. If he conceals himfelf behind the printer, and you can neverthelefs difcover who he is, you may, in like manner way-lay him in the night, attack him behind, and give him a good drubbing. If your adverfary hires better writers than himfelf, to abufe you more effec-tually, you may hire brawney porters, ftronger than yourfelf, to affift you in giving him a more effeétual drubbing. Thus far goes my projeét, as to *private* refentment and retribution. But if the public fhould ever happen to be affronted, as it ought to be, with the conduét of fuch writers, I would not advife proceeding immediately to thefe extremities, but that we fhould in moderation content ourfelves with tarring and feathering, and tofling them in a blanket.

If, however, it fhould be thought that this propofal of mine may difturb the public peace, I fhould then humbly recommend to our legiflators to take up the confideration of both liberties, that of the prefs, and that of the cudgel ; and by an explicit law mark their extent and limits : and at the fame time that they fecure the perfon of a citizen from affaults, they would likewife provide for the fecurity of his reputation.

PAPER

PAPER: A POEM.

Some wit of old—such wits of old there were—
Whose hints show'd meaning, whose allusions care,
By one brave stroke to mark all human-kind,
Call'd clear blank paper ev'ry infant mind;
When still, as opening sense her dictates wrote,
Fair virtue put a seal, or vice a blot.

The thought was happy, pertinent, and true;
Methinks a genius might the plan pursue.
I (can you pardon my presumption), I—
No wit, no genius, yet for once will try.

Various the papers various wants produce,
The wants of fashion, elegance, and use,
Men are as various: and, if right I scan,
Each sort of *paper* represents some *man*.

Pray note the fop—half powder and half lace—
Nice, as a bandbox were his dwelling-place:
He's the *gilt-paper*, which apart you store,
And lock from vulgar hands in the 'scrutoire.

Mechanics, servants, farmers, and so forth,
Are *copy-paper*, of inferior worth;
Less priz'd, more useful, for your desk decreed,
Free to all pens, and prompt at ev'ry need.

The wretch whom av'rice bids to pinch and spare,
Starve, cheat, and pilfer, to enrich an heir,
Is coarse *brown paper*; such as pedlars choose
To wrap up wares, which better men will use.

Take next the miser's contrast, who destroys
Health, fame, and fortune, in a round of joys.
Will any paper match him? Yes, throughout,
He's a true *sinking-paper*, past all doubt.

The

The retail politician's anxious thought
Deems *this* fide always right, and *that* ftark nought;
He foams with cenfure; with applaufe he raves—.
A dupe to rumours, and a tool of knaves;
He'll want no type his weaknefs to proclaim,
While fuch a thing as *fools-cap* has a name.

The hafty gentleman, whofe blood runs high,
Who picks a quarrel, if you ftep awry,
Who can't a jeft, or hint, or look endure:
What's he? What? *Touch-paper* to be fure.

What are our poets, take them as they fall,
Good, bad, rich, poor, much read, not read at all?
Them and their works in the fame clafs you'll find;
They are the mere *wafte-paper* of mankind.

Obferve the maiden, innocently fweet,
She's fair *white-paper*, an unfullied fheet;
On which the happy man whom fate ordains,
May write his *name*, and take her for his pains.

One inftance more, and only one I'll bring;
Tis the *great man* who fcorns a little thing,
Whofe thoughts, whofe deeds, whofe maxims are his own,
Form'd on the feelings of his heart alone:
True genuine *royal-paper* is his breaft;
Of all the kinds moft precious, pureft, beft.

ON

IN ANSWER TO SOME ENQUIRIES OF M. DUBOURG* ON THE SUBJECT.

I AM apprehensive that I shall not be able to find leisure for making all the disquisitions and experiments which would be desirable on this subject. I must, therefore, content myself with a few remarks.

The specific gravity of some human bodies, in comparison to that of water, has been examined by M. Robinson, in our philosophical Transactions, volume 50, page 30, for the year 1757. He asserts, that fat persons with small bones float most easily upon water.

The diving bell is accurately described in our Transactions.

When I was a boy, I made two oval pallets, each about ten inches long, and six broad, with a hole for the thumb, in order to retain it fast in the palm of my hand. They much resemble a painter's pallets. In swimming I pushed the edges of these forward, and I struck the water with their flat surfaces as I drew them back. I remember I swam faster by means of these pallets, but they fatigued my wrists.—I also fitted to the soles of my feet a kind of sandals; but I was not satisfied with them, because I observed that the stroke is partly given by the inside of the feet and the ancles, and not entirely with the soles of the feet.

We have here waistcoats for swimming, which are made of double sail-cloth, with small pieces of cork quilted in between them.

* Translator of Dr. Franklin's works into French.

I know

I know nothing of the *scaphandre* of M. de la Chapelle.

I know by experience that it is a great comfort to a swimmer, who has a considerable distance to go, to turn himself sometimes on his back, and to vary in other respects the means of procuring a progressive motion.

When he is seized with the cramp in the leg, the method of driving it away is to give to the parts affected a sudden, vigorous, and violent shock; which he may do in the air as he swims on his back.

During the great heats of summer there is no danger in bathing, however warm we may be, in rivers which have been thoroughly warmed by the sun. But to throw oneself into cold spring water, when the body has been heated in the sun, is an imprudence which may prove fatal. I once knew an instance of four young men, who having worked at harvest in the heat of the day, with a view of refreshing themselves plunged into a spring of cold water: two died upon the spot, a third the next morning, and the fourth recovered with great difficulty. A copious draught of cold water, in similar circumstances, is frequently attended with the same effect in North America.

The exercise of swimming is one of the most healthy and agreeable in the world. After having swam for an hour or two in the evening, one sleeps coolly the whole night, even during the most ardent heat of summer. Perhaps the pores being cleansed, the insensible perspiration increases and occasions this coolness.—It is certain that much swimming is the means of stopping a diarrhœa, and even of producing a constipation. With respect to those who do not know how to swim;

swim, or who are affected with a diarrhœa at a season which does not permit them to use that exercise, a warm bath, by cleansing and purifying the skin, is found very salutary, and often effects a radical cure. I speak from my own experience, frequently repeated, and that of others to whom I have recommended this .

You will not be displeased if I conclude these hasty remarks by informing you, that as the ordinary method of swimming is reduced to the act of rowing with the arms and legs, and is consequently a laborious and fatiguing operation when the space of water to be crossed is considerable; there is a method in which a swimmer may pass to great distances with much facility, by means of a sail. This discovery I fortunately made by accident, and in the following manner.

When I was a boy I amused myself one day with flying a paper kite; and approaching the bank of a pond, which was near a mile broad, I tied the string to a stake, and the kite ascended to a very considerable height above the pond, while I was swimming. In a little time, being desirous of amusing myself with my kite, and enjoying at the same time the pleasure of swimming, I returned; and loosing from the stake the string with the little stick which was fastened to it, went again into the water, where I found, that, lying on my back and holding the stick in my hands, I was drawn along the surface of the water in a very agreeable manner. Having then engaged another boy to carry my clothes round the pond, to a place which I pointed out to him on the other side, I began to cross the pond with my kite, which carried me quite over without the least fatigue, and with the greatest pleasure imaginable. I was only obliged occasionally to halt a little in my course, and resist its progress,

when

when it appeared that, by following too quick, I lowered the kite too much; by doing which occafionally I made it rife again.—I have never fince that time practifed this fingular mode of fwimming, though I think it not impoffible to crofs in this manner from Dover to Calais. The packet-boat, however, is ftill preferable.

NEW

NEW MODE OF BATHING.

EXTRACTS OF LETTERS TO M. DUBOURG.

London, July 28, 1768.

I GREATLY approve the epithet which you give, in your letter of the 8th of June, to the new method of treating the fmall pox, which you call the *tonic* or bracing method : I will take occafion, from it, to mention a practice to which I have accuftomed myfelf. You know the cold bath has long been in vogue here as a tonic ; but the fhock of the cold water has always appeared to me, generally fpeaking, as too violent, and I have found it much more agreeable to my conftitution to bathe in another element, I mean cold air. With this view I rife early almoft every morning, and fit in my chamber without any clothes whatever, half an hour or an hour, according to the feafon, either reading or writing. This practice is not in the leaft painful, but, on the contrary, agreeable ; and if I return to bed afterwards, before I drefs myfelf, as fometimes happens, I make a fupplement to my night's reft of one or two hours of the moft pleafing fleep that can be imagined. I find no ill confequences whatever refulting from it, and that at leaft it does not injure my health, if it does not in fact contribute much to its prefervation.—I fhall therefore call it for the future a *bracing* or *tonic* bath.

March

March 10, 1773.

I shall not attempt to explain why damp
clothes occasion colds, rather than wet ones, because I doubt the fact; I imagine that neither
the one nor the other contribute to this effect,
and that the causes of colds are totally independent of wet and even of cold. I propose writing a short paper on this subject, the first moment of leisure I have at my disposal.—In the
mean time I can only say, that having some sus-
picions that the common notion, which attributes
to cold the property of stopping the pores and
obstructing perspiration, was ill founded, I engaged a young physician, who is making some
experiments with Sanctorius's balance, to esti-
mate the different proportions of his perspiration,
when remaining one hour quite naked, and another warmly clothed. He pursued the experiment in this alternate manner for eight hours
successively, and found his perspiration almost
double during those hours in which he was
naked.

OBSERVATIONS ON THE GENERALLY PREVAILING DOCTRINES OF LIFE AND DEATH.

TO THE SAME.

YOUR obfervations on the caufes of death, and the experiments which you propofe for recalling to life thofe who appear to be. killed by lightning, demonftrate equally your fagacity and humanity. It appears that the doctrines of life and death, in general, are yet but little underftood.

A toad buried in fand will live, it is faid, until the fand becomes petrified; and then, being inclofed in the ftone, it may ftill live for we know not how many ages. The facts which are cited in fupport of this opinion, are too numerous and too circumftantial not to deferve a certain degree of credit. As we are accuftomed to fee all the animals with which we are acquainted eat and drink, it appears to us difficult to conceive how a toad can be fupported in fuch a dungeon. But if we reflect, that the neceffity of nourifhment, which animals experience in their ordinary ftate, proceeds from the continual wafte of their fubftance by perfpiration; it will appear lefs incredible, that fome animals in a torpid ftate, perfpiring lefs becaufe they ufe no exercife, fhould have lefs need of aliment; and that others, which are covered with fcales or fhells, which ftop perfpiration, fuch as land and fea turtles, ferpents, and fome fpecies of fifh, fhould be able to fubfift a confiderable time without
out

out any nourifhment whatever.—A plant, with
its flowers, fades and dies immediately, if expofed to the air without having its roots immerfed in a humid foil, from which it may draw
a fufficient quantity of moifture, to fupply that
which exhales from its fubftance, and is carried
off continually by the air. Perhaps, however,
if it were buried in quickfilver, it might preferve,
for a confiderable fpace of time, its vegetable
life, its fmell and colour. If this be the cafe, it
might prove a commodious method of tranfporting from diftant countries thofe delicate plants
which are unable to fuftain the inclemency of
the weather at fea, and which require particular
care and attention.

I have feen an inftance of common flies preferved in a manner fomewhat fimilar. They
had been drowned in Madeira wine, apparently
about the time when it was bottled in Virginia,
to be fent to London. At the opening of one
of the bottles, at the houfe of a friend where I
was, three drowned flies fell into the firft glafs
which was filled. Having heard it remarked
that drowned flies were capable of being revived
by the rays of the fun, I propofed making the
experiment upon thefe. They were therefore
expofed to the fun, upon a fieve which had been
employed to ftrain them out of the wine. In
lefs than three hours two of them began by degrees to recover life. They commenced by fome
convulfive motions in the thighs, and at length
they raifed themfelves upon their legs, wiped
their eyes with their fore feet, beat and brufhed
their wings with their hind feet, and foon after
began to fly, finding themfelves in Old England,
without knowing how they came thither. The
third continued lifelefs until fun-fet, when, lofing all hopes of him, he was thrown away.

I wifh

I wifh it were poffible, from this inftance, to invent a method of embalming drowned perfons, in fuch a manner that they might be recalled to life at any period, however diftant; for having a very ardent defire to fee and obferve the ftate of America an hundred years hence, I fhould prefer, to an ordinary death, the being immerfed in a cafk of Madeira wine, with a few friends, until that time, then to be recalled to life by the folar warmth of my dear country! But fince, in all probability, we live in an age too early, and too near the infancy of fcience, to fee fuch an art brought in our time to its perfection, I muft, for the prefent, content myfelf with the treat, which you are fo kind as to promife me, of the refurrection of a fowl or a turkey-cock.

PRE-

PRECAUTIONS TO BE USED BY THOSE WHO ARE ABOUT TO UNDERTAKE A SEA VOYAGE.

WHEN you intend to take a long voyage, nothing is better than to keep it a fecret till the moment of your departure. Without this, you will be continually interrupted and tormented by vifits from friends and acquaintances, who not only make you lofe your valuable time, but make you forget a thoufand things which you wifh to remember; fo that when you are em-barked, and fairly at fea, you recollect, with much uneafinefs, affairs which you have not ter-minated, accounts that you have not fettled, and a number of things which you propofed to carry with you, and which you find the want of every moment. Would it not be attended with the beft confequences to reform fuch a cuftom, and to fuffer a traveller, without deranging him, to make his preparations in quietnefs, to fet apart a few days, when thefe are finifhed, to take leave of his friends, and to receive their good wifhes for his happy return?

It is not always in one's power to choofe a captain; though great part of the pleafure and happinefs of the paffage depends upon this choice, and though one muft for a time be confined to his company, and be in fome meafure under his command. If he is a focial fenfible man, oblig-ing, and of a good difpofition, you will be fo much the happier. One fometimes meets with people of this defcription, but they are not com-mon; however, if yours be not of this number, if he be a good feaman, attentive, careful, and

active

active in the management of his veffel, you muft difpenfe with the reft, for thefe are the moft ef-fential qualities.

Whatever right you may have, by your agree-ment with him, to the provifions he has taken on board for the ufe of the paffengers, it is always proper to have fome private ftore, which you may make ufe of occafionally. You ought, there-fore, to provide good water, that of the fhip being often bad; but you muft put it into bottles, without which you cannot expect to preferve it fweet. You ought alfo to carry with you good tea, ground coffee, chocolate, wine of that fort which you like beft, cyder, dried raifins, almonds, fugar, capillaire, citrons, rum, eggs dipped in oil, portable foup, bread twice baked. With re-gard to poultry, it is almoft ufelefs to carry any with you, unlefs you refolve to undertake the office of feeding and fattening them yourfelf. With the little care which is taken of them on board fhip, they are almoft all fickly, and their flefh is as tough as leather.

All failors entertain an opinion, which has un-doubtedly originated formerly from a want of water, and when it has been found neceffary to be fparing of it, that poultry never know when they have drank enough; and that when water is given them at difcretion, they generally kill themfelves by drinking beyond meafure. In con-fequence of this opinion, they give them water only once in two days, and even then in fmall quantities: but as they pour this water into troughs inclining on one fide, which occafions it to run to the lower part, it thence it happens that they are obliged to mount one upon the back of another in order to reach it; and there are fome which cannot even dip their beaks in it. Thus continually tantalized and tormented by

Q   thirft,

thirft, they are unable to digeft their food, which is very dry, and they foon fall fick and die. Some of them are found thus every morning, and are thrown into the fea ; whilft thofe which are killed for the table are fcarcely fit to be eaten. To remedy this inconvenience, it will be neceffary to divide their troughs into fmall compartments, in fuch a manner that each of them may be capable of containing water; but this is feldom or never done. On this account, fheep and hogs are to be confidered as the beft frefh provifion that one can have at fea ; mutton there being in general very good, and pork excellent.

It may happen that fome of the provifions and ftores which I have recommended may become almoft ufelefs, by the care which the captain has taken to lay in a proper ftock; but in fuch a cafe you may difpofe of it to relieve the poor paffengers, who, paying lefs for their paffage, are ftowed among the common failors, and have no right to the captain's provifions, except fuch part of them as is ufed for feeding the crew. Thefe paffengers are fometimes fick, melancholy, and dejected ; and there are often women and children among them, neither of whom have any opportunity of procuring thofe things which I have mentioned, and of which, perhaps, they have the greateft need. By diftributing amongft them a part of your fuperfluity, you may be of the greateft affiftance to them. You may reftore their health, fave their lives, and in fhort render them happy ; which always affords the livelieft fenfation to a feeling mind.

The moft difagreeable thing at fea is the cookery ; for there is not, properly fpeaking, any profeffed cook on board. The worft failor is generally chofen for that purpofe, who for the moft part is equally dirty. Hence comes the proverb

ufed

used among the English sailors, that *God sends meat, and the Devil sends cooks.* Those, however, who have a better opinion of Providence, will think otherwise. Knowing that sea air, and the exercise or motion which they receive from the rolling of the ship, have a wonderful effect in whetting the appetite, they will say, that Providence has given sailors bad cooks to prevent them from eating too much; or that knowing they would have bad cooks, he has given them a good appetite to prevent them from dying with hunger. However, if you have no confidence in these succours of Providence, you may yourself, with a lamp and a boiler, by the help of a little spirits of wine, prepare some food, such as soup, hash, &c. A small oven made of tin-plate is not a bad piece of furniture : your servant may roast in it a piece of mutton or pork. If you are ever tempted to eat salt beef, which is often very good, you will find that cyder is the best liquor to quench the thirst generally caused by salt meat or salt fish. Sea-biscuit, which is too hard for the teeth of some people, may be softened by steeping it; but bread double baked is the best; for being made of good loaf-bred cut into slices, and baked a second time, it readily imbibes water, becomes soft, and is easily digested : it consequently forms excellent nourishment, much superior to that of biscuit, which has not been fermented.

I must here observe, that this double-baked bread was originally the real biscuit prepared to keep at sea; for the word *biscuit*, in French, signifies twice baked *. Pease often boil badly, and do not become soft; in such a case, by putting a two-pound shot into the kettle, the rolling of the vessel, by means of this bullet, will convert the pease into a kind of porridge, like mustard.

* It is derived from *bis* again, and *cuit* baked.

Q 2   Having

Having often feen foup, when put upon the table at fea in broad flat difhes, thrown out on every fide by the rolling of the veffel, I have wifhed that our tin-men would make our foup-bafons with divifions or compartments; forming fmall plates, proper, for containing foup for one perfon only. By this difpofition, the foup, in an extraordinary roll, would not be thrown out of the plate, and would not fall into the breafts of thofe who are at table, and fcald them.—Having entertained you with thefe things of little impor-tance, permit me now to conclude with fome general reflections upon navigation.

When navigation is employed only for tranf-porting neceffary provifions from one country, where they abound, to another where they are wanting; when by this it prevents famines which were fo frequent and fo fatal before it was inven-ted and became fo common; we cannot help con-fidering it as one of thofe arts which contribute moft to the happinefs of mankind.—But when it is employed to tranfport things of no utility, or articles merely of luxury, it is uncertain whether the advantages refulting from it are fufficient to counterbalance the misfortunes it occafions, by expofing the lives of fo many individuals upon the vaft ocean. And when it is ufed to plunder veffels and tranfport flaves, it is evidently only the dreadful means of increafing thofe calamities which afflict human nature.

One is aftonifhed to think on the number of veffels and men who are daily expofed in going to bring tea from China, coffee from Arabia, and fugar and tobacco from America; all commodi-ties which our anceftors lived very well without. The fugar trade employs nearly a thoufand vef-fels; and that of tobacco almoft the fame number.

ber. With regard to the utility of tobacco, little can be faid; and, with regard to fugar, how much more meritorious would it be to facrifice the momentary pleafure which we receive from drinking it once or twice a-day in our tea, than to encourage the numberlefs cruelties that are continually exercifed in order to procure it us?

A celebrated French moralift faid, that, when he confidered the wars which we foment in Africa to get negroes, the great number who of courfe perifh in thefe wars, the multitude of thofe wretches who die in their paffage, by difeafe, bad air, and bad provifions; and laftly, how many perifh by the cruel treatment they meet with in a ftate of flavery; when he faw a bit of fugar, he could not help imagining it to be covered with fpots of human blood. But, had he added to thefe confiderations the wars which we carry on againft one another, to take and retake the iflands that produce this commodity, he would not have feen the fugar fimply *fpotted* with blood, he would have beheld it entirely tinged with it.

Thefe wars make the maritime powers of Europe, and the inhabitants of Paris and London, pay much dearer for their fugar than thofe of Vienna, though they are almoft three hundred leagues diftant from the fea. A pound of fugar, indeed, cofts the former not only the price which they give for it, but alfo what they pay in taxes, neceffary to fupport thofe fleets and armies which ferve to defend and protect the countries that produce it.

ON LUXURY, IDLENESS, AND INDUSTRY:

From a Letter to Benjamin Vaughan, Efq. *
written in 1784.

IT is wonderful how prepofteroufly the affairs of this world are managed. Naturally one would imagine, that the intereft of a few individuals fhould give way to general intereft ; but individuals manage their affairs with fo much more application, induftry, and addrefs, than the public do theirs, that general intereft moft commonly gives way to particular. We affemble parliaments and councils, to have the benefit of their collected wifdom ; but we neceffarily have, at the fame time, the inconvenience of their collected paffions, prejudices, and private interefts. By the help of thefe, artful men overpower their wifdom, and dupe its poffeffors : and if we may judge by the acts, arrets, and edicts, all the world over, for regulating commerce, an affembly of great men is the greateft fool upon earth.

I have not yet, indeed, thought of a remedy for luxury. I am not fure that in a great ftate it is capable of a remedy ; nor that the evil is in itfelf always fo great as it is reprefented. Suppofe we include in the definition of luxury all unneceffary expence, and then let us confider whether laws to prevent fuch expence are poffible to be executed in a great country, and whether,

---

* Prefent member of parliament for the borough of Calne, in Wiltfhire, between whom and our author there fubfifted a very clofe friendfhip.

if

if they could be executed, our people generally would be happier, or even richer. Is not the hope of being one day able to purchafe and enjoy luxuries, a great fpur to labour and induftry? May not luxury therefore produce more than it confumes, if, without fuch a fpur, people would be, as they are naturally enough inclined to be, lazy and indolent? To this purpofe I remember a circumftance. The fkipper of a fhallop, employed between Cape-May and Philadelphia, had done us fome fmall fervice, for which he refufed to be paid. My wife underftanding that he had a daughter, fent her a prefent of a new-fafhioned cap. Three years after, this fkipper being at my houfe with an old farmer of Cape-May, his paffenger, he mentioned the cap, and how much his daughter had been pleafed with it. "But " (faid he) it proved a dear cap to our congre-. " gation."—How fo?—" When my daughter " appeared with it at meeting, it was fo much " admired, that all the girls refolved to get fuch " caps from Philadelphia; and my wife and I " computed that the whole could not have coft " lefs than a hundred pounds."—" True (faid " the farmer), but you do not tell all the ftory. " I think the cap was neverthelefs an advantage " to us; for it was the firft thing that put our " girls upon knitting worfted mittens for fale at " Philadelphia, that they might have where- " withal to buy caps and ribbons there; and " you know that that induftry has continued, " and is likely to continue and increafe to a " much greater value, and anfwer better pur- " pofes."—Upon the whole, I was more reconciled to this little piece of luxury, fince not only the girls were made happier by having fine caps, but the Philadelphians by the fupply of warm mittens.

In

In our commercial towns upon the fea-coaft, fortunes will occafionally be made. Some of thofe who grow rich will be prudent, live within bounds, and preferve what they have gained for their pofterity: others, fond of fhewing their wealth, will be extravagant, and ruin themfelves. Laws cannot prevent this: and perhaps it is not always an evil to the public. A fhilling fpent idly by a fool, may be picked up by a wifer perfon, who knows better what to do with it. It is therefore not loft. A vain, filly fellow builds a fine houfe, furnifhes it richly, lives in it expenfively, and in a few years ruins himfelf: but the mafons, carpenters, fmiths, and other honeft tradefmen, have been by his employ affifted in maintaining and raifing their families; the farmer has been paid for his labour, and encouraged, and the eftate is now in better hands.—In fome cafes, indeed, certain modes of luxury may be a public evil, in the fame manner as it is a private one. If there be a nation, for inftance, that exports its beef and linen, to pay for the importation of claret and porter, while a great part of its people live upon potatoes, and wear no fhirts; wherein does it differ from the fot who lets his family ftarve, and fells his clothes to buy drink? Our American commerce is, I confefs, a little in this way. We fell our victuals to the iflands for rum and fugar; the fubftantial neceffaries of life for fuperfluities. But we have plenty, and live well neverthelefs; though, by being foberer, we might be richer.

The vaft quantity of foreft land we have yet to clear, and put in order for cultivation, will for a long time keep the body of our nation laborious and frugal. Forming an opinion of our people and their manners, by what is feen among the inhabitants of the fea-ports, is judging from
an

an improper sample. The people of the trading towns may be rich and luxurious, while the country poffeffes all the virtues that tend to promote happinefs and public profperity. Thofe towns are not much regarded by the country; they are hardly confidered as an effential part of the States; and the experience of the laft war has fhewn, that their being in the poffeffion of the enemy did not neceffarily draw on the fubjection of the country; which bravely continued to maintain its freedom and independence notwithftanding.

It has been computed by fome political arithmetician, that if every man and woman would work for four hours each day on fomething ufeful, that labour would produce fufficient to procure all the neceffaries and comforts of life; want and mifery would be banifhed out of the world, and the reft of the twenty-four hours might be leifure and pleafure.

What occafions then fo much want and mifery? It is the employment of men and women in works that produce neither the neceffaries nor conveniences of life, who, with thofe who do nothing, confume neceffaries raifed by the laborious. To explain this:

The firft elements of wealth are obtained by labour, from the earth and waters. I have land, and raife corn. With this, if I feed a family that does nothing, my corn will be confumed, and at the end of the year I fhall be no richer than I was at the beginning. But if, while I feed them, I employ them, fome in fpinning, others in making bricks, &c. for building, the value of my corn will be arrefted and remain with me, and at the end of the year we may all be better clothed and better lodged. And if, inftead of employing a man I feed in making bricks,

bricks, I employ him in fiddling for me, the corn he eats is gone, and no part of his manufacture remains to augment the wealth and convenience of the family: I fhall therefore be the poorer for this fiddling man, unlefs the reft of my family work more, or eat lefs, to make up the deficiency he occafions.

Look round the world, and fee the millions employed in doing nothing, or in fomething that amounts to nothing, when the neceffaries and conveniences of life are in queftion. What is the bulk of commerce, for which we fight and deftroy each other, but the toil of millions for fuperfluities, to the great hazard and lofs of many lives, by the conftant dangers of the fea? How much labour is fpent in building and fitting great fhips, to go to China and Arabia for tea and coffee, to the Weft Indies for fugar, to America for tobacco? Thefe things cannot be called the neceffaries of life, for our anceftors lived very comfortably without them.

A queftion may be afked: Could all thefe people now employed in raifing, making, or carrying fuperfluities, be fubfifted by raifing neceffaries? I think they might. The world is large, and a great part of it ftill uncultivated. Many hundred millions of acres in Afia, Africa and America, are ftill in a foreft; and a great deal even in Europe. On a hundred acres of this foreft a man might become a fubftantial farmer; and a hundred thoufand men employed in clearing each his hundred acres, would hardly brighten a fpot big enough to be vifible from the moon, unlefs with Herfchel's telefcope; fo vaft are the regions ftill in wood.

It is however fome comfort to reflect, that, upon the whole, the quantity of induftry and prudence among mankind exceeds the quantity

of

of idlenefs and folly. Hence the increafe of good buildings, farms cultivated, and populous cities filled with wealth, all over Europe, which a few ages fince were only to be found on the coafts of the Mediterranean; and this notwithftanding the mad wars continually raging, by which are often deftroyed in one year the works of many years peace. So that we may hope, the luxury of a few merchants on the coaft will not be the ruin of America.

One reflection more, and I will end this long rambling letter. Almoft all the parts of our bodies require fome expence. The feet demand fhoes; the legs ftockings; the reft of the body clothing; and the belly a good deal of victuals. Our eyes, though exceedingly ufeful, afk when reafonable, only the cheap affiftance of fpectacles, which could not much impair our finances. But the eyes of other people are the eyes that ruin us. If all but myfelf were blind, I fhould want neither fine clothes, fine houfes, nor fine fur-niture.

ON

READING in the newspapers the speech of Mr. Jackson in congress, against meddling with the affair of slavery, or attempting to mend the condition of slaves, it put me in mind of a similar speech, made about one hundred years since, by Sidi Mehemet Ibrahim, a member of the Divan of Algiers, which may be seen in Martin's account of his consulship, 1687. It was against granting the petition of the sect called *Erika*, or *Purists*, who prayed for the abolition of piracy and slavery as being unjust.—Mr. Jackson does not quote it; perhaps he has not seen it. If, therefore, some of its reasonings are to be found in his eloquent speech, it may only shew that men's interests operate, and are operated on, with surprising similarity, in all countries and climates, whenever they are under similar circumstances. The African speech, as translated, is as follows:

" Alla Bismillah, &c. God is great, and Mahomet is his prophet.

" Have these Erika considered the consequences of granting their petition? If we cease our cruises against the Christians, how shall we be furnished with the commodities their countries produce, and which are so necessary for us? If we forbear to make slaves of their people, who, in this hot climate, are to cultivate our lands? Who are to perform the common labours of our city, and of our families? Must we not then be our own slaves? And is there not more compassion and more favour due to us Mussulmen, than to those Christian dogs?—We have now above fifty thousand slaves in and near Algiers. This
number,

number, if not kept up by fresh supplies, will
soon diminish, and be gradually annihilated. If,
then, we cease taking and plundering the infidel
ships, and making slaves of the seamen and passen-
gers, our lands will become of no value, for want
of cultivation ; the rents of houses in the city
will sink one half ; and the revenues of government, arising from the share of prizes, must be
totally destroyed.—And for what ? To gratify
the whim of a whimsical sect, who would have
us not only forbear making more slaves, but even
manumit those we have. But who is to indemni-
fy their masters for the loss ? Will the state do it ;
Is our treasury sufficient ? Will the Erika do it ?
Can they do it ? Or would they, to do what they
think justice to the slaves, do a greater injustice
to the owners ? And if we set our slaves free,
what is to be done with them ? Few of them
will return to their native countries ; they know
too well the greater hardships they must there
be subject to. They will not embrace our holy
religion : they will not adopt our manners : our
people will not pollute themselves by intermarry-
ing with them. Must we maintain them as beg-
gars in our streets ? or suffer our properties to be
the prey of their pillage ? for men accustomed to
slavery will not work for a livelihood, when not
compelled.—And what is there so pitiable in their
present condition ? Were they not slaves in their
own countries ? Are not Spain, Portugal, France,
and the Italian states, governed by despots, who
hold all their subjects in slavery, without excep-
tion ? Even England treats her sailors as slaves,
for they are, whenever the government pleases,
seized and confined in ships of war, condemned
not only to work, but to fight for small wages,
or a mere subsistence, not better than our slaves
are allowed by us. Is their condition then made

worse

worfe by their falling into our hands? No; they have only exchanged one flavery for another; and I may fay a better: for here they are brought into a land where the fun of Iflamifm gives forth its light, and fhines in full fplendour, and they have an opportunity of making themfelves acquainted with the true doctrine, and thereby faving their immortal fouls. Thofe who remain at home, have not that happinefs. Sending the flaves home, then, would be fending them out of light into darknefs.

"I repeat the queftion, what is to be done with them? I have heard it fuggefted, that they may be planted in the wildernefs, where there is plenty of land for them to fubfift on, and where they may flourifh as a free ftate.—But they are, I doubt, too little difpofed to labour without compulfion, as well as too ignorant to eftablifh good government: and the wild Arabs would foon moleft and deftroy, or again enflave them. While ferving us, we take care to provide them with every thing; and they are treated with humanity. The labourers in their own countries are, as I am informed, worfe fed, lodged, and clothed. The condition of moft of them is therefore already mended, and requires no farther improvement. Here their lives are in fafety. They are not liable to be impreffed for foldiers, and forced to cut one another's Chriftian throats, as in the wars of their own countries. If fome of the religious mad bigots, who now teafe us with their filly petitions, have, in a fit of blind zeal, freed their flaves, it was not generofity, it was not humanity that moved them to the action; it was from the confcious burthen of a load of fins, and hope, from the fuppofed merits of fo good a work, to be excufed from damnation—How grofsly are they miftaken, in
imagining

imagining flavery to be difavowed by the Alcoran! Are not the two precepts, to quote no more, " Mafters, treat your flaves with kindnefs—Slaves, ferve your mafters with cheerfulnefs and fidelity," clear proofs to the contrary? Nor can the plundering of infidels be in that facred book forbidden? fince it is well known from it that God has given the world, and all that it contains, to his faithful Muffulmen, who are to enjoy it, of right, as faft as they can conquer it. Let us then hear no more of this deteftable propofition, the manumiffion of Chriftian flaves, the adoption of which would, by depreciating our lands and houfes, and thereby depriving fo many good citizens of their properties, create univerfal difcontent, and provoke infurrections, to the endangering of government, and producing general confufion. I have, therefore, no doubt that this wife council will prefer the comfort and happinefs of a whole nation of true believers, to the whim of a few Erika, and difmifs their petition."

The refult was, as Martin tells us, that the Divan came to this refolution: " That the doctrine, " that the plundering and enflaving the Chriftians " is unjuft, is at beft problematical; but that it " is the intereft of this ftate to continue the prac- "tice, is clear; therefore, let the petition be re- " jected."——And it was rejected accordingly.

And fince like motives are apt to produce, in the minds of men, like opinions and refolutions, may we not venture to predict, from this account, that the petitions to the parliament of England for abolifhing the flave trade, to fay nothing of other legiflatures, and the debates upon them, will have a fimilar conclufion.

HISTORICUS.

March 23, 1790.

OBSER-

OBSERVATIONS ON WAR.

BY the original law of nations, war and extir-
pation were the punifhment of injury. Huma-
nizing by degrees, it admitted flavery inftead of
death: a farther ftep was, the exchange of prifoners inftead of flavery: another, to refpect more
the property of private perfons under conqueft,
and be content with acquired dominion. Why
fhould not this law of nations go on improving?
Ages have intervened between its feveral fteps:
but as knowledge of late increafes rapidly, why
fhould not thofe fteps be quickened? Why fhould
it not be agreed to, as the future law of nations,
that in any war hereafter the following defcription
of men fhould be undifturbed, have the protection of both fides, and be permitted to follow
their employments in fecnrity? viz.

1. Cultivators of the earth, becaufe they labour
for the fubfiftence of mankind.

2. Fifhermen, for the fame reafon.

3. Merchants and traders in unarmed fhips,
who accommodate different nations by commu-
nicating and exchanging the neceffaries and conveniencies of life.

4. Artifts and mechanics, inhabiting and
working in open towns.

It is hardly neceffary to add, that the hofpitals
of enemies fhould be unmolefted—they ought to
be affifted. It is for the intereft of humanity in
general, that the occafions of war, and the inducements to it, fhould be diminifhed. If rapine
be abolifhed, one of the encouragements to war
is taken away; and peace therefore more likely to
continue and be lafting.

The

The practice of robbing merchants on the high feas—a remnant of the antient piracy—though it may be accidentally beneficial to particular perfons, is far from being profitable to all engaged in it, or to the nation that authorifes it. In the beginning of a war fome rich fhips are furprized and taken. This encourages the firft adventurers to fit out more armed veffels; and many others to do the fame. But the enemy at the fame time become more careful; arm their merchant fhips better, and render them not fo eafy to be taken: they go alfo more under the protection of convoys. Thus, while the privateers to take them are multiplied, the veffels fubject to be taken, and the chances of profit, are diminifhed; fo that many cruifes are made wherein the expences overgo the gains; and, as is the cafe in other lotteries, though particulars have got prizes, the mafs of adventurers are lofers, the whole expence of fitting out all the privateers during a war being much greater than the whole amount of goods taken.

Then there is the national lofs of all the labour of fo many men during the time they have been employed in robbing; who befides fpend what they get in riot, drunkennefs, and debauchery; lofe their habits of induftry; are rarely fit for any fober bufinefs after a peace, and ferve only to increafe the number of highwaymen and houfebreakers. Even the undertakers who have been fortunate, are, by fudden wealth, led into expenfive living, the habit of which continues when the means of fupporting it ceafe, and finally ruins them: a juft punifhment for their having wantonly and unfeelingly ruined many honeft, innocent traders and their families, whofe fubftance was employed in ferving the common intereft of mankind.

R

ON

ON THE

IMPRESS OF SEAMEN.

Notes copied from Dr. Franklin's writing in pencil in the margin of Judge Foster's celebrated argument in favour of the IMPRES-SING OF SEAMEN *(published in the folio edition of his works.)*

JUDGE Foster, p. 158. " Every Man."—The conclusion here from the *whole to a part*, does not seem to be good logic. If the alphabet should say, Let us all fight for the defence of the whole; that is equal, and may. therefore, be just. But if they should say, Let A B C and D go out and fight for us, while we stay at home and sleep in whole skins; that is not equal, and therefore can-not be just.

Ib.   " Employ."—If you please. The word signifies engaging a man to work for me, by of-fering him such wages as are sufficient to induce him to prefer my service. This is very different from compelling him to work on such terms as I think proper.

Ib.   " This service and employment, &c."—These are false facts. His employments and ser-vice are not the same.—Under the merchant he goes in an unarmed vessel, not obliged to fight, but to transport merchandize. In the king's service he is obliged to fight, and to hazard all the dan-gers of battle. Sickness on board of king's ships is also more common and more mortal. The merchant's service too he can quit at the end of the voyage; not the king's. Also, the merchant's wages are much higher.

Ib.

Ib. " I am very fenfible, &c"—Here are two
things put in comparifon that are not compara-
ble: viz. injury to feamen, and inconvenience
to trade. Inconvenience to the whole trade of
a nation will not juftify injuftice to a fingle feaman. If the trade would fuffer without his fervice, it is able and ought to be willing to offer
him fuch wages as may induce him to afford his
fervice voluntarily.

Page 159. " Private mifchief muft be borne
" with patience, for preventing a national cala-
" mity."—Where is this maxim in law and good
policy to be found? And how can that be a maxim which is not confiftent with common fenfe?
If the maxim had been, that private mifchiefs,
which prevent a national calamity, ought to be
generoufly compenfated by the nation, one might
underftand it: but that fuch private mifchiefs
are only to be borne with patience, is abfurd!

Ib. " The expedient, &c. And, &c." (Paragraphs 2 and 3).—Twenty ineffectual or inconvenient fchemes will not juftify one that is unjuft.

Ib. " Upon the foot of, &c."—Your reafoning,
indeed, like a lie, ftands but upon one *foot ;* truth
upon two.

Page 160. " Full wages."—Probably the fame
they had in the merchant's fervice.

Page 174. " I hardly admit, &c." (Paragraph
5).——When this author fpeaks of impreffing,
page 158, he diminifhes the horror of the practice
as much as poffible, by prefenting to the mind
one failor only fuffering a " *hardfhip*" (as he ten-
derly calls it) in fome " *particular cafes*" only ;
and he places againft this private mifchief the inconvenience to the trade of the kingdom.—But
if, as he fuppofes is often the cafe, the failor who
is preffed, and obliged to ferve for the defence of
trade, at the rate of twenty-five fhillings a month,

could

could get three pounds fifteen fhillings in the merchant's fervice, you take from him fifty fhillings
a month; and if you have a 100,000 in your fervice, you rob this honeft induftrious part of fociety and their poor families of 250,000l. per
month, or three millions a year, and at the fame
time oblige them to hazard their lives in fighting
for the defence of your trade; to the defence of
which all ought indeed to contribute (and failors
among the reft) in proportion to their profits by
it; but this three millions is more than their
fhare, if they did not pay with their perfons; but
when you force that, methinks you fhould excufe the other.

But it may be faid, to give the king's feamen
merchant's wages would coft the nation too
much, and call for more taxes. The queftion
then will amount to this: whether it be juft in a
community, that the richer part fhould compel
the poorer to fight in defence of them and their
properties, for fuch wages as they think fit to allow, and punifh them if they refufe? Our author
tells us that it is " *legal*." I have not law enough
to difpute his authorities, but I cannot perfuade
myfelf that it is equitable. I will, however,
own for the prefent, that it may be lawful when
neceffary; but then I contend that it may be ufed
fo as to produce the fame good effects—*the public
fecurity*, without doing fo much intolerable injuftice as attends the impreffing common feamen.
—In order to be better underftood I would pre-
mife two things; Firft, that voluntary feamen
may be had for the fervice, if they were fufficiently paid. The proof is, that to ferve in the
fame fhip, and incur the fame dangers, you have
no occafion to imprefs captains, lieutenants, fecond lieutenants, midfhipmen, purfers, nor many other officers. Why, but that the profits of
                                                their

their places, or the emoluments expected, are
fufficient inducements? The bufinefs then is, to
find money, by impreffing, fufficient to make
the failors all volunteers, as well as their officers;
and this without any frefh burthen upon trade.
—The fecond of my premifes is, that twenty-five
fhillings a month, with his fhare of the falt beef,
pork, and peas-pudding, being found fufficient for the fubfiftence of a hard-working feaman, it will certainly be fo for a fedentary fcholar
or gentleman. I would then propofe to form a
treafury, out of which encouragements to feamen
fhould be paid. To fill this treafury, I would imprefs a number of civil officers who at prefent
have great falaries, oblige them to ferve in their
refpective offices for twenty-five fhillings a month
with their fhares of mefs provifions, and throw
the reft of their falaries into the feamen's
treafury. If fuch a prefs-warrant were given
me to execute, the firft I would prefs fhould be
a Recorder of Briftol, or a Mr. Juftice Fofter,
becaufe I might have need of his edifying example, to fhow how much impreffing ought to be
borne with; for he would certainly find, that
though to be reduced to twenty-five fhillings a
month might be a "*private mifchief,*" yet that,
agreeably to his maxim of law and good policy,
it "*ought to be borne with patience,*" for preventing a national calamity. Then I would prefs the
reft of the Judges; and, opening the red book,
I would prefs every civil officer of government
from 50l. a year falary, up to 50,000l. which
would throw an immenfe fum into our treafury:
and thefe gentlemen could not complain, fince
they would receive twenty-five fhillings a month,
and their rations: and this without being obliged
to fight. Laftly, I think I would imprefs ***

ON THE CRIMINAL LAWS, AND THE PRACTICE
OF PRIVATEERING.

LETTER TO BENJAMIN VAUGHAN, ESQ.

March 14th, 1785.

MY DEAR FRIEND,

AMONG the pamphlets you lately fent me, was one, entitled, *Thoughts on Executive Juſtice.* In return for that, I fend you a French one on the fame fubject, *Obſervations concernant l'Exécution de l'Article II. de la Déclaration ſur le Vol.* They are both addreſſed to the judges, but written, as you will fee, in a very different fpirit. The Engliſh author is for hanging *all* thieves. The French-man is for proportioning puniſhments to offences.

If we really believe, as we profeſs to believe, that the law of Mofes was the law of God, the dictate of divine wifdom, infinitely fuperior to human; on what principles do we ordain death as the puniſhment of an offence, which, according to that law, was only to be puniſhed by a reſtitution of fourfold? To put a man to death for an offence which does not deferve death, is it not a murder? And, as the French writer fays, *Doit-on punir un délit contre la focieté par un crime contre la nature?*

Superfluous property is the creature of fociety. Simple and mild laws were fufficient to guard the property that was merely neceſſary. The favage's bow, his hatchet, and his coat of fkins, were fufficiently fecured, without law, by the fear of perſonal refentment and retaliation. When, by virtue of the firſt laws, part of the fociety accumulated

mulated wealth and grew powerful, they enacted others more fevere, and would protect their property at the expence of humanity. This was abufing their power, and commencing a tyranny. If a favage, before he entered into fociety, had been told—" Your neighbour, by this means, " may become owner of an hundred deer; but if " your brother, or your fon, or yourfelf, having " no deer of your own, and being hungry, " fhould kill one, an infamous death muft be the " confequence:" he would probably have preferred his liberty, and his common right of killing any deer, to all the advantages of fociety that might be propofed to him.

That it is better a hundred guilty perfons fhould efcape, than that one innocent perfon fhould fuffer, is a maxim that has been long and generally approved; never, that I know of, controverted. Even the fanguinary author of the *Thoughts* agrees to it, adding well, " that the very thought of " *injured* innocence, and much more that of *fuffer-* " *ing* innocence, muft awaken all our tendereft " and moft compaffionate feelings, and at the " fame time raife our higheft indignation againft " the inftruments of it. But," he adds, " there " is no danger of *either*, from a ftrict adherence " to the laws."—Really!—Is it then impoffible to make an unjuft law? and if the law itfelf be unjuft, may it not be the very " inftrument" which ought " to raife the author's, and every " body's higheft indignation?" I fee, in the laft newfpapers from London, that a woman is capitally convicted at the Old Bailey, for privately ftealing out of a fhop fome gauze, value fourteen fhillings and three-pence: Is there any proportion between the injury done by a theft, value fourteen fhillings and three-pence, and the punifhment of a human creature, by death, on a gibbet?

Might

Might not that woman, by her labour, have made the reparation ordained by God, in paying four-fold? Is not all punishment inflicted beyond the merit of the offence, so much punishment of innocence? In this light, how vast is the annual quantity, of not only *injured* but *suffering* innocence, in almost all the civilized states of Europe!

But it seems to have been thought, that this kind of innocence may be punished by way of *preventing* crimes. I have read, indeed, of a cruel Turk in Barbary, who, whenever he bought a new Christian slave, ordered him immediately to be hung up by the legs, and to receive a hundred blows of a cudgel on the soles of his feet, that the severe sense of the punishment, and fear of incurring it thereafter, might prevent the faults that should merit it. Our author himself would hardly approve entirely of this Turk's conduct in the government of slaves; and yet he appears to recommend something like it for the government of English subjects, when he applauds the reply of Judge Burnet to the convict horse-stealer; who being asked what he had to say why judgment of death should not pass against him, and answering, that it was hard to hang a man for *only* stealing a horse, was told by the judge, " Man, thou art " not to be hanged *only* for stealing a horse, but " that horses may not be stolen." The man's answer, if candidly examined, will, I imagine, appear reasonable, as being founded on the eternal principle of justice and equity, that punishments should be proportioned to offences; and the judge's reply brutal and unreasonable, though the writer " wishes all judges to carry it with them " whenever they go the circuit, and to bear it in " their minds, as containing a wise reason for all " the penal statutes which they are called upon to " put in execution. It at once illustrates," says

he,

he, " the true grounds and reasons of all capital
" punishments whatsoever, namely, that every
" man's property, as well as his life, may be held
" sacred and inviolate." Is there then no difference in value between property and life? If I
think it right that the crime of murder should be
punished with death, not only as an equal punishment of the crime, but to prevent other murders,
does it follow that I must approve of inflicting
the same punishment for a little invasion on my
property by theft? If I am not myself so barbarous, so bloody-minded, and revengeful, as to
kill a fellow-creature for stealing from me fourteen
shillings and three-pence, how can I approve of a
law that does it? Montesquieu, who was himself
a judge, endeavours to impress other maxims.
He must have known what humane judges feel on
such occasions, and what the effects of those
feelings; and, so far from thinking that severe
and excessive punishments prevent crimes, he
asserts, as quoted by our French writer, that

" *L'atrocité des loix en empêche l'exécution.*

" *Lorsque la peine est sans mesure, on est souvent*
" *obligé de lui préférer l'impunité.*

" *La cause de tous les relâchemens vient de l'impu-*
" *nité des crimes, et non de la modération des peines.*"

It is said by those who know Europe generally,
that there are more thefts committed and punished annually in England, than in all the other
nations put together. If this be so, there must
be a cause or causes for such depravity in our
common people. May not one be the deficiency of
justice and morality in our national government,
manifested in our oppressive conduct to subjects,
and unjust wars on our neighbours? View the
long-persisted in, unjust, monopolizing treatment
of Ireland, at length acknowledged! View the
plundering

plundering government exercifed by our merchants in the Indies; the confifcating war made
upon the American colonies; and, to fay nothing
of thofe upon France and Spain, view the late
war upon Holland, which was feen by impartial
Europe in no other light than that of a war of
rapine and pillage; the hopes of an immenfe and
cafy prey being its only apparent, and probably
its true and real motive and encouragement.
Juftice is as ftrictly due between neighbour nations
as between neighbour citizens. A highway-man
is as much a robber when he plunders in a gang,
as when fingle; and a nation that makes an unjuft
war is only a great gang. After employing your
people in robbing the Dutch, 'is it ftrange that,
being put out of that employ by peace, they ftill
continue robbing, and rob one another? *Pira-
terie*, as the French call it, or privateering, is the
univerfal bent of the Englifh nation, at home and
abroad, wherever fettled. No lefs than feven
hundred privateers were, it is faid, commiffioned
in the laft war! Thefe were fitted out by merchants, to prey upon other merchants, who had
never done them any injury. Is there probably
any one of thofe privateering merchants of London, who were fo ready to rob the merchants of
Amfterdam, that would not as readily plunder
another London merchant of the next ftreet, if
he could do it with the fame impunity! The
avidity, the *alieni appetens* is the fame; it is the
fear alone of the gallows that makes the difference. How then can a nation, which, among
the honefteft of its people, has fo many thieves
by inclination, and whofe government encouraged
and commiffioned no lefs than feven hundred
gangs of robbers; how can fuch a nation have
the face to condemn the crime in individuals, and
hang up twenty of them in a morning! It naturally

rally puts one in mind of a Newgate anecdote. One of the prifoners complained, that in the night fomebody had taken his buckles out of his fhoes. "What the devil!" fays another, "have "we then *thieves* amongft us? It muft not be "fuffered. Let us fearch out the rogue, and "pump him to death."

There is, however, one late inftance of an Englifh merchant who will not profit by fuch ill-gotten gain. He was, it feems, part-owner of a fhip, which the other owners thought fit to employ as a letter of marque, and which took a number of French prizes. The booty being fhared, he has now an agent here enquiring, by an advertifement in the Gazette, for thofe who fuffered the lofs, in order to make them, as far as in him lies, reftitution. This confcientious man is a quaker. The Scotch prefbyterians were formerly as tender; for there is ftill extant an ordinance of the town-council of Edinburgh, made foon after the Reformation, "forbidding the "purchafe of prize goods, under pain of lofing "the freedom of the burgh for ever, with other "punifhment at the will of the magiftrate; the "practice of making prizes being contrary to "good confcience, and the rule of treating Chrif- "tian brethren as we would wifh to be treated; "and fuch goods *are not to be fold by any godly men* "*within this burgh.*" The race of thefe godly men in Scotland is, probably extinct, or their principles are abandoned fince, as far as that nation had a hand in promoting the war againft the colonies, prizes and confifcations are believed to have been a confiderable motive.

It has been for fome time a generally-received opinion, that a military man is not to enquire whether a war be juft or unjuft; he is to execute his orders. All princes who are difpofed to be-

come

come tyrants, muft probably approve of this opinion, and be willing to eftablifh it ; but is it not
a dangerous one ? fince, on that principle, if the
tyrant commands his army to attack and deftroy,
not only an unoffending neighbour nation, but
even his own fubjects, the army is bound to obey.
A negro flave, in our colonies, being commanded
by his mafter to rob or murder a neighbour, or
do any other immoral act, may refufe ; and the
magiftrate will protect him in his refufal. The
flavery then of a foldier is worfe than that of a
negro ! A confcientious officer, if not reftrained
by the apprehenfion of its being imputed to another caufe, may indeed refign, rather than be employed in an unjuft war ; but the private men are
flaves for life ; and they are perhaps incapable of
judging for themfelves. We can only lament
their fate, and ftill more that of a failor, who is
often dragged by force from his honeft occupation,
and compelled to imbrue his hands in perhaps
innocent blood. But methinks it well behoves
merchants (men more enlightened by their education, and perfectly free from any fuch force or
obligation) to confider well of the juftice of a
war, before they voluntarily engage a gang of
ruffians to attack their fellow-merchants of a
neighbouring nation, to plunder them of their
property, and perhaps ruin them and their families, if they yield it ; or to wound, maim, and
murder them, if they endeavour to defend it.
Yet thefe things are done by Chriftian merchants,
whether a war be juft or unjuft ; and it can hardly
be juft on both fides. They are done by Englifh
and American merchants, who, neverthelefs,
complain of private theft, and hang by dozens
the thieves they have taught by their own example.

It

It is high time, for the fake of humanity, that a ftop were put to this enormity. The United States of America, though better fituated than any European nation to make profit by privateering (moft of the trade of Europe, with the Weft Indies, paffing before their doors), are, as far as in them lies, endeavouring to abolifh the practice, by offering, in all their treaties with other powers, an article, engaging folemnly, that, in cafe of future war, no privateer fhall be commiffioned on either fide ; and that unarmed merchant-fhips, on both fides, fhall purfue their voyages unmolefted*. This will be a happy improvement of the law

* This offer having been accepted by the late king of Pruffia, a treaty of amity and commerce was concluded between that monarch and the United States, containing the following humane, philanthropic article ; in the formation of which Dr. Franklin, as one of the American plenipotentiaries, was principally concerned, viz.

ART. XXIII.

If war fhould arife between the two contracting parties, the merchants of either country, then refiding in the other, fhall be allowed to remain nine months to collect their debts and fettle their affairs, and may depart freely, carrying off all their effects without moleftation or hindrance : and all women and children, fcholars of every faculty, cultivators of the earth, artifans, manufacturers, and fifhermen, unarmed and inhabiting unfortified towns, villages, or places, and in general all others whofe occupations are for the common fubfiftence and benefit of mankind, fhall be allowed to continue their refpective employments, and fhall not be molefted in their perfons, nor fhall their houfes or goods be burnt, or otherwife deftroyed, nor their fields wafted, by the armed force of the enemy into whofe power, by the events of war, they may happen to fall ; but if any thing is neceffary to be taken from them for the ufe of fuch armed force, the fame fhall be paid for at a reafonable price. And all merchant and trading veffels employed in exchanging the products of different places, and thereby rendering the neceffaries, conveniences, and comforts

law of nations. The humane and the juſt cannot but wiſh general ſucceſs to the propoſition.

With unchangeable eſteem and affection,

I am, my dear friend,

Ever yours.

forts of human life more eaſy to be obtained, and more gene ral, ſhall be allowed to paſs free and unmoleſted ; and neither of the contracting powers ſhall grant or iſſue any commiſſion to any private armed veſſels, empowering them to take or deſtroy ſuch trading veſſels, or interrupt ſuch commerce.

REMARKS

REMARKS CONCERNING THE SAVAGES OF
NORTH-AMERICA.

SAVAGES we call them, becaufe their
manners differ from ours, which we think the
perfection of civility; they think the fame of
theirs.

Perhaps, if we could examine the manners of
different nations with impartiality, we fhould find
no people fo rude as to be without any rules of
politenefs; nor any fo polite as not to have fome
remains of rudenefs.

The Indian men, when young, are hunters and
warriors; when old, counfellors; for all their
government is by the counfel or advice of the
fages; there is no force, there are no prifons, no
officers to compel obedience, or inflict punifhment.
Hence they generally ftudy oratory; the beft
fpeaker having the moft influence. The Indian
women till the ground, drefs the food, nurfe and
bring up the children, and preferve and hand
down to pofterity the memory of public tranfactions. Thefe employments of men and women
are accounted natural and honourable. Having
few artificial wants, they have abundance of leifure for improvement by converfation. Our
laborious manner of life, compared with theirs,
they efteem flavifh and bafe; and the learning on
which we value ourfelves, they regard as frivo-
lous and ufelefs. An inftance of this occurred at
the treaty of Lancafter, in Pennfylvania, anno
1744, between the government of Virginia and
the Six Nations. After the principal bufinefs was
fettled, the commiffioners from Virginia acquainted the Indians by a fpeech, that there was at Wil-
liamfburg

liamſburg a college, with a fund, for educating
Indian youth; and that if the chiefs of the Six
Nations would ſend down half a dozen of their
ſons to that college, the government would take
care that they ſhould be well provided for, and
inſtructed in all the learning of the white people.
It is one of the Indian rules of politeneſs not to
anſwer a public propoſition the ſame day that it is
made; they think it would be treating it as a light
matter; and that they ſhew it reſpect by taking
time to conſider it, as of a matter important.
They therefore deferred their anſwer till the day
following; when their ſpeaker began, by expreſſ-
ing their deep ſenſe of the kindneſs of the Virginia government, in making them that offer;
" for we know," ſays he, " that you highly
" eſteem the kind of learning taught in thoſe
" colleges, and that the maintenance of our
" young men, while with you, would be very
" expenſive to you. We are convinced, there-
" fore, that you mean to do us good by your
" propoſal; and we thank you heartily. But
" you who are wiſe muſt know, that different
" nations have different conceptions of things;
" and you will therefore not take it amiſs, if our
" ideas of this kind of education happen not to
" be the ſame with yours. We have had ſome
" experience of it: ſeveral of our young people
" were formerly brought up at the colleges of
" the northern provinces; they were inſtructed
" in all your ſciences; but when they came back
" to us, they were bad runners; ignorant of every
" means of living in the woods; unable to bear
" either cold or hunger; knew neither how to
" build a cabin, take a deer, or kill an enemy;
" ſpoke our language imperfectly; were there-
" fore neither fit for hunters, warriors, or coun-
" ſellors; they were totally good for nothing.
                                        " We

" We are however not the less obliged by your
" kind offer, though we decline accepting it;
" and to show our grateful sense of it, if the
" gentlemen of Virginia will send us a dozen of
" their sons, we will take great care of their edu-
" cation, instruct them in all we know, and make
" *men* of them."

Having frequent occasions to hold public councils, they have acquired great order and decency
in conducting them. The old men sit in the fore-
most ranks, the warriors in the next, and the
women and children in the hindmost. The business of the women is to take exact notice of what
passes, imprint it in their memories, for they
have no writing, and communicate it to their
children. They are the records of the council,
and they preserve tradition of the stipulations in
treaties a hundred years back; which, when we
compare with our writings, we always find exact.
He that would speak, rises. The rest observe a
profound silence. When he has finished, and sits
down, they leave him five or six minutes to recollect, that, if he has omitted any thing he intended
to say, or has any thing to add, he may rise again
and deliver it. To interrupt another, even in
common conversation, is reckoned highly inde-
cent. How different this is from the conduct of
a polite British House of Commons, where scarce
a day passes without some confusion, that makes
the speaker hoarse in calling *to order;* and how
different from the mode of conversation in many
polite companies of Europe, where, if you do
not deliver your sentence with great rapidity,
you are cut off in the middle of it by the impatient loquacity of those you converse with, and
never suffered to finish it!

The politeness of these savages in conversation,
is, indeed, carried to excess; since it does not

permit

permit them to contradict or deny the truth of what is afferted in their prefence. By this means they indeed avoid difputes; but then it becomes difficult to know their minds, or what impreffion you make upon them. The miffionaries who have attempted to convert them to Chriftianity, all complain of this as one of the great difficulties of their miffion. The Indians hear with patience the truths of the gofpel explained to them, and give their ufual tokens of affent and approbation: you would think they were convinced. No fuch matter. It is mere civility.

A Swedifh minifter having affembled the chiefs of the Safquehannah Indians, made a fermon to them, acquainting them with the principal hifto-rical facts on which our religion is founded; fuch as the fall of our firft parents by eating an apple; the coming of Chrift to repair the mifchief; his miracles and fuffering, &c.——When he had finifhed, an Indian orator ftood up to thank him. " What you have told us," fays he, " is all very " good. It is indeed bad to eat apples. It is " better to make them all into cyder. We are " much obliged by your kindnefs in coming fo " far, to tell us thofe things which you have " heard from your mothers. In return, I will " tell you fome of thofe we have heard from " ours.

" In the beginning, our fathers had only the " flefh of animals to fubfift on; and if their " hunting was unfuccefsful, they were ftarving. " Two of our young hunters having killed a deer, " made a fire in the woods to broil fome parts of " it. When they were about to fatisfy their hun- " ger, they beheld a beautiful young woman de- " fcend from the clouds, and feat herfelf on that " hill which you fee yonder among the Blue " Mountains. They faid to each other, it is a
" fpirit

" fpirit that perhaps has fmelt our broiling veni-
" fon, and wifhes to eat of it : let us offer fome
" to her. They prefented her with the tongue :
" fhe was pleafed with the tafte of it, and faid,
" Your kindnefs fhall be rewarded. Come to
" this place after thirteen moons, and you fhall
" find fomething that will be of great benefit in
" nourifhing you and your children to the lateft
" generations. They did fo, and to their fur-
" prife, found plants they had never feen before ;
" but which, from that ancient time, have been
" conftantly cultivated among us, to our great
" advantage. Where her right hand had touched
" the ground, they found maize; where her left
" hand had touched it they found kidney-beans;
" and where her backfide had fat on it, they
" found tobacco." The good miffionary, dif-
gufted with this idle tale, faid, " What I deliver-
" ed to you were facred truths ; but what you
" tell me is mere fable, fiction, and falfehood."
The Indian, offended, replied, " My brother, it
" feems your friends have not done you juftice
" in your education; they have not well inftruct-
" ed you in the rules of common civility. You
" faw that we, who underftand and practife thofe
" rules, believed all your ftories, why do you
" refufe to believe ours?"

When any of them come into our towns, our
people are apt to crowd round them, gaze upon
them, and incommode them where they defire to
be private ; this they efteem great rudenefs, and
the effect of the want of inftruction in the rules
of civility and good manners. " We have," fay
they, " as much curiofity as you, and when you
" come into our towns, we wifh for opportunities
" of looking at you; but for this purpofe we
" hide ourfelves behind bufhes where you are to

" pafs,

" pafs, and never intrude ourfelves into your
" company."

Their manner of entering one another's villages
has likewife its rules. It is reckoned uncivil in
travelling ftrangers to enter a village abruptly,
without giving notice of their approach. Therefore, as foon as they arrive within hearing, they
ftop and hollow, remaining there till invited to
enter. Two old men ufually come out to them,
and lead them in. There is in every village a
vacant dwelling, called the ftranger's houfe. Here
they are placed, while the old men go round
from hut to hut, acquainting the inhabitants that
ftrangers are arrived, who are probably hungry
and weary; and every one fends them what he
can fpare of victuals, and fkins to repofe on.
When the ftrangers are refrefhed, pipes and tobacco are brought; and then, but not before,
converfation begins, with enquiries who they are,
whither bound, what news, &c. and it ufually
ends with offers of fervice; if the ftrangers have
occafion of guides, or any neceffaries for continuing their journey; and nothing is exacted for
the entertainment.

The fame hofpitality, efteemed among them as
a principal virtue, is practifed by private perfons;
of which *Conrad Weifer*, our interpreter, gave me
the following inftance. He had been naturalized
among the Six Nations, and fpoke well the Mo-
huck language. In going through the Indian
country, to carry a meffage from our govenor to
the council at *Onondaga*, he called at the habita-
tion of *Canaffetego*, an old acquaintance, who embraced him, fpread furs for him to fit on, placed
before him fome boiled beans and venifon, and
mixed fome rum and water for his drink. When
he was well refrefhed, and had lit his pipe,
Canaffetego began to converfe with him : afked

how

how he had fared the many years since they had
seen each other, whence he then came, what occasioned the journey, &c. ,Conrad answered all
his questions; and when the discourse began to
flag, the Indian, to continue it, said, " Conrad,
" you have lived long among the white people,
" and know something of their customs; I have
" been sometimes at Albany, and have observed,
" that once in seven days they shut up their
" shops, and assemble all in the great house; tell
" me what it is for? What do they do there?"
" They meet there," says Conrad, " to hear and
" learn *good things.*" " I do not doubt," says the
Indian, " that they tell you so; they have told
" me the same: but I doubt the truth of what
" they say, and I will tell you my reasons. I
" went lately to Albany to sell my skins and buy
" blankets, knives, powder, rum, &c. You
" know I used generally to deal with Hans Han-
" son; but I was a little inclined this time to try
" some other merchants. However, I called first
" upon Hans, and asked him what he would
" give for beaver. He said he could not give
" more than four shillings a pound: but, says he,
" I cannot talk on business now; this is the day
" when we meet together to learn *good things,* and
" I am going to the meeting. So I thought to
" myself, since I cannot do any business to-day,
" I may as well go to the meeting too, and I went
" with him. There stood up a man in black,
" and began to talk to the people very angrily.
" I did not understand what he said; but per-
" ceiving that he looked much at me, and at
" Hanson, I imagined he was angry at seeing me
" there; so I went out, sat down near the house,
" struck fire, and lit my pipe, waiting till the
" meeting should break up. I thought too that
" the man had mentioned something of beaver,
" and

" and I fufpected it might be the fubject of their
" meeting. So when they came out I accofted
" my merchant. Well, Hans, fays I, I hope
" you have agreed to give more than four fhil-
" lings a pound." " No," fays he, " I cannot
" give fo much, I cannot give more than three
" fhillings and fixpence." I then fpoke to feve-
" ral other dealers, but they all fung the fame
" fong, three and fixpence, three and fixpence.
" This made it clear to me that my fufpicion
" was right; and that whatever they pretended
" of meeting to learn *good things*, the real pur-
" pofe was to confult how to cheat Indians in the
" price of beaver. Confider but a little, Conrad,
" and you muft be of my opinion. If they meet
" fo often to learn *good things*, they would cer-
" tainly have learned fome before this time.
" But they are ftill ignorant. You know our
" practice. If a white man, in travelling through
" our country, enters one of our cabins, we all
" treat him as I do you; we dry him if he is
" wet, we warm him if he is cold, and give him
" meat and drink, that he may allay his thirft
" and hunger; and we fpread foft furs for him
" to reft and fleep on: we demand nothing in
" return*. But if I go into a white man's houfe
" at Albany, and afk for victuals and drink,
" they fay, Where is your money; and if I have

---

* It is remarkable, that in all ages and countries, hofpitality has been allowed as the virtue of thofe, whom the civilized were pleafed to call Barbarians; the Greeks celebrated
the Scythians for it. The Saracens poffeffed it eminently;
and it is to this day the reigning virtue of the wild Arabs,
St. Paul too, in the relation of his voyage and fhipwreck, on
the ifland of Melita, fays, " The barbarous people fhewed
" us no little kindnefs; for they kindled a fire, and received
" us every one, becaufe of the prefent rain, and becaufe of
" the cold." This note is taken from a fmall collection of
Franklin's papers, printed for Dilly.

" none,

" none, they fay, Get out, you Indian dog.
" You fee they have not yet learned thofe little
" *good things* that we need no meetings to be in-
" ftructed in, becaufe our mothers taught them
" to us when we were children ; and therefore it
" is impoffible their meetings fhould be, as they
" fay, for any fuch purpofe, or have any fuch
" effect ; they are only to contrive *the cheating of*
" *Indians in the price of beaver.*"

TO

TO MR. DUBOURG,

CONCERNING THE DISSENSIONS BETWEEN ENGLAND AND AMERICA.

London, October 2, 1770.

I SEE with pleasure that we think pretty much alike on the subjects of English America. We of the colonies have never insisted that we ought to be exempt from contributing to the common expences necessary to support the prosperity of the empire. We only assert, that having parliaments of our own, and not having representatives in that of Great Britain, our parliaments are the only judges of what we can and what we ought to contribute in this case; and that the English parliament has no right to take our money without our consent. In fact the British empire is not a single state; it comprehends many; and though the parliament of Great-Britain has arrogated to itself the power of taxing the colonies, it has no more right to do so, than it has to tax Hanover. We have the same king, but not the same legislatures.

The dispute between the two countries has already lost England many millions sterling, which it has lost in its commerce, and America has in this respect been a proportionable gainer. This commerce consisted principally of superfluities; objects of luxury and fashion, which we can well do without; and the resolution we have formed of importing no more till our grievances are redressed, has enabled many of our infant manufactures to take root; and it will not be easy to

make

make our people abandon them in future, even should a connection more cordial then ever succeed the prefent troubles.—I have, indeed, no doubt that the parliament of England will finally abandon its prefent pretenfions, and leave us to the peaceable enjoyment of our rights and privileges.

B. FRANKLIN.

A Comparison of the Conduct of the Ancient JEWS, *and of the* ANTIFEDERALISTS *in the United States of* AMERICA.

A ZEALOUS advocate for the proposed Federal Constitution in a certain public assembly, said, that " the repugnance of a great part of mankind " to good government was such, that he believ- " ed, that if an angel from heaven was to bring " down a constitution formed there for our use, it " would nevertheless meet with violent oppositi- " on."—He was reproved for the supposed extravagance of the sentiment; and he did not justify it. —Probably it might not have immediately occurred to him that the experiment had been tried, and that the event was recorded in the most faithful of all histories, the Holy Bible; otherwise he might, as it seems to me, have supported his opinion by that unexceptionable authority.

The Supreme Being had been pleased to nourish up a single family, by continued acts of his attentive Providence, 'till it became a great people: and having rescued them from bondage by many miracles performed by his servant Moses, he personally delivered to that chosen servant, in presence of the whole nation, a constitution and code of laws for their observance; accompanied and sanctioned with promises of great rewards, and threats of severe punishments, as the consequence of their obedience or disobedience.

This constitution, though the Deity himself was to be at its head (and it is therefore called by political writers a Theocracy) could not be carried into execution but by the means of his ministers; Aaron and his sons were therefore commissioned

commiffioned to be, with Mofes, the firſt eſtabliſhed miniſtry of the new government.

One would have thought, that the appointment of men who had diſtinguiſhed themſelves
in procuring the liberty of their nation, and had
hazarded their lives in openly oppoſing the will
of a powerful monarch who would have retained
that nation in ſlavery, might have been an appointment acceptable to a grateful people; and
that a conſtitution, framed for them by the Deity
himſelf, might on that account have been ſecure
of an univerſal welcome reception. Yet there
were, in every one of the thirteen tribes, ſome
diſcontented, reſtleſs ſpirits, who were continually exciting them to reject the propoſed new government, and this from various motives.

Many ſtill retained an affection for Egypt, the
land of their nativity, and theſe, whenever they
felt any inconvenience or hardſhip, though the
natural and unavoidable effect of their change of
ſituation, exclaimed againſt their leaders as the
authors of their trouble; and were not only for
returning into Egypt, but for ſtoning their deli-
verers *. Thofe inclined to idolatry were diſ-
pleaſed that their golden calf was deſtroyed. Many of the chiefs thought the new conſtitution
might be injurious to their particular intereſts,
that the profitable places would be *engroffed by the
families and friends of Mofes and Aaron*, and others
equally well-born excluded †.—In Jofephus, and
the Talmud, we learn ſome particulars, not
ſo fully narrated in the ſcripture. We are there

---

* Numbers, chap. xiv.

† Numbers, chap. xvi. ver. 3. " And they gathered
" themſelves together againſt Mofes and againſt Aaron, and
" faid unto them, ye take too much upon you, feeing all the
" congregations are holy, every one of them,—wherefore
" then lift ye up yourſelves above the congregation."

told,

told, " that, Corah was ambitious of the prieſt-
" hood; and offended that it was conferred on
" Aaron; and this, as he ſaid, by the authority of
" Moſes only, *without the conſent of the people*. He
" accuſed Moſes of having, by various artifices,
" fraudulently obtained the government, and de-
" prived the people of their liberties; and of con-
" ſpiring with Aaron to perpetuate the tyranny
" in their family. Thus, though Corah's real
" motive was the ſupplanting of Aaron, he per-
" ſuaded the people that he meant only the pub-
" lic good; and they, moved by his inſinuations,
" began to cry out,—' Let us maintain the com-
" mon liberty of our *reſpective tribes*; we have
" freed ourſelves from the ſlavery impoſed upon
" us by the Egyptians, and ſhall we ſuffer our-
" ſelves to be made ſlaves by Moſes? If we muſt
" have a maſter, it were better to return to
" Pharaoh, who at leaſt fed us with bread and oni-
" ons, than to ſerve this new tyrant, who has
" brought us into danger of famine.' Then they
" called in queſtion the *reality of his conference*
" with God; and objected to the privacy of the
" meetings, and the preventing any of the peo-
" ple from being preſent at the colloquies, or even
" approaching the place, as grounds of great
" ſuſpicion. They accuſed Moſes alſo of *pecula-*
" *tion;* as embezzling part of the golden ſpoons
" and the ſilver chargers, that the princes had
" offered at the dedication of the altar *, and the
" offerings of gold by the common people †, as
" well as moſt of the poll tax ‡; and Aaron they
" accuſed of pocketing much of the gold of which
" he pretended to have made a molten calf. Be-
" ſides peculation, they charged Moſes with *am-*

* Numbers, chap. vii.
† Exodus, chapter xxxv. ver. 22.
‡ Numbers, chap. iii. and Exodus, chap. xxx.

" *bition,*

" *bition ;* to gratify which paſſion, he had, they
" ſaid, deeived the people, by promiſing to bring
" them to a land flowing with milk and honey ;
" inſtead of doing which, he had brought them
" *from* ſuch a land ; and that he thought light of
" all this miſchief, provided he could make him-
" ſelf an *abſolute prince **. That, to ſupport the
" new dignity with ſplendour in his family, the
" partial poll tax already levied and given to
" Aaron † was to be followed by a general one ‡,
" which would probably be augmented from
" time to time, if he were ſuffered to go on pro-
" mulgating new laws, on pretence of new occa-
" ſional revelations of the Divine Will, till their
" whole fortunes were devoured by that ariſto-
" cracy."

Moſes denied the charge of peculation ; and
his accuſers were deſtitute of proofs to ſupport it ;
though *facts,* if real, are in their nature capable
of proof. " I have not," ſaid he (with holy confidence in the preſence of God), " I have not ta-
" ken from this people the value of an aſs, nor
" done them any other injury." But his enemies had made the charge, and with ſome ſucceſs
among the populace ; for no kind of accuſation
is ſo readily made, or eaſily believed, by knaves,
as the accuſation of knavery.

In fine, no leſs than two hundred and fifty of
the principal men " famous in the congregation,
men of renown §," heading and exciting the mob,
worked them up to ſuch a pitch of phrenſy, that

* Numbers, chap. xvi. ver. 13. " Is it a ſmall thing that
" thou haſt brought us up out of a land flowing with milk
" and honey, to kill us in this wilderneſs, except thou make
" thyſelf altogether a prince over us ?"
† Numbers. chap. iii.
‡ Exodus, chap. xxx.
§ Numbers, chap. xvi.

they

they called out, stone 'em, stone 'em, and thereby secure our liberties; and let us choose other captains that may lead us back into Egypt, in cafe we do not succeed in reducing the Canaanites.

On the whole, it appears that the Israelites were a people jealous of their newly acquired liberty, which jealousy was in itself no fault; but that, when they suffered it to be worked upon by artful men, pretending public good, with nothing really in view but private interest, they were led to oppose the establishment of the new constitution, whereby they brought upon themselves much inconvenience and misfortune. It farther appears from the fame inestimable history, that when, after many ages, the constitution had become old and much abused, and an amendment of it was proposed, the populace as they had accused Moses of the ambition of making himself a prince, and cried out, stone him, stone him; so, excited by their high-priests and scribes, they exclaimed against the Messiah, that he aimed at becoming king of the Jews, and cried, crucify him, crucify him. From all which we may gather, that popular opposition to a public measure is no proof of its impropriety, even though the opposition be excited and headed by men of distinction.

To conclude, I beg I may not be understood to infer, that our general convention was divinely inspired when it formed the new federal constitution, merely because that constitution has been unreasonably and vehemently opposed: yet, I must own, I have so much faith in the general government of the world by Providence, that I can hardly conceive a transaction of such momentous importance to the welfare of millions now existing, and to exist in the posterity of a

great

great nation, fhould be fuffered to pafs with-out being in fome degree influenced, guided, and governed by that omnipotent, omnipre-fent and beneficent Ruler, in whom all inferi-or fpirits live, and move, and have their be-ing.

THE

THE INTERNAL STATE OF AMERICA:

BEING A TRUE DESCRIPTION OF THE INTEREST
AND POLICY OF THAT VAST CONTINENT.

THERE is a tradition, that, in the planting of
New-England, the firſt ſettlers met with many
difficulties and hardſhips; as is generally the caſe
when a civilized people attempt eſtabliſhing themſelves in a wilderneſs country. Being piouſly
diſpoſed, they ſought relief from Heaven, by
laying their wants and diſtreſſes before the Lord,
in frequent ſet days of faſting and prayer. Con-
ſtant meditation and diſcourſe on theſe ſubjects
kept their minds gloomy and diſcontented; and,
like the children of Iſrael, there were many diſpoſed to return to that Egypt which perſecution
had induced them to abandon. At length, when
it was propoſed in the aſſembly to proclaim another faſt, a farmer of plain ſenſe roſe, and remarked, that the inconveniencies they ſuffered,
and concerning which they had ſo often wearied
Heaven with their complaints, were not ſo great
as they might have expected, and were diminiſh-
ing every day as the colony ſtrengthened; that
the earth began to reward their labour, and to
furniſh liberally for their ſubſiſtence; that the
ſeas and rivers were found full of fiſh, the air
ſweet, the climate healthy; and, above all, that
they were there in the full enjoyment of liberty,
civil and religious: he therefore thought, that
reflecting and converſing on theſe ſubjects would
be more comfortable, as tending more to make
them contented with their ſituation; and that it
would

would be more becoming the gratitude they owed to the Divine Being, if, inftead of a faft, they fhould proclaim a thankfgiving. His advice was taken; and from that day to this they have, in every year, obferved circumftances of public felicity fufficient to furnifh employment for a thankfgiving day; which is therefore conftantly ordered and religioufly obferved.

I fee in the public newfpapers of different ftates frequent complaints of *hard times, deadnefs of trade, fcarcity of money*, &c. It is not my intention to affert or maintain that thefe complaints are entirely without foundation. There can be no country or nation exifting, in which there will not be fome people fo circumftanced as to find it hard to gain a livelihood; people who are not in the way of any profitable trade, and with whom money is fcarce, becaufe they have nothing to give in exchange for it; and it is always in the power of a fmall number to make a great clamour. But let us take a cool view of the general ftate of our affairs, and perhaps the profpect will appear lefs gloomy than has been imagined.

The great bufinefs of the continent is agriculture. For one artifan, or merchant, I fuppofe, we have at leaft one hundred farmers, by far the greateft part cultivators of their own fertile lands, from whence many of them draw not only food neceffary for their fubfiftence, but the materials of their clothing, fo as to need very few foreign fupplies; while they have a furplus of productions to difpofe of, whereby wealth is gradually accumulated. Such has been the goodnefs of Divine Providence to thefe regions, and fo favourable the climate, that, fince the three or four years of hardfhip in the firft fettlement of our fathers here, a famine or fcarcity has never been heard of among us; on the contrary, though

T

fome

some years may have been more, and others less
plentiful, there has always been provision enough
for ourselves, and a quantity to spare for expor-
tation. And although the crops of last year
were generally good, never was the farmer better
paid for the part he can spare commerce, as the
published price currents abundantly testify. The
lands he possesses are also continually rising in
value with the increase of population; and, on
the whole, he is enabled to give such good wages
to those who work for him, that all who are
acquainted with the old world must agree, that
in no part of it are the labouring poor so generally well fed, well clothed, well lodged, and
well paid, as in the United States of America.

If we enter the cities, we find that, since the
revolution, the owners of houses and lots of
ground have had their interest vastly augmented
in value; rents have risen to an astonishing height,
and thence encouragement to increase building,
which gives employment to an abundance of
workmen, as does also the increased luxury and
splendour of living of the inhabitants thus made
richer. These workmen all demand and obtain
much higher wages than any other part of the
world would afford them, and are paid in ready
money. This rank of people therefore do not,
or ought not, to complain of hard times; and
they make a very considerable part of the city
inhabitants.

At the distance I live from our American fish-
eries, I cannot speak of them with any degree of
certainty; but I have not heard that the labour
of the valuable race of men employed in them is
worse paid, or that they meet with less success,
than before the revolution. The whale-men indeed have been deprived of one market for their
oil; but another, I hear, is opening for them,
which

which it is hoped may be equally advantageous; and the demand is conſtantly increaſing for their ſpermaceti candles, which therefore bear a much higher price than formerly.

There remain the merchants and ſhopkeepers. Of theſe, though they make but a ſmall part of the whole nation, the number is conſiderable, too great indeed for the buſineſs they are employed in; for the conſumption of goods in every country has its limits; the faculties of the people, that is, their ability to buy and pay, is equal only to a certain quantity of merchandize. If merchants calculate amiſs on this proportion, and import too much, they will of courſe find the ſale dull for the overplus, and ſome of them will ſay that trade languiſhes. They ſhould, and doubtleſs will, grow wiſer by experience, and import leſs. If too many artificers in town, and farmers from the country, flattering themſelves with the idea of leading eaſier lives, turn ſhopkeepers, the whole natural quantity of that buſineſs divided among them all may afford too ſmall a ſhare for each, and occaſion complaints that trading is dead; theſe may alſo ſuppoſe that it is owing to ſcarcity of money, while, in fact, it is not ſo much from the fewneſs of buyers, as from the exceſſive number of ſellers, that the miſchief ariſes; and, if every ſhopkeeping farmer and mechanic would return to the uſe of his plough and working tools, there would remain of widows, and other women, ſhopkeepers ſufficient for the buſineſs, which might then afford them a comfortable maintenance.

Whoever has travelled through the various parts of Europe, and obſerved how ſmall is the proportion of the people in affluence or eaſy circumſtances there, compared with thoſe in poverty and miſery; the few rich and haughty landlords, the

multitude

multitude of poor, abject, rack-rented, tythe-paying tenants, and half-paid and half-ftarved ragged labourers ; and views here the happy mediocrity that fo generally prevails throughout thefe ftates, where the cultivator works for himfelf, and fupports his family in decent plenty ; will, methinks, fee abundant reafon to blefs Divine Providence for the evident and great difference in our favour, and be convinced that no nation known to us enjoys a greater fhare of human felicity.

It is true, that in fome of the ftates there are parties and difcords ; but let us look back, and afk if we were ever without them ? Such will exift wherever there is liberty ; and perhaps they help to preferve it. By the collifion of different fentiments, fparks of truth are ftruck out, and political light is obtained. The different factions, which at prefent divide us, aim all at the public good ; the differences are only about the various modes of promoting it. Things, actions, meafures, and objects of all kinds, prefent themfelves to the minds of men in fuch a variety of lights, that it is not poffible we fhould all think alike at the fame time on every fubject, when hardly the fame man retains at all times the fame ideas of it. Parties are therefore the common lot of humanity ; and ours are by no means more mifchievous or lefs beneficial than thofe of other countries, nations, and ages, enjoying in the fame degree the great blefling of political liberty.

Some indeed among us are not fo much grieved for the prefent ftate of our affairs, as apprehenfive for the future. The growth of luxury alarms them, and they think we are from that alone in the high road to ruin. They obferve, that no revenue is fufficient without œconomy, and that the moft plentiful income of a whole people from
the

the natural productions of their country may be diffipated in vain and needlefs expences, and poverty be introduced in the place of affluence.— This may be poffible. It however rarely happens: for there feems to be in every nation a greater proportion of induftry and frugality, which tend to enrich, than of idlenefs and prodigality, which occafion poverty; fo that upon the whole there is a continual accumulation.   Reflect what Spain, Gaul, Germany, and Britain were in the time of the Romans, inhabited by people little richer than our favages, and confider the wealth they at prefent poffefs, in numerous well-built cities, improved farms, rich moveables, magazines ftocked with valuable manufactures, to fay nothing of plate, jewels, and coined money; and all this, notwithftanding their bad, wafteful, plundering governments, and their mad, deftructive wars; and yet luxury and extravagant living has never fuffered much reftraint in thofe countries. Then confider the great proportion of induftrious frugal farmers inhabiting the interior parts of thefe American ftates, and of whom the body of our nation confifts, and judge whether it is poffible that the luxury of our fea-ports can be fufficient to ruin fuch a country.—If the importation of foreign luxuries could ruin a people, we fhould probably have been ruined long ago; for the Britifh nation claimed a right, and practifed it, of importing among us not only the fuperfluities of their own production, but thofe of every nation under heaven; we bought and confumed them, and yet we flourifhed and grew rich. At prefent our independent governments may do what we could not then do, difcourage by heavy duties, or prevent by heavy prohibitions, fuch importations, and thereby grow richer;—if, indeed, which may admit of difpute, the defire of

adorning

adorning ourfelves with fine clothes, poffeffing fine furniture, with elegant houfes, &c. is not, by ftrongly inciting to labour and induftry, the occafion of producing a greater value than is con- fumed in the gratification of that defire.

The agriculture and fifheries of the United States are the great fources of our increafing wealth. He that puts a feed into the earth is re- compenced, perhaps, by receiving forty out of it; and he who draws a fifh out of our water, draws up a piece of filver.

Let us (and there is no doubt but we fhall) be attentive to thefe, and then the power of rivals, with all their reftraining and prohibiting acts, cannot much hurt us. We are fons of the earth and feas, and, like Antæus in the fable, if in wreftling with a Hercules we now and then receive a fall, the touch of our parents will communicate to us frefh ftrength and vigour to renew the conteft.

INFOR-

INFORMATION TO THOSE WHO WOULD REMOVE TO AMERICA.

MANY perfons in Europe having, directly or by letters, expreffed to the writer of this, who is well acquainted with North-America, their defire of tranfporting and eftablifhing themfelves in that country; but who appear to him to have formed, through ignorance, miftaken ideas and expectations of what is to be obtained there; he thinks it may be ufeful, and prevent inconvenient, expenfive, and fruitlefs removals and voyages of improper perfons, if he gives fome clearer and truer notions of that part of the world than appear to have hitherto prevailed.

He finds it is imagined by numbers, that the inhabitants of North-America are rich, capable of rewarding, and difpofed to reward, all forts of ingenuity; that they are at the fame time ignorant of all the fciences, and confequently that ftrangers, poffeffing talents in the belles-lettres, fine arts, &c. muft be highly efteemed, and fo well paid as to become eafily rich themfelves; that there are alfo abundance of profitable offices to be difpofed of, which the natives are not qualified to fill; and that having few perfons of family among them, ftrangers of birth muft be greatly refpected, and of courfe eafily obtain the beft of thofe offices, which will make all their fortunes: that the governments too, to encourage emigrations from Europe, not only pay the expence of perfonal tranfportation, but give lands gratis to ftrangers, with negroes to work for them, utenfils of hufbandry, and ftocks of cattle. Thefe are all wild imaginations; and thofe who go to America with expectations

founded

founded upon them, will furely find themfelves difappointed.

The truth is, that though there are in that country few people fo miferable as the poor of Europe, there are alfo very few that in Europe would be called rich : it is rather a general happy mediocrity that prevails. There are few great proprietors of the foil, and few tenants; moft people cultivate their own lands, or follow fome handicraft or merchandife; very few rich enough to live idly upon their rents or incomes, or to pay the high prices given in Europe for painting, ftatues, architecture, and the other works of art that are more curious than ufeful. Hence the natural geniufes that have arifen in America, with fuch talents, have uniformly quitted that country for Europe, where they can be more fuitably rewarded. It is true that letters and mathematical knowledge are in efteem there, but they are at the fame time more common than is apprehended; there being already exifting nine colleges, or univerfities, viz. four in New-England, and one in each of the provinces of New-York, New-Jerfey, Pennfylvania, Maryland, and Virginia, all furnifhed with learned profeffors ; befides a number of fmaller academies : thefe educate many of their youth in the languages, and thofe fciences that qualify men for the profeffions of divinity, law, or phyfic. Strangers indeed are by no means excluded from exercifing thofe profeffions; and the quick increafe of inhabitants every where gives them a chance of employ, which they have in common with the natives. Of civil offices, or employments, there are few; no fuperfluous ones as in Europe; and it is a rule eftablifhed in fome of the ftates, that no office fhould be fo profitable as to make it defirable. The 36th article of the conftitution of Pennfylvania

vania runs exprefsly in thefe words : " As every
" freeman, to preferve his independence (if he
" has not a fufficient eftate), ought to have fome
" profeffion, calling, trade, or farm, whereby
" he may honeftly fubfift, there can be no necef-
" fity for, nor ufe in, eftablifhing offices of pro-
" fit; the ufual effects of which are dependence
" and fervility, unbecoming freemen, in the
" poffeffors and expectants; faction, contention,
" corruption and diforder among the people.
" Wherefore, whenever an office, through in-
" creafe of fees or otherwife, becomes fo profita-
" ble as to occafion many to apply for it, the
" profits ought to be leffened by the legiflature."
These ideas prevailing more or lefs in all the
United States, it cannot be worth any man's
while, who has a means of living at home, to
expatriate himfelf in hopes of obtaining a profitable civil office in America; and as to military
offices, they are at an end with the war, the armies being difbanded. Much lefs is it advifeable
for a perfon to go thither, who has no other
quality to recommend him but his birth. In
Europe it has indeed its value ; but it is a commodity that cannot be carried to a worfe market
than to that of America, where people do not
enquire concerning a ftranger, *What is he?* but
What can he do? If he has any ufeful art he is
welcome; and if he exercifes it, and behaves
well, he will be refpected by all that know him ;
but a mere man of quality, who on that account
wants to live upon the public by fome office or
falary, will be defpifed and difregarded. The
hufbandman is in honour there, and even the
mechanic, becaufe their employments are ufeful.
The people have a faying, that God Almighty is
himfelf a mechanic, the greateft in the univerfe;
and he is refpected and admired more for the
variety,

variety, ingenuity, and utility of his handiworks, than for the antiquity of his family. They are pleafed with the obfervation of a negro, and frequently mention it, that Boccarorra (meaning the white man) make de black man workee, make de horfe workee, make de ox workee, make ebery ting workee; only de hog. He de hog, no workee; he eat, he drink, he walk about, he go to fleep when he pleafe, he libb like a gentleman. According to thefe opinions of the Americans, one of them would think himfelf more obliged to a genealogift, who could prove for him that his anceftors and relations for ten generations had been ploughmen, fmiths, carpenters, turners, weavers, tanners, or even fhoemakers, and confequently that they were ufeful members of fociety; than if he could only prove that they were gentlemen, doing nothing of value, but living idly on the labour of others, mere *fruges confumere nati* *, and otherwife *good* for *nothing*, till by their death their eftates, like the carcafe of the negro's gentleman-hog, come to be *cut up*.

With regard to encouragements for ftrangers from government, they are really only what are derived from good laws and liberty. Strangers are welcome, becaufe there is room enough for them all, and therefore the old inhabitants are not jealous of them ; the laws protect them fufficiently, fo that they have no need of the patronage of great men; and every one will enjoy fecurely the profits of his induftry. But if he does not bring a fortune with him, he muft work and be induftrious to live. One or two years refidence give him all the rights of a citizen;

---

* . . . . born

Merely to eat up the corn. Watts.

but

but the government does not at prefent, whatever it may have done in former times, hire
people to become fettlers, by paying their paffages, giving land, negroes, utenfils, ftock, or
any other kind of emolument whatfoever. In
fhort, America is the land of labour, and by no
means what the Englifh call *Lubberland*, and the
French *Pays de Cocagne*, where the ftreets are
faid to be paved with half-peck loaves, the houfes
tiled with pancakes, and where the fowls fly
about ready roafted, crying, *Come eat me!*

Who then are the kind of perfons to whom
an emigration to America may be advantageous?
And what are the advantages they may reafona-
bly expect?

Land being cheap in that country, from the
vaft forefts ftill void of inhabitants, and not likely
to be occupied in an age to come, infomuch that
the propriety of an hundred acres of fertile foil
full of wood may be obtained near the frontiers,
in many places, for eight or ten guineas, hearty
young labouring men, who underftand the hufbandry of corn and cattle, which is nearly the
fame in that country as in Europe, may eafily
eftablifh themfelves there. A little money faved
of the good wages they receive there while they
work for others, enables them to buy the land
and begin their plantation, in which they are
affifted by the good-will of their neighbours, and
fome credit. Multitudes of poor people from
England, Ireland, Scotland, and Germany, have
by this means in a few years become wealthy
farmers, who in their own countries, where all
the lands are fully occupied, and the wages of
labour low, could never have emerged from the
mean condition wherein they were born.

From the falubrity of the air, the healthinefs
of the climate, the plenty of good provifions,
and

and the encouragement to early marriages, by the certainty of fubfiftence in cultivating the earth, the increafe of inhabitants by natural generation is very rapid in America, and becomes ftill more fo by the acceffion of ftrangers ; hence there is a continual demand for more artifans of all the neceffary and ufeful kinds, to fupply thofe cultivators of the earth with houfes, and with furniture and utenfils of the groffer forts, which cannot fo well be brought from Europe. Tolerably good workmen in any of thofe mechanic arts, are fure to find employ, and to be well paid for their work, there being no reftraints preventing ftrangers from exercifing any art they underftand, nor any permiffion neceffary. If they are poor, they begin firft as fervants or journeymen ; and if they are fober, induftrious, and frugal, they foon become mafters, eftablifh themfelves in bufinefs, marry, raife families, and become refpectable citizens.

Alfo, perfons of moderate fortunes and capitals, who having a number of children to provide for, are defirous of bringing them up to induftry, and to fecure eftates for their pofterity, have opportunities of doing it in America, which Europe does not afford. There they may be taught and practife profitable mechanic arts, without incurring difgrace on that account; but on the contrary acquiring refpect by fuch abilities. There fmall capitals laid out in lands, which daily become more valuable by the increafe of people, afford a folid profpect of ample fortunes thereafter for thofe children. The writer of this has known feveral inftances of large tracts of land, bought on what was then the frontier of Pennfylvania, for ten pounds per hundred acres, which, after twenty years, when the fettlements had been extended far beyond them,

fold

fold readily, without any improvement made upon them for three pounds per acre. The acre in America is the fame with the Englifh acre, or the acre of Normandy.

Thofe who defire to underftand the ftate of government in America, would do well to read the conftitutions of the feveral ftates, and the articles of confederation that bind the whole together for general purpofes, under the direction of one affembly, called the Congrefs. Thefe conftitutions have been printed, by order of Congrefs, in America; two editions of them have alfo been printed in London; and a good tranflation of them into French, has lately been publifhed at Paris.

Several of the princes of Europe having of late, from an opinion of advantage to arife by producing all commodities and manufactures within their own dominions, fo as to diminifh or render ufelefs their importations, have endeavoured to entice workmen from other countries, by high falaries, privileges, &c. Many perfons pretending to be fkilled in various great manufactures, imagining that America muft be in want of them, and that the Congrefs would probably be difpofed to imitate the princes above mentioned, have propofed to go over, on condition of having their paffages paid, lands given, falaries appointed, exclufive privileges for terms of years, &c. Such perfons, on reading the articles of confederation, will find that the Congrefs have no power committed to them, or money put into their hands, for fuch purpofes; and that if any fuch encouragement is given, it muft be by the government of fome feparate ftate. This, however, has rarely been done in America; and when it has been done, it has rarely fucceeded, fo as to eftablifh a manufacture,

facture, which the country was not yet fo ripe for as to encourage private perfons to fet it up; labour being generally too dear there, and hands difficult to be kept together, every one defiring to be a mafter, and the cheapnefs of land inclining many to leave trades for agriculture. Some indeed have met with fuccefs, and are carried on to advantage; but they are generally fuch as require only a few hands, or wherein great part of the work is performed by machines. Goods that are bulky, and of fo fmall value as not well to bear the expence of freight, may often be made cheaper in the country than they can be imported; and the manufacture of fuch goods will be profitable wherever there is a fufficient demand. The farmers in America produce indeed a good deal of wool and flax; and none is exported, it is all worked up; but it is in the way of domeftic manufacture, for the ufe of the family. The buying up quantities of wool and flax, with the defign to employ fpinners, weavers, &c. and form great eftablifhments, producing quantities of linen and woollen goods for fale, has been feveral times attempted in different provinces; but thofe projects have generally failed, goods of equal value being imported cheaper. And when the governments have been folicited to fupport fuch fchemes by encouragements, in money, or by impofing duties on importation of fuch goods, it has been generally refufed, on this principle, that if the country is ripe for the manufacture, it may be carried on by private perfons to advantage; and if not, it is a folly to think of forcing nature. Great eftablifhments of manufacture, require great numbers of poor to do the work for fmall wages; thofe poor are to be found in Europe, but will not be found in America, till the lands are all taken up and cultivated, and the

excefs

excefs of people who cannot get land want employment. The manufacture of filk, they fay, is natural in France, as that of cloth in England, becaufe each country produces in plenty the firft material : but if England will have a manufacture of filk as well as that of cloth, and France of cloth as well as that of filk, thefe unnatural operations muft be fupported by mutual prohibitions, or high duties on the importation of each other's goods ; by which means the workmen are enabled to tax the home confumer by greater prices, while the higher wages they receive make them neither happier nor richer, fince they only drink more and work lefs. Therefore the governments in America do nothing to encourage fuch projects. The people, by this means, are not impofed on either by the merchant or mechanic : if the merchant demands too much profit on imported fhoes, they buy of the fhoemaker ; and if he afks too high a price, they take them of the merchant : thus the two profeffions are checks on each other. The fhoemaker, however, has, on the whole, a confiderable profit upon his labour in America, beyond what he had in Europe, as he can add to his price a fum nearly equal to all the expences of freight and commiffion, rifque or infurance, &c. neceffarily charged by the merchant. And the cafe is the fame with the workmen in every other mechanic art. Hence it is, that artifans generally live better and more eafily in America than in Europe ; and fuch as are good œconomifts make a comfortable provifion for age, and for their children. Such may, therefore, remove with advantage to America.

In the old long-fettled countries of Europe, all arts, trades, profeffions, farms, &c. are fo full, that it is difficult for a poor man who has children to place them where they may gain, or learn to
gain,

gain, a decent livelihood. The artifans, who fear creating future rivals in bufinefs, refufe to take apprentices, but upon conditions of money, maintenance, or the like, which the parents are unable to comply with. Hence the youth are dragged up in ignorance of every gainful art, and obliged to become foldiers, or fervants, or thieves, for a fubfiftence. In America, the rapid increafe of inhabitants takes away that fear of rivalfhip, and artifans willingly receive apprentices from the hope of profit by their labour, during the remainder of the time ftipulated, after they fhall be inftructed. Hence it is eafy for poor families to get their children inftructed; for the artifans are fo defirous of apprentices, that many of them will even give money to the parents, to have boys from ten to fifteen years of age bound apprentices to them, till the age of twenty-one; and many poor parents have, by that means, on their arrival in the country, raifed money enough to buy land fufficient to eftablifh themfelves, and to fubfift the reft of their family by agriculture. Thefe contracts for apprentices are made before a magiftrate, who regulates the agreement according to reafon and juftice; and having in view the formation of a future ufeful citizen, obliges the mafter to engage by a written indenture, not only that, during the time of fervice ftipulated, the apprentice fhall be duly provided with meat, drink, apparel, wafhing, and lodging, and at its expiration with a complete new fuit of clothes, but alfo that he fhall be taught to read, write, and caft accounts; and that he fhall be well inftructed in the art or profeffion of his mafter, or fome other, by which he may afterwards gain a livelihood, and be able in his turn to raife a family. A copy of this indenture is given to the apprentice or his friends, and the magiftrate keeps
a record

a record of it, to which recourse may be had, in case of failure by the master in any point of performance. This desire among the masters to have more hands employed in working for them, induces them to pay the passages of young persons, of both sexes, who, on their arrival, agree to serve them one, two, three, or four years; those who have already learned a trade, agreeing for a shorter term, in proportion to their skill, and the consequent immediate value of their service; and those who have none, agreeing for a longer term, in consideration of being taught an art their poverty would not permit them to acquire in their own country.

The almost general mediocrity of fortune that prevails in America, obliging its people to follow some business for subsistence, those vices that arise usually from idleness, are in a great measure prevented. Industry and constant employment are great preservatives of the morals and virtue of a nation. Hence bad examples to youth are more rare in America, which must be a comfortable consideration to parents. To this may be truly added, that serious religion, under its various denominations, is not only tolerated, but respected and practised. Atheism is unknown there; infidelity rare and secret; so that persons may live to a great age in that country without having their piety shocked by meeting with either an atheist or an infidel. And the Divine Being seems to have manifested his approbation of the mutual forbearance and kindness with which the different sects treat each other, by the remarkable prosperity with which he has been pleased to favour the whole country.

U   FINAL

FINAL SPEECH OF DR. FRANKLIN IN THE
LATE FEDERAL CONVENTION *.

MR. PRESIDENT,

I CONFESS that I do not entirely approve of
this conftitution at prefent: but, Sir, I am not fure
I fhall never approve it; for having lived fo long,
I have experienced many inftances of being obliged by better information, or fuller confideration, to change opinions even on important fubjects, which I once thought right, but found to
be otherwife. It is, therefore, that the older I
grow, the more apt I am to doubt my own
judgment, and to pay more refpect to the judgment of others. Moft men, indeed, as well as
moft fects in religion, think themfelves in poffeffion of all truth, and that whenever others differ
from them, it is fo far error. Steele, a proteftant,
in a dedication, tells the pope, that " the only
" difference between our two churches, in their
" opinions of the certainty of their doctrines, is,
" the Romifh church is infallible, and the church
" of England never in the wrong." But, though
many private perfons think almoft as highly of
their own infallibility as of that of their fect, few
exprefs it fo naturally as a certain French lady,
who, in a little difpute with her fifter, faid, I
don't know how it happens, fifter, but I meet
with nobody but myfelf that is always in the right.
Il n'y a que moi qui a toujours raifon. In thefe fentiments, Sir, I agree to this conftitution, with all

* Our reafons for afcribing this fpeech to Dr. Franklin,
are its internal evidence, and its having appeared with his
name, during his life-time, uncontradicted, in an American
periodical publication.

its faults, if they are fuch; becaufe I think a general government neceffary for us, and there is
no form of government but what may be a bleffing, if well adminiftered; and I believe farther,
that this is likely to be well adminiftered for a
courfe of years, and can only end in defpotifm, as
other forms have done before it, when the people
fhall become fo corrupted as to need defpotic government, being incapable of any other. I doubt,
too, whether any other convention we can obtain, may be able to make a better conftitution.
For when you affemble a number of men, to have
the advantage of their joint wifdom, you inevitably affemble with thofe men, all their prejudices,
their paffions, their errors of opinion, their local
interefts, and their felfifh views. From fuch an
affembly can a perfect production be expected? It
therefore aftonifhes me, Sir, to find this fyftem
approaching fo near to perfection as it does; and
I think it will aftonifh our enemies, who are waiting with confidence, to hear that our councils are
confounded, like thofe of the builders of Babylon,
and that our ftates are on the point of feparation,
only to meet hereafter for the purpofe of cutting
each other's throats.

Thus I confent, Sir, to this conftitution, becaufe I expect no better, and becaufe I am not
fure that this is not the beft. The opinions I have
had of its errors, I facrifice to the public good.
I have never whifpered a fyllable of them abroad.
Within thefe walls they were born; and here they
fhall die. If every one of us, in returning to our
conftituents, were to report the objections he has
had to it, and endeavour to gain partifans in fupport of them, we might prevent its being generally received, and thereby lofe all the falutary
effects and great advantages refulting naturally in
our favour among foreign nations, as well as

U 2   among

among ourfelves, from our real or apparent unanimity. Much of the ftrength and efficiency of
any government, in procuring and fecuring happinefs to the people, depends on opinion ; on the
general opinion of the goodnefs of that government, as well as of the wifdom and integrity of
its governors.

I hope, therefore, that for our own fakes as a
part of the people, and for the fake of our pofterity, we fhall act heartily and unanimoufly in re-
commending this conftitution, wherever our influence may extend, and turn our future thoughts
and endeavours to the means of having it well adminiftered.

On the whole, Sir, I cannot help expreffing a
wifh, that every member of the convention, who
may ftill have objections, would with me, on
this occafion, doubt a little of his own infallibility,
and, to make manifeft our unanimity, put his
name to this inftrument.

[The motion was then made for adding the laft
formula, viz.

Done in Convention, by the unanimous confent, &c. : which was agreed to, and added accordingly.]

SKETCH

SKETCH OF AN ENGLISH SCHOOL:

FOR THE CONSIDERATION OF THE TRUSTEES OF
THE PHILADELPHIA ACADEMY *.

I T is expected that every fcholar to be admitted
into this fchool, be at leaft able to pronounce and
divide the fyllables in reading, and to write a legible hand. None to be received that are under
years of age.

FIRST, OR LOWEST CLASS.

Let the firft clafs learn the Englifh Grammar
rules, and at the fame time let particular care be
taken to improve them in orthography. Perhaps
the latter is beft done by pairing the fcholars; two
of thofe neareft equal in their fpelling to be put
together. Let thefe ftrive for victory; each pro-
pounding ten words every day to the other to be
fpelled. He that fpells truly moft of the other's
words, is victor for that day; he that is victor
moft days in a month, to obtain a prize, a pretty
neat book of fome kind, ufeful in their future
ftudies. This method fixes the attention of children extremely to the orthography of words, and
makes them good fpellers very early. It is a
fhame for a man to be fo ignorant of this little
art, in his own language, as to be perpetually
confounding words of like found and different
fignifications; the confcioufnefs of which defect

---

* This piece did not come to hand till the volume had been
fome time at the prefs. This was the cafe alfo with feveral
other papers, and muft be our apology for any defect that
may appear in the arrangement.

makes

makes fome men, otherwife of good learning and underftanding, averfe to writing even a common letter.

Let the pieces read by the fcholars in this clafs be fhort; fuch as Croxal's fables and little ftories. In giving the leffon, let it be read to them; let the meaning of the difficult words in it be explained to them; and let them con over by themfelves before they are called to read to the mafter or ufher; who is to take particular care that they do not read too faft, and that they duly obferve the ftops and paufes. A vocabulary of the moft ufual difficult words might be formed for their ufe, with explanations; and they might daily get a few of thofe words and explanations by heart, which would a little exercife their memories; or at leaft they might write a number of them in a fmall book for the purpofe, which would help to fix the meaning of thofe words in their minds, and at the fame time furnifh every one with a little dictionary for his future ufe.

THE

THE SECOND CLASS

TO be taught reading with attention, and with proper modulations of the voice; according to the sentiment and the subject.

Some short pieces, not exceeding the length of a Spectator, to be given this class for lessons (and some of the easier Spectators would be very suitable for the purpose). These lessons might be given every night as tasks; the scholars to study them against the morning. Let it then be required of them to give an account, first of the parts of speech, and construction of one or two sentences. This will oblige them to recur frequently to their grammar, and fix its principal rules in their memory. Next, of the intention of the writer, or the scope of the piece, the meaning of each sentence, and of every uncommon word. This would early acquaint them with the meaning and force of words, and give them that most necessary habit, of reading with attention.

The master then to read the piece with the proper modulations of voice, due emphasis, and suitable action, where action is required; and put the youth on imitating his manner.

Where the author has used an expression not the best, let it be pointed out; and let his beauties be particularly remarked to the youth.

Let the lessons for reading be varied, that the youth may be made acquainted with good styles of all kinds in prose and verse, and the proper manner of reading each kind—sometimes a well-told story, a piece of a sermon, a general's speech to his soldiers, a speech in a tragedy, some part

of

of a comedy, an ode, a satire, a letter, blank verse, Hudibrastic, heroic, &c. But let such lessons be chosen for reading, as contain some useful instruction, whereby the understanding or morals of the youth may at the same time be improved.

It is required that they should first study and understand the lessons, before they are put upon reading them properly to which end each boy should have an English dictionary, to help him over difficulties. When our boys read English to us, we are apt to imagine they understand what they read, because we do, and because it is their mother tongue. But they often read, as parrots speak, knowing little or nothing of the meaning. And it is impossible a reader should give the due modulation to his voice, and pronounce properly, unless his understanding goes before his tongue, and makes him master of the sentiment. Accustoming boys to read aloud what they do not first understand, is the cause of those even set tones so common among readers, which, when they have once got a habit of using, they find so difficult to correct; by which means, among fifty readers we scarcely find a good one. For want of good reading, pieces published with a view to influence the minds of men, for their own or the public benefit, lose half their force. Were there but one good reader in a neighbourhood, a public orator might be heard throughout a nation with the same advantages, and have the same effect upon his audience, as if they stood within the reach of his voice.

THE

THE THIRD CLASS

TO be taught speaking properly and gracefully; which is near a-kin to good reading, and naturally follows it in the studies of youth. Let the scholars of this class begin with learning the elements of rhetoric from some short system, so as to be able to give an account of the most useful tropes and figures. Let all their bad habits of speaking, all offences against good grammar, all corrupt or foreign accents, and all improper phrases, be pointed out to them. Short speeches from the Roman or other history, or from the parliamentary debates, might be got by heart, and delivered with the proper action, &c. Speeches and scenes in our best tragedies and comedies (avoiding every thing that could injure the morals of youth) might likewise be got by rote, and the boys exercised in delivering or acting them; great care being taken to form their manner after the truest models.

For their farther improvement, and a little to vary their studies, let them now begin to read history, after having got by heart a short table of the principal epochas in chronology. They may begin with Rollin's ancient and Roman histories, and proceed at proper hours, as they go through the subsequent classes, with the best histories of our own nation and colonies. Let emulation be excited among the boys, by giving, weekly, little prizes, or other small encouragements to those who are able to give the best account of what they have read, as to times, places, names of persons, &c. This will make them read with attention, and imprint the history well in their memories.

In

In remarking on the hiſtory, the maſter will have fine opportunities of inſtilling inſtructions of various kinds, and improving the morals, as well as the underſtandings, of youth.

The natural and mechanic hiſtory, contained in the *Spectacle de la Nature*, might alſo be begun in this claſs, and continued through the ſubſequent claſſes, by other books of the ſame kind; for, next to the knowledge of duty, this kind of knowledge is certainly the moſt uſeful, as well as the moſt entertaining. The merchant may thereby be enabled better to underſtand many commodities in trade; the handicraftſman to improve his buſineſs by new inſtruments, mixtures and materials; and frequently hints are given for new manufactures, or new methods of improving land, that may be ſet on foot greatly to the advantage of a country.

THE

THE FOURTH CLASS

TO be taught compofition. Writing one's own language well, is the next neceffary accomplifhment after good fpeaking. It is the writingmafter's bufinefs to take care that the boys make fair characters, and place them ftraight and even in the lines : but to form their ftyle, and even to take care that the ftops and capitals are properly difpofed, is the part of the Englifh mafter. The boys fhould be put on writing letters to each other on any common occurrences, and on various fubjects, imaginary bufinefs, &c. containing little ftories, accounts of their late reading, what parts of authors pleafe them, and why ; letters of congratulation, of compliment, of requeft, of thanks, of recommendation, of admonition, of confolation, of expoftulation, excufe, &c. In thefe they fhould be taught to exprefs themfelves clearly, concifely and naturally, without affected words or high-flown phrafes. All their letters to pafs through the mafter's hand, who is to point out the faults, advife the corrections, and commend what he finds right. Some of the beft letters publifhed in our own language, as Sir William Temple's, thofe of Pope and his friends, and fome others, might be fet before the youth as models, their beauties pointed out and explained by the mafter, the letters themfelves tranfcribed by the fcholar.

Dr. Johnfon's *Ethices Elementa*, or Firft Principles of Morality, may now be read by the fcholars, and explained by the mafter, to lay a folid foundation of virtue and piety in their minds.

And

And as this clafs continues the reading of hiftory, let them now, at proper hours, receive fome farther inftruction in chronology, and in that part of geography (from the mathematical mafter) which is neceffary to underftand the maps and globes. They fhould alfo be acquainted with the modern names of the places they find mentioned in ancient writers. The exercifes of good reading, and proper fpeaking, ftill continued at fuitable times.

THE

THE FIFTH CLASS.

TO improve the youth in compofition, they may now, befides continuing to write letters, begin to write little effays in profe, and fometimes in verfe; not to make them poets, but for this reafon, that nothing acquaints a lad fo fpeedily with variety of expreffion, as the neceffity of finding fuch words and phrafes as will fuit the meafure, found and rhime of verfe, and at the fame time well exprefs the fentiment. Thefe effays fhould all pafs under the mafter's eye, who will point out their faults, and put the writer on correcting them. Where the judgment is not ripe enough for forming new effays, let the fentiments of a Spectator be given, and required to be clothed in the fcholar's own words; or the circumftances of fome good ftory; the fcholar to find expreffion. Let them be put fometimes on abridging a paragraph of a diffufe author: fometimes on dilating or amplifying what is wrote more clofely. And now let Dr. Johnfon's *Noetica*, or Firft Principles of Human Knowledge, containing a logic, or art of reafoning, &c. be read by the youth, and the difficulties that may occur to them be explained by the mafter. The reading of hiftory, and the exercifes of good reading and juft fpeaking, ftill continued.

THE SIXTH CLASS.

IN this clafs, befides continuing the ftudies of the preceding in hiftory, rhetoric, logic, moral and natural philofophy, the beft Englifh authors may be read and explained ; as Tillotfon, Milton, Locke, Addifon, Pope, Swift, the higher papers in the Spectator and Guardian, the beft tranf- lations of Homer, Virgil and Horace, of Telema- chus, Travels of Cyrus, &c.

Once a year let there be public exercifes in the hall ; the truftees and citizens prefent. Then let fine gilt books be given as prizes to fuch boys as diftinguifh themfelves, and excel the others in any branch of learning, making three degrees of com- parifon : giving the beft prize to him that performs beft ; a lefs valuable one to him that comes up next to the beft : and another to the third. Commendations, encouragement, and advice to the reft ; keeping up their hopes, that, by in- duftry, they may excel another time. The names of thofe that obtain the prize, to be yearly printed in a lift.

The hours of each day are to be divided and difpofed in fuch a manner as that fome claffes may be with the writing-mafter, improving their hands ; others with the mathematical mafter, learning arithmetic, accounts, geography, ufe of the globes, drawing, mechanics, &c. ; while the reft are in the Englifh fchool, under the Englifh mafter's care.

Thus inftructed, youth will come out of this fchool fitted for learning any bufinefs, calling, or profeffion, except fuch wherein languages are required ; and though unacquainted with any

ancient

ancient or foreign tongue, they will be masters of their own, which is of more immediate and general use; and withal will have attained many other valuable accomplishments: the time usually spent in acquiring those languages, often without success, being here employed in laying such a foundation of knowledge and ability, as, properly improved, may qualify them to pass through and execute the several offices of civil life, with advantage and reputation to themselves and country.

F I N I S.